Kendra Fortmeyer grew up in the lushly magic swamp-woods of North Carolina. She now lives and writes in Austin, Texas, where she received an MFA in fiction from the New Writer's Project. A former teacher and youth librarian (and forever feminist), she's had the great joy of working with heaps of hilarious, brilliant and wonderful teens, and is passionate about giving their voices a home in her work. She's worked as a wilderness ranger in the Blue Ridge Mountains, tried her hand at blacksmithing, and drinks an absurd amount of tea.

A recipient of a grant from the Elizabeth George Foundation, Kendra won a 2017 Pushcart Prize for her story 'Things I Know to Be True' and she is a graduate of the Clarion Science Fiction and Fantasy Writers' Workshop class of 2016.

HOLE
IN THE
MIDDLE

Kendra Fortmeyer

ATOM

ATOM

First published in Great Britain in 2017 by Atom

1 3 5 7 9 10 8 6 4 2

Copyright © 2017 by Kendra Fortmeyer

The moral right of the author has been asserted.

A CIP catalogue record for this book
is available from the British Library.

ISBN 978-0-349-00275-0

Typeset in Janson by M Rules
Printed and bound in Great Britain by
Clays Ltd, St Ives plc

Papers used by Atom are from well-managed forests
and other responsible sources.

Atom
An imprint of
Little, Brown Book Group
Carmelite House
50 Victoria Embankment
London EC4Y 0DZ

An Hachette UK Company
www.hachette.co.uk

www.atombooks.co.uk

For all the hole kids –
you're not alone.

1

Here are the options for a girl like me.

Option A: Not mention it on the first date, or the second or third. We get to know each other, laugh, accidentally-on-purpose brush each other's shoulders as we walk. We go to a movie and say stupid things during the dramatic scenes, and I look over and notice that you're crying, and you look over and notice me noticing you crying, and we both pretend not to notice that the other person is noticing these things, but you take my hand, quietly and gratefully.

A fondness begins to well. A language begins to form, a gauze-webbed network of inside jokes. We text each other and are paralysed with terror from the moment we hit send until the phone buzzes back and our hearts begin to beat again. Our friends get sick of us. The world takes on a brightness that it only does for the specially loved. I start to wonder if you are The One, and I can see, gleaming in your eyes, the kernel of the notion that I am The One, too.

At some point you want to take the next step. The Big

Step. Maybe we are at your parents' house; maybe they are out of town; maybe you make some transparent excuse about showing me something in your bedroom and I say something brilliant like 'OK', and my heart is pounding, and I don't know how to speak and it's not until you close the door behind us with a faint click that I can say,

'Um, Hypothetical Person?'

And you, running your hands down my sides hazily, fingers curling up through my blouse, murmur into my hair, 'Mmm?'

'There's something I have to tell you,' I say.

I lift up my shirt and you see it. It is egg-shaped, the Hole: an imperfect oblong just to the lower right of my navel, about the size of peach or a fist. It is perfectly smooth, sealed: a toroid tunnel of white skin. Peering through it, you can see the room behind me. You can read the titles on the bookshelf.

'Whoa,' you say.

'Yeah,' I say.

'Holy shit,' you say.

'Yep,' I say.

'Does it hurt?' you say.

'No,' I say.

'What happened?' you say.

'Nothing,' I say. 'I don't know. I was born with it.'

And this is the moment I lose you.

Option B: I tell you up front.

I'm that semi-cute, flat-chested girl bagging groceries at the

2

co-op: quiet, sarcastic, INTJ. I love biking and slushies and talking during movies. I've been drawing since I was little, and my mom's a manic home DVD celebrity. Also, I have a giant, hermetically sealed hole in my torso that you could stick a fist through. Seventeen, non-smoker, virgin.

I don't get many takers.

2

My best friend and roommate Caroline sprawls over the edge of my bed, upside-down, pulling pastries one by one from a white paper bag. She's stopped back at our apartment between her morning shift at Java Jane and our senior year kick-off beach party. It's the Saturday before school begins, a humid North Carolina scorcher. Although it's barely 9 a.m., Caro's delicate skin is flushed from biking home in the punishing August heat, her hair a matted blonde mess of sweat and flyaways.

'It's not too late for you to come, you know,' Caro says. 'We could sneak you in. Emmeline's dad does construction – we'll build a wooden horse, Odysseus-style. Or tie you to the bottom of a sheep.'

'Or just tie me to Emmeline.'

Caro eyes me.

'Because she's a sheep.'

Caro sticks her tongue out at me, upside-down. Thing 387 I love about Caro: her proclivity for dangling. Her mother tried for years to push her into gymnastics, trapeze, space camp, but Caro wasn't interested. 'I don't want to make it a *job*,' she said at age nine, hanging from the sofa with her hands on her small, plump hips. 'I just like the way it makes my face feel.' But this is still not compelling enough for me to spend eight sandy, miserable hours on a school-sponsored beach trip, hunched in a huge T-shirt while people I have classes with cavort half-naked in the water.

Caro sighs.

'I wish you were coming,' she says. 'It's only eight hours, and I want you to hang out with me. Me, your best friend Caroline, who you love the most.'

'I do love you the most. But that is still eight hours longer than I want to be at the beach,' I say, climbing on the bed beside her. I hang back over the edge, crane my neck toward the unvacuumed carpet, feel my spine slowly uncurling. 'Fun and happiness are the polar opposite of everything I stand for. I might explode from sheer cognitive dissonance. Besides, Todd's coming, and I don't want to feel like a third wheel.'

'You're never a third wheel,' Caro protests. 'Todd loves you.'

'I am a third wheel. Who also really hates the beach.'

'What if,' Caro says, 'you came and spontaneously combusted from fun but timed it with the music so that it was the most epic beat drop of all time?'

'Tempting,' I muse. 'But somehow not enough to make me violate my moral code.'

Caro begins sorting the day-old pastries onto our stomachs: three muffins, a broken cookie, too many scones. 'Morgs, you won't be a third wheel for ever. There's someone out there who's a perfect match for you.'

I resist the urge to roll my eyes. 'I told you, this isn't about not having a date.'

'I'm just saying,' she tells me. 'A little optimism never killed anybody.'

I don't respond. One of the awkward things about being permasingle is how it makes other people feel bad for you. I mean, sure. Sometimes, when I'm passing the make-out stairwell at school, or when I see couples smiling at each other on billboards advertising Mentos or whatever, I get this little aching twinge, sneeze-quick. The word, *oh*. Just that. As in, *oh, wouldn't it be nice*. But it usually fades pretty fast. The thing is, I like me. I've been me my whole life, and I'm going to keep on doing it.

Caro's phone chimes and she spills herself upward, hair and crumbs curling onto my duvet. 'Hey,' she says, brightly. 'Yum Yum Situation is throwing an anti-back-to-school party tonight. Morgs, this is perfect! Come to this. You have to come to this.'

Yum Yum Situation is a local college band that special-ises in power pop songs with atonal bass lines and tortured, insightful lyrics like *'It's not the size of the boat, it's the motion of the— oh-oh!'* Her extremely boring boyfriend Todd, a fresh-man at NC State, plays the keyboard. They have parties in somebody's dilapidated off-campus house every week, and every week I end up third-wheeling with Caro and Todd, or

6

listening to somebody's drunk girlfriend talk about how much she loves her boyfriend.

Caro snorts at my expression and bumps me with her hip. A muffin rolls off of her stomach and slides into the well where my black T-shirt stretches taut over the Hole.

'Dear Morgs. Kindly come to this party because you're getting that glassy, I-haven't-interacted-with-humans-in-three-days look in your eye. Love, Caroline.'

'Dear Caroline,' I say. 'I've interacted with, like, four humans already today.'

'P.S. Not counting me.'

'Three humans.'

'Not counting your mother calling to yell at you about getting your shit together.'

'In my defence,' I say, 'she counts as at least sixteen people.'

Caro checks her watch and sits up, scattering crumbs. 'I've got to go catch the bus. I promised Angela I'd sit with her,' she says. She points to my forehead. 'Party. Think about it.'

'Thinking,' I say. 'Bye.'

I lie on the bed for a long time after the door clicks shut, ears ringing in the sudden hush. Our empty apartment smells of turpentine, hollow and grey. Outside, distant traffic thrums through the August afternoon like a pulse. I sigh and push myself upright, brushing away cake and crumbs. Two days before senior year, when everyone else my age is loading up on school supplies and wondering if their crush will notice them this year and saying to each other *'We're seniors, I can't believe we're seniors'*, I quietly collect myself off and drive, alone, to the medical clinic.

My social calendar is packed. Liaisons with old men in lab coats. Hot dates with cold exam tables. I have a pulmonologist, a cardiologist, a dermatologist, a gynaecologist, a renal specialist, a radiologist, a phlebotomist, a chiropractor and a host of wisecracking X-ray technicians, not to mention a general practitioner.

The Hole is nestled below and to the right of my navel. Its lip is soft and rubbery, lined with smooth, hairless flesh, my organs shifted neatly up and down and to the left, rearranged around the absence at my core. My posture could be better, and I think I'm missing a few abdominal muscles, but in nearly every regard, I've led a normal, healthy life: no broken bones, no cavities, no stints in an iron lung. The worst thing that's happened to me health-wise was the time I contracted chicken pox and couldn't find a way to scratch the bit between my descending colon and my small intestine in polite society.

I've been with my primary doctor, Dr Takahashi, for nearly ten years. We've been through everything together: I've cried about bad grades on this examination table, brought him drawings. He patiently gave me the facts when I was eleven and thought the fat little lumps of my breasts were cancer, and lost sleep when I hit a growth spurt at thirteen that we feared would stretch the Hole out until it exposed my spine, dissolving me into a human stew of raw nerves and vertebrae. He's the only person I trust to touch the Hole – not my other doctors, not Caro, not even Mother since I was six and began to bathe alone.

Even so, there's a barrier between us. He's always washing his hands, donning gloves, never letting me in on his true thoughts or feelings. I sometimes want to say, 'You know more about me than ninety-nine point nine per cent of my schoolmates, can't we just hang out?' But I guess that's not the point.

'How's it going today, Morgan?' Taka asks as he washes his hands. I roll my eyes. I know it's standard practice, but come on, it's not like you can catch Hole. Although I like this idea: Dr Takahashi starting awake in the night next to some shadowy-faced wife, lifting his hands from his bedspread and seeing— ... no! *No!* The beginnings of little pits, burrowing through his skin like worms! Holding them up to the moonlit window and seeing through them like lace! A swelling of music. And then, black screen: THE HOLE. Coming to theatres in October.

'What?' I ask.

'I said, has your menstrual cycle evened out?'

I don't even talk to my mom this much about my period. 'It's okay,' I say. 'It was kind of weird for a while.'

Taka's eyes flicker over the screen, through electronic charts and notes. 'You said it had been sporadic.'

I normally menstruate once every two months. Something about the way my internal organs have rearranged to accommodate the Hole. Things aren't quite where they should be. My life lacks normal flow.

'Oh, yeah,' I say. 'For a while I was on this new brand of tampons. I think it dried me out.'

Dr Takahashi doesn't blink. Nor, to his credit, does he acknowledge this obvious bullshit. 'Have you thought about going on birth control?' he asks.

I watch him as he prepares a needle for a blood draw. I've never had the luxury of being afraid of needles. It's all part of getting better, maybe, ultimately. I haven't given up hope. Being afraid of needles would be like a drowning person being afraid of the lifeboat.

I watch, detached, as my blood beads darkly in the syringe. Some days, my body just feels like meat.

'Please,' I say. 'Like I'm ever going to need it.'

Because Caro is right, I am categorically terrible at meeting people. Call it self-preservation, call it being anti-social; call it whatever you like. If I had it my way, no one would get close enough to know my name, let alone learn that I've got a great big unholey secret. My report cards from kindergarten: *good vocabulary*, *mediocre penmanship*, *DOES NOT PLAY WELL WITH OTHERS*. And in grades 8–12, when Mother shipped me off to a series of expensive boarding schools: *Morgan seems resistant to integrating into the community*. Liberal upper-middle-class code for, *she seems like kind of a bitch?*

I thought things would change at every new school – that I would finally find my super-close, college-brochure-diverse,

Girls-esque group of friends who I would share clothes with and pee in front of. People who would finally make me feel at home. But somehow I've always remained awkwardly on the periphery. It's like normal life is a code I never learned quite how to crack. I grew up with doctors, with Mother – in and out of school, obsessing over X-rays, gulping down pills and hopping on one rattling bandwagon of miracle cures after another, while other kids my age watched anime and worried about whether they could actually get cooties from their gym lockers. Even with a decade of sweet, weirdly anomalous Caro telling me otherwise, it feels too late to catch up.

I'm pulling out of the parking lot of Taka's clinic when my phone jumps in my lap. I fumble with my earpiece and hit Accept. 'Hello?'

There's an awkward pause. I try again, 'Hel—'

'Would you buy a fragrance called *Lambence*?' my mother asks.

I frown at the road, hearing, now, the vague moth-wing static of overseas air. 'Isn't that a kind of eel?'

'That's what I told Srivani,' she mutters. 'That idiot.'

'What are ... why are you naming fragrances?'

'Christine wants me to launch a limited spa line for Christmas,' she says drily. 'Ayogatherapy. Like *aromatherapy*. It's clever. How are your college applications coming? Did you look at the brochures Tabitha sent you?'

'Great, yeah,' I say, and instantly feel bad. The packet from Mother's assistant has been sitting unopened on the kitchen counter for the last week, getting Jackson Pollocked with oil stains. Something about college puts me in a blind panic. I barely know who I am half the time. How am I supposed to go somewhere else for four years to become *more* of it? But somehow, *tell Mother I'm planning to take a gap year* has never made it to the top of my to-do list.

'You know what would be a great perfume name?' I blurt. '*Defenestrate.*'

'I'm glad to hear you're on track,' she says. 'I put in a word with Tony about a letter of recommendation; you should touch base with him on Thursday. Also, your extracurriculars are lacking. I set up a meeting for you at Loblolly.'

'A strip club?' I ask.

'A gallery,' she says, brusquely.

'Another one?' I groan. 'Mother. Not that I don't love getting patted patronisingly on the head and told to come back when I'm old enough to vote, really, it's just that I'm super busy getting ready for senior year and—'

'Morgan Adina Stone,' Mother interrupts. 'I locked in my first commercial spot when I was six years old. Six. By the time I was eighteen, I launched my first product line. Do you think the first investors I approached took me seriously? Of course they did. Because I made them. It's all about presentation, Morgan. It's about confidence.'

I sigh and it disappears into the crisp silence of overseas airwaves. I picture Mother in my mind's eye; headset looped through a perfect ponytail, abs oiled and gleaming as she power-stalks down the halls of the luxury gym where she's filming her latest fitness video – something with a vaguely torture-porn title, like *The Hard Core* or *Rip/Tuck*.

Here's a punchline for a girl with a deformed body: your mother is a celebrity fitness guru!

Ha! Ha! Ha!

By all accounts, she's a beautiful and terrifying woman. She jet-sets around the world, terrifying the rich and famous. She's made two different James Bonds weep. They optioned her for *The Biggest Loser* before going with Jillian Michaels instead. Apparently, they thought Jillian was more likeable.

I think my broken body must drive her mad on some level: its persistent, relentless inability to conform to the conventional beauty standards she's spent her life selling to cable networks. If I can't be fixed, I must make something of myself. I've been drawing since I was little? Go Forth, Young Morgan, and Have a Career.

'You know what would be a great perfume? *Galatea*.'

'Too new-age,' Mother says. 'What's that noise? Where are you, a bar?'

'A bar, Mother? Really? It's two in the afternoon and I hate people.'

'You're still doing that?' she asks with a sigh.

'Misanthropy isn't a phase. It's a way of life.'

'Then learn to fake it,' she says. 'Particularly tomorrow morning. At Loblolly. Where you're going to convince a woman named Karen that despite your questionable shoes you're a prodigy, and it's in her best interest to let you display some art.'

'I'm not ready for a gallery show.'

'That,' she says, 'is exactly what you won't say to Karen at Loblolly.'

I grit my teeth and brake for a yellow light.

'I'm not going to let you waste your life, Morgan,' she says.

'I'm not wasting it,' I say. 'I'm just figuring things out.'

'You're bagging groceries.'

'While I'm figuring things out.'

'I just don't want you to believe you're a failure.'

'*I* don't believe that.'

The phone is silent for a moment.

'I'm getting you a life coach. What's your schedule look like?'

'Full of doctors.'

There's a staticky burst behind her: a faint, cringing voice asking for a signature. 'Tomorrow,' my mother says. 'Loblolly, off of Capital. A dusting of gold-toned bronzer will make you look like you go outdoors occasionally. So that's a no on *Lambence*?'

'Mother—' I begin, and I'm not sure if the next words will be *please let me handle my life on my own* or *you know I don't own bronzer*, but there's a sharp click, and my mother and her high-powered world drain from my ear.

I know, deep down, that Mother pushes me because she loves me. But I also worry that she loves me for all the wrong

14

reasons. Guilt, mostly: my dad left when I was four. It's the one thing Caro and I don't talk about. We discuss: poop, boys, French literature, lunch, whose turn it is to buy dish soap, solving world hunger, if it's worse to die alone or in a loveless marriage, acne and art. But we don't talk about my dad. That is the gaping hole in our conversations, the one we step around so deftly and silently now that is has become a habit. Brokenness is a taboo subject to people from happy families.

Mother says it isn't my fault that he left. Half of me knows she's lying, and half of me doesn't care. I remember only two things from that time. One is a secret, and the other is this: waking up from my first failed surgery to my parents arguing with a doctor at the foot of my bed. My father glanced up at me, and the expression on his face was panic, sheer and blinding: like when you glance into a puddle just as it catches the sun, and your whole vision sears white.

A nurse whisked the teddy-bear-print curtain closed. And when he opened it again, my father was gone for good. My mother loved me twice as fiercely to make up for it, but her weeping crept through my bedroom wall some grey nights, saturating the life we'd propped up together.

I've collected scraps from Mother over the years: *he was an idiot*, she told me when I was too old for a simple *he's gone away*. On my fourteenth birthday, staring after a drink-sodden afternoon into the ripening dusk, all merlot lips and lidded eyes: *I used to think about telling you he was dead*. And finally, simply: *he was afraid, Morgan*. Afraid of raising a kid with a hole in her core, like it would grow and grow and swallow our family whole.

I try not to think about it. What can you do with a man who won't love you because you're a broken thing? Try to be less broken?

3

I go home, make a lonely dinner. Caro and I got our apartment at the start of junior year after a full summer of working
crappy jobs and begging our parents. When we moved in, it
felt like the start of everything we'd ever wanted: a canvas
where we could paint our own kind of life. It's low-ceilinged
and smells perennially like mould, and the refrigerator howls
in the night and there's an almost-definitely drug dealer
named George who's always hanging around in the back
stairwell. But after years of Caro sharing a too-small bedroom
with too many siblings, and of me tiptoeing through Mother's
freezing, marble house, empty except for the latest in a series
of terrified maids, we could open the door to a space with my
art on the walls, Caro's books and craft supplies everywhere,
dishes in the sink caked with the remnants of weird recipes
Caro finds on the internet: lively and busy and ours.

Most nights, anyway.

My Facebook and Instagram feeds are already flooded
with photos of the beach trip: groups of girls in string

bikinis pretending to kiss, the bright slices of people's smiles in the surf, Claire Chong finishing a huge sandcastle just as Jeremy Waldeman comes Godzilla-ing through it. Someone named Aurelis has tagged Caro in a picture with Boring Todd. They're standing in the soft line where the water meets the sand, talking quietly to each other and holding hands. There's a flush of real happiness on her cheeks.

I know everyone feels like a misfit in high school. But for one magic moment, everyone in these pictures looks completely, perfectly like they belong, and I feel like more of an outsider than ever.

I pull out my sketchpad, the big one that takes up my whole lap. What Mother and my art teacher don't know is that I have been working on a project. A secret one, that I'm not ready to show anyone yet. I call it *Erasures*: a series of careful charcoal drawings of people I see in the waiting rooms of my radiologist's and gynaecologist's and doctors' offices, each with something missing. There's a runner without legs leaning pensively against a building, and a handless businesswoman staring at a pile of money, unable to touch it. I scroll through the cascading beach photos, this live feed of the life I'm not living, looking for an image: something that would show me that I'm not alone in feeling like an outsider. Someone on the edge of things. A smile that doesn't quite stick. But all I see is Caro with a huge group of healthy, happy people, Todd doing something that looks like the Robot, Emmeline and Angela shrieking and playing chicken with two boys I don't know. Nowhere do I see a space for myself.

I pick up my charcoal pencil and draw a slender nude, small and frail, with a dark pixie cut and a hint of a scowl in a blurred face. Then I pick up a black Sharpie and trace a hole like a howl over the figure's body: the lines thick and circling dark, sucking the entire drawing into the Hole and down, down.

4

Caro bounces into my room at five the next morning, a cloud of sunscreen and sweat and leftover salt. 'Morgs,' she whispers. 'Are you awake?'

I groan, and she flings herself into my desk chair. 'The beach. Was. Amazing!' she whisper-shouts. 'You should have come. Everyone asked about you.'

'That is a very nice lie,' I say, squinting with one eye in the gloom. She's glowing in the blue ambient light of my charging phone, the salt-dried curls straggling out of her hair. Someone's drawn a heart on her cheek: all the lingering detritus of a night fully lived. I remember my sorry sketch, and that ache pings through me, quick and twinging.

'One: it is the truth, whole truth, and nothing but. Two: you would have loved Anti-School Back-to-School. It was at this anarchist commune in west Raleigh with a Food Not Bombs in the basement, where they give out donated food to homeless people, and everyone there was so cool and smart, and political, and engaged. Todd and I ended up talking to

Gwynn's roommate Sierra for hours about body acceptance and fat activism. It was amazing.'

'Awesome,' I croak into the pillow. She kicks her feet, sending herself spinning.

'It *is* awesome,' her voice says in every dark direction. 'She just sent me links to all these amazing blogs. Did you know forty per cent of American women would give up three years of their life in exchange for reaching their ideal weight? Isn't that insane?'

'Did you know that ninety-six per cent of best-friend homicides are provoked by too much enthusiasm before breakfast?'

She bounces up. 'I'm good for you,' she says. 'I'm like vitamins.'

'Vitamins are toxic in high doses,' I tell my pillow.

'Not the water-soluble ones,' she says brightly. 'B and C are fine. C, like Caroline. See? No problem.'

'Is this going to be a campaign?'

'Campaigns are good for you.'

'Just don't sticky-note the toilet this time.'

She musses my hair. 'I make no promises.'

I roll, sigh. Caro's self-improvement campaigns are famously relentless – and since we got the apartment, she's generously expanded them into self-plus-Morgan improvement: filling our pantry with chia seeds, stocking the bathroom with thick Great Novels, and papering all available space with motivational notes. For the past month, Russian verbs have marched in Post-its down the stairwell like Cyrillic ants.

By the time I come down to breakfast, ripe clumps of STOP HATING YOURSELF FOR WHAT YOU AREN'T AND START LOVING YOURSELF FOR WHAT YOU ARE and I AM BEAUTIFUL have massed in the kitchen like body-positive fruit flies. I bat them away, pour own-brand Lucky Charms into a mug that reads KISS ME, I'M CONTAGIOUS. Caro sits at the table in yoga pants and a light sheen of sweat, eating steel-cut oatmeal with local honey and raw almonds I smuggled home from Simple Earth.

'What would you think if I did burlesque?' She looks bright-eyed and disgustingly well-rested.

'Do you want to do burlesque?'

Caro narrows her eyes, tilts her chin toward the ceiling.

'I don't know,' she says. 'But if I did, would you be shocked?'

'Probably,' I say, curling into a chair. 'You don't usually take off your clothes in front of strangers.'

She flicks an almond at me. 'I mean because Americans aren't accustomed to seeing normative sexualisation of fat bodies.'

'You're not fat,' I say, reflexively. I pick the marshmallows out of my cereal and line them up on the table, one of each colour.

'I am fat, actually,' she says. 'You can say it. It's not a bad word. In fact, saying I'm not fat just contributes to the stigma of fatness. It's counter-productive.'

Okay, the thing is, Caro is fat. She's also blonde and very pretty, all three of which she's been as long as I've known her (except that military-grade awkward period in middle school, when literally nobody is pretty). But it's one of those unspoken rules of Girl Code: *never tell your friend she's fat.* Even if she is. I don't know. It's pretty dumb. 'You're counter-productive,' I say. She flicks another almond at me. It sticks to the wall for a moment, then flops to the floor, organic and defeated.

'Not cleaning it,' I say.

'Me neither.'

'Fine,' I say. 'Now there's oatmeal on our wall for ever. I hope you're proud of yourself.'

'I'd be prouder of myself if I loved my body.'

'You already love your body,' I say, rising with my mug. 'You just think you don't so that you can feel empowered when you accept it all over again.'

'Stop pseudo-understanding me,' she calls after me. 'Where are you going?'

I fill my mouth with cereal. 'A gallery,' I mumble.

'Oh God,' she says. 'For fun or for your mother?'

I take eight thousand years to swallow. 'Definitely fun,' I lie.

She gets up and peels the almond off the wall. 'Morgs, you don't have to do everything your mother tells you to.'

I lift my hands and point at my entire life like, *I know.*

'Did she blackmail you? What was it this time?'

I run my hand through my hair, already exhausted, and just shake my head.

'You always come home from these things feeling like shit

23

and then lock yourself in your room and paint angry squares for days.'

'Sometimes circles,' I argue. 'Even rhombuses. I'm diverse.'

'It's our last day of freedom,' she argues. 'Just hang out with me today. Cinda's mom just harvested their whole herb garden and we're going to make vegan herb ice cream. And then YYS are opening for Sex Hiatus tonight at the Mansion.' She perks up as she goes, a juggernaut of optimism. 'Their new bassist is super adorable. I think you'd really like him.'

'I never thought I'd have to tell *you* this, but we kind of have school tomorrow.'

'They're going on early. Come on, you haven't been to a show in ages.'

'You always tell me they aren't fun,' I say.

'That's because you're not there,' she says. 'Come on. Wheaton is like, edgy-cute. He just moved here from Brooklyn.'

'His name is Wheaton?' I say.

'Morgs, come on,' she says. 'You never go out.'

'That is categorically untrue,' I say.

'Out-out.'

'I hate out-out,' I groan. 'It's only fun if you like being ground on by creepy old dudes.'

'No one will grind on you,' she says. 'Come on. I need you. Todd's ex is going.'

'Sheila Super Tits?'

'Exactly.'

I let out a long, slow sigh.

'I'll think about it,' I say.

'Glory hallelujah,' she says. 'Now, can I convince you to come to Cinda's? Basil ice cream is supposed to be seriously tasty.'

'Tempting,' I say. 'But I've got to go make something of myself.' She opens her mouth, and I cut her off. 'Caro, it's fine. Mother just wants what's best for me,' I say.

'Yeah,' she says, troubled. 'But I'm not sure she knows what that is.'

The Loblolly Gallery is far north of town, where the city crumbles away into the kudzu vine-draped countryside. I wind down a quiet drive through a rain-heavy apple orchard, until the trees part and reveal a magnificent, peeling barn with a sign in mod block print: lob.lolly.

There are a few other cars in the gravel parking lot. I step inside with my portfolio under my arm, heart hammering.

Inside, the barn is vast and sterile, the floor a slab of cement so white it sends electric feather curls sparking through my vision. There's an installation in the centre of the floor; a series of sculptures tumbling after a taxidermied elephant, rearing into the air. Alcoves run down the shadowy sides of the enormous room: the old horse stalls, cleaned out and turned into individual artists' display spaces. It's one of these that Mother wants me to gun for.

A group of kids from school emerges from one of the horse stalls, laughing. This black girl named Celeste looks up, and in the second before our eyes meet we both realise it's way too late to pretend we don't recognise each other, and so we both wave awkwardly and put on big smiles like *this is really cool! You! A person I know! In public!* I pray to God that they'll keep walking, but instead they turn and come my way, which, given the number of times I've gone to synagogue in the last decade, is probably deserved.

'Hey, guys,' I say. 'What's up?'

'Hey,' Celeste says. She eyes my portfolio, but doesn't say anything about it, which makes me like her more. 'Guys, do you know Morgan? She was in my art class last year.'

'Hi,' I say, like I don't recognise every single one of them from AP Government, from freshman bio, from home-room – classes during which I kept myself carefully apart, waiting for the day to end. They smile and nod back, a smat-tering of *hey*s.

'We're checking out the new exhibit,' Celeste says. She hesitates, then says, as if it's the easiest thing in the world to bat away years of social awkwardness, 'You wanna join us?'

I waver for a second, then open my mouth to say that scar-iest word in the world, *yes*. Yes to an afternoon with people my age, doing regular people things. *Yes* to looking at art with this girl who's a scary-good painter, and might someday want to do critiques with me, to these casually cute boys with nerdy glasses and comic book T-shirts and easy laughs. Then a voice says,

'Morgan Stone?' There's a clack of heels on the floor. A

26

polished woman appears from one of the alcoves. 'You must be my ten o'clock.'

I shrink like a Doritos bag tossed in the microwave. I risk a glance at Celeste & Co. They are staring at me in surprise. It's like looking over a wall. I am suddenly a thing apart. I want to torch my gigantic portfolio, Viking-funeral style.

'Yeah,' I say, reluctantly.

'I didn't mean to interrupt,' Celeste says. She glances from me to the gallery owner, curiosity written all over her face. Also respect. And a little thing like – my heart sinks – awe. The same look as every new surgeon Mother's ever trotted me out in front of.

'No, it's cool,' I say. 'Can I – I'll come with you another time?'

'Sure, of course,' she says. But she and her friends are already trading glances, already retreating. 'Bye.'

I follow the impeccably groomed woman (*Karen*, I remind myself) to her office on numb feet, wanting to say *wait*. But it's already past too late.

I stand with Karen over a desk of rough-hewn slate that shimmers like crushed velvet as she thumbs through my portfolio. I've always been top of my art classes at school, but now, in the expensively curated light of this gallery, all I can see is my inadequacy. The rough lines. The sloppy mark-making. All the ways in which this is a perfectly excellent high school portfolio and how little that means in the hard cold adult world.

Karen makes polite noises from time to time, but they puddle limply in the air between us, convincing no one.

'I'm sorry about my mother,' I say at last.

'It's fine,' Karen answers, but her smile seems copied-and-pasted. 'Do you . . . ' she begins, and then falls silent.

It's the drawing I began last night: the waif-thin girl with the hole in her gut. It seems even more of a howl today: a dark whirlpool, sucking up her life.

'Oh,' I say startled. 'That's not supposed to be here.'

Karen says nothing. She studies the picture. My heart gives a painful thump as she turns and looks at my own body.

'What's going on in this one?' she asks.

It would be so easy, in this moment, to tell this stranger the truth. To lift my shirt. But all I can hear in my thundering pulse is Mother's voice: *don't tell don't tell don't tell.* The blinding flash of my father leaving.

'It's about anorexia,' I say, smoothly. 'It's commentary. About how it consumes more than just you. You know?' I want to go back and delete the *you know?* from the air, but I can't, so I barrel on. 'It consumes your world.'

'Mmm,' she says. She sits on the edge of the table, stares up at me, hard. 'Do you have an eating disorder?'

'No,' I say, knocked off guard.

She aligns the edges of the papers with a finger, and slides the portfolio closed.

'I'll be straight with you,' she says, looking me in the eye. 'You're talented. But—'

'But I have to keep practising,' I finish. The same thing they told me at Five Finger. At Redbud.

'No,' she says. 'Yes. But you also have some living to do. You're seventeen. Don't be political about things you've read on the internet. Art comes from experience. Go have some.'

When I step back into the gallery, Celeste and her friends are in the parking lot. I can see them through the glass, jumping off of the low stone wall, posing for pictures against the gleaming-leaved apple trees. *You're not like them*, Mother always told me when I was a kid. *You can be so much more*. One more brick in the tower she built for me.

Shame-faced, I wander through the hall. The taxidermied elephant is part of an enormous installation, a full-scale circus parade of frozen figures: dogs and strongmen, a gorgeous trapeze artist in peacock feathers, brightly-clad limbs in the process of spilling from a clown car. **The Greatest Show**, reads a moodily lit sign in Helvetica on the floor. In small font, below:

A full-scale, plaster-cast circus parade that challenges the function of linear time, allowing the viewer to walk the length of the parade forwards or backwards – speeding up, reversing or pausing this childhood experience as he or she chooses.

I stare up at the elephant, his trunk raised in triumph. I wonder how heavy it must be, what a strain to keep that face

29

aloft in the lonely nights after the gallery lights go out. His glass eyes glitter in his face. I turn away from them and walk the length of the frozen parade – the silk-suited acrobats, the dancing girls, the lions – and I feel a sudden, desperate urge to run. To fling myself backward, past the balloonist, past the popcorn man, to the moment when this kind-hearted stranger looked at my body, and to say, instead, *yes, this is me.* Instead, I just keep walking the length of the line like everything inside of me isn't screaming, and let the frozen parade of life stream silently by.

On the way home, I call Caro. 'Don't try to set me up with anybody.'

'Are you coming tonight?'

I watch the country retreat under its blanket of concrete as I approach the city, the sun catching the windshields of passing cars like gold.

'Yes.'

She squeals. 'I love you,' she says.

'You owe me,' I say.

But I feel a secret flush of excitement. I know, after a lifetime of aborted romances and crushing social failure, that you're not supposed to hope any more, that some part of you is just supposed to shut down. But there is that terrible little piece inside that still hopes, even when the rest of your brain is shouting *you idiot, give it up, you know more than anyone how love is a steamroller that will crush you to a pulp of human mess on asphalt and never look back*, and it is that stupid little part that rolls down the window now and lets the hot summer wind catch my hair, heart pounding, wondering if maybe this time, maybe.

5

Caro gets home from Cinda's at six, and by eight we're in her room, getting dressed to go out. Or, rather, I am getting dressed to go out. Caro bounces around for the first hour in nervous excitement, chattering about plus-sized model campaigns before finally, nervously, donning a honey-coloured dress with a swooping décolletage.

'Look at my body!' she proclaims. The shimmering fabric outlines her in small geometries: arcs and curves and ellipticals. 'Aren't I magnificent? Aren't I punching preconceived notions of fatness equalling lazy, ugly and unlovable in the *face*?'

But forty-five minutes later, she's lying listlessly on her bed, reading *Lolita* in full eyeliner while I stand at the mirror, paralysed with dread. I own three nice tops and hate them all. Two make me look frumpy. The other makes me look green.

'This is the *worst*,' I groan, for the sixth time in an hour.

Caroline squints a dark-fringed eye at me, turns a page.

'Has he killed the mom yet?' I ask.

She sits up. 'Damn it, Morgan.'

'Sorry,' I say. 'Be honest, does this make me look like a grandma?'

She sighs. 'By the time we leave, you might be. Scoot your boot, Granny.'

I tug at the hem, evaluating octogenerianism. Caro's notes flutter above the mirror:

GENDER OPPRESSION IS PERPETUATED
BY BODY OPPRESSION.

RIOT NOT DIET.

START A REVOLUTION:
STOP HATING YOUR BODY.

'Let me look through your stuff,' I say.

'Go for it,' she says, picking up her phone.

I dig through Caro's closet, plunging my hand deep into the curtains of fabric, and emerge clutching a small cerulean T-shirt. It's a child's souvenir tee, sporting a picture of an orca and the legend MY GRANDMA WENT TO SEA WORLD AND ALL I GOT WAS THIS STUPID T-SHIRT. 'Grandma' has been crossed out, and **BEST FRIEND** carefully Sharpied in. The 'I' is dotted with a heart. I feel a little rush of warmth.

'Why do you still have this?' I ask.

'Because you gave it to me,' Caroline says, not looking up.

'When we were eleven,' I say.

'Because I'm a sentimental fool,' she says.

'That's for sure,' I say. I hold the T-shirt up against my chest, and smile despite myself, remembering the first time I saw Caroline, when we were six. She charged up to me on my first day at my new school and informed me I was sleeping over at her house on Friday. *Why?* I asked. *Because you're the new kid*, she answered. *And being the new kid sucks, so I'm going to be your friend.*

I tug the T-shirt over my head. The armpits pinch, and the whale warps across my chest, but it's a beautiful colour – one of the primaries, my favourite, the hue simultaneously bright and deep. I turn to Caro, grinning. 'Hey, bestie,' I sing-song.

She rolls her eyes and checks her phone. 'Hey, gonna-make-us-latie. Come on, get dressed. They're going on in ten minutes.'

I catch a glimpse in the mirror as I turn back to the closet, and freeze. The Hole peeks out from beneath the shirt's hem, which ends just below my ribcage. I see it every day – I painstakingly clean it every time I shower – but suddenly it's just there. On display. It is startling, eye-catching against the blue. I glimpse pieces of Caro through it – the ripple of blonde as she sits up, suddenly paying attention; a flicker of hand laying the book down on the comforter, Lolita an afterthought.

I half want her to say, *do it. You look gorgeous, embrace your*

34

non-normative body, get out there. I found some articles about Hole acceptance, didn't I tell you? Here, let me send you a link.

Instead, she just sighs. 'Morgs, quit screwing around. We'll miss their set. Just wear the purple one; it wasn't that bad.' Something in me quietly crumbles with relief, or disappointment, or both. Caro collects her phone and rises from the bed, flipping off the light. 'I'll wait for you downstairs, okay?'

I linger in the room a moment after she goes, illuminated only by the orphaned light of the stairs. The blue of the shirt is washed to a dusky graphite in the half-light, the puff-painted orca glowing eerily. I raise my arms, and the air of the bedroom threads cool and velvet through the Hole. I look like a bead that's lost its necklace.

I've been hiding for so long. Behind floppy T-shirts, one-piece swimsuits, a protective scowl. The records live in a hushed drawer in one of Mother's offices, eighteen separate counts of failure and disappointment. The doctors took grafts from my buttocks, from Mother's, from anonymous donors who I realised, upon passing my driving test at sixteen and ticking the organ donor box, had probably died on highways, whole and healthy blood gushing out onto distant asphalt.

But each time the implanted flesh shrank from mine, drawing thin and translucent around the edges. I found dead transplants shrivelled in my bed sheets; they dropped with flaccid *glop*s to the floor of the shower, quivering like jellyfish on the drain.

A note over the mirror reminds me to STARt A

REVOLUTION: STOP HATING YOUR BODY. I swallow down my fast-beating heart. Then I cover the shirt with a bulky sweater and head down the stairs.

Caro's fussing with her swooping décolletage when I drop into view. She lets her hand fall and looks up at me, the anxiety on her face laced through with hope. 'Ready?'

'Yeah.'

'Don't crap out on me, Morgan, please,' she says, earnestly. 'Sheila's probably going to show up in mirrored hot pants or something.'

'I'm fine,' I lie. 'Don't worry about Disco Ball Butt. She'll be first against the wall in your glorious body revolution.'

'That wasn't hypothetical,' she says as we clatter out into the stairwell. 'Those pants are real. They used to call her the Ass-tronaut.'

'Trust me,' I say. 'Tonight, she's the least of our worries.'

6

The Mansion is in a darkened part of town that I never visit, tucked away in its own lot past a row of old warehouses, far from the bright downtown. Caroline eases the car into a parallel-parking space as a group of girls totters past in three-inch heels and painted-on dresses. For half a second, I think about staying in the car, feigning sickness. But somehow I'm on my feet, and Caro and I are flowing like liquid through the street, through a gate, handing fake IDs to a bouncer who sees nothing but our shining eyes and Caro's breasts, and we're in.

I take a breath, willing my heartbeat to slow as I look around. I've only heard about this place by name. I hadn't realised that it actually is an old mansion: crumbling Southern Gothic complete with sagging porch and gabled roof with rusting iron railings. The interior walls have been gutted, carving the entire building into a high-ceilinged cavern packed densely with bodies. Soundproofing is nailed around an old, dusty cornice carved with cherub heads and grape leaves. Lights drench the bouncing crowd and empty stage like neon water. I realise that the music flooding around and through us is recorded: we've missed the first set.

'Come on,' Caroline screams in my ear, tugging me towards the bar. I make out the dim shape of Boring Todd leaning against the bar with a drink in each hand, and a black-lit smile that I want to pretend includes me, but I know is for Caroline alone. I shake my head and gently pour out of my best friend's grip. *Go on*, I wave. Everything pounds – my blood, the bass, the spaces in and between the molecules that make up my humming body. I let the pulsing of everything pull me to the dance floor. No: this is not true. I choose. I go.

If it were a movie, silence would fall when I step onto the floor. But instead, the music is so loud I'm drowning in it, sinking to my eye teeth, my body ripped away in the howl of sound and dark. The flashing lights swim over the mad pulse of torsos, of hands. Anonymous faces appear and disappear in the snapshots of strobe lights, Cheshire-cat smiles flashing and gone.

Beat by beat I let the music erase me until I am nothing but the bassline in my bones, and then, in the throbbing heat of this crowd of strangers, I drop my sweater to the ground.

Something in my body begins to hum.

I lift my arms.

And I'm dancing.

If people notice the Hole, they aren't immediately obvious about it. And probably, they don't. The Mansion is a mess of sweat and bodies, a thousand tricks of half-light. Even if they did see, everyone is so drunk and stoned and high on music that what would they say? The steamy hot air slides around and through my torso, the filmy cotton shirt clinging almost immediately to my skin, shrivelling. Around me, strangers grind and I wind my hands into the air and grind with them. I give myself over to the music. I am painting the dark and pulsing air with the colours that are me.

A guy dances up on me, grabs my hips. I let him, and we swing together. The beat shifts and he does too, to my front. There is a double-take, a startled yelp I can barely hear – an offbeat in the music. I close my eyes, feel him vanish into the dark. I don't care. I let my body unfurl. I am electric. I am fluid. I dance and I dance and I dance.

I'm completely useless at school the next morning because Caro and I stay up half the night screaming *oh my God* and *are you insane?* and *yes, this is awesome, yes.* Fortunately, since it's the first day of school, I'm able to sleepwalk through the haze of syllabi and ice-breaker games with kids I've known since I was six. My voice is nearly gone, my body aching and crusted in a skin of dried sweat. I'm still wearing the little blue shirt beneath my sweater, sticky and rank now. I thought, when I fell asleep, that I could get up today and live the rest of my life like I did last night: wild and free, secret-less beneath the bare and certain sky. But in the flat light of day, everything feels anticlimactic. Ordinary. The cafeteria still smells like rotting tomatoes, Principal Crowell still uptalks through the morning announcements ('And the chess club? Will meet? In room three-o-one?'), I still get a lecture from Coach Machlan for not changing for gym. I feel like Difference must be radiating from my pores, my body shining bright with everything that I know I can be. I keep glancing behind me, at desktops and pens, half-expecting to see dusty silver fingerprints lingering behind, evidence of this new magic. But there is nothing but crude graffiti and the freshmen getting lost in the hallways and teachers pushing us to fill our brains so that we can graduate, please, just graduate and get out of here.

When I get home, I grab Caro's sewing scissors and fling open my closet door.

I go back to the Mansion almost every night after that. I don't meet the bassist. I don't need to meet the bassist. It's as though dropping that first sweater has unleashed a hunger in me that my old existence can't fill. My collection of belly shirts grows, becoming increasingly elaborate. I favour spangles, sparkles and fringe. And people respond. After the first few awkward questions from the first few awkward guys, the word spreads – oh yeah, the girl with the hole in her middle. Not that people get it. Not that they aren't freaked out. But everyone pretends they're okay with it. And so everyone's okay.

Caroline is torn at first between worry and support. Finally, though, she caves: picks out outfits with me, rushes to the Mansion night after night and then makes us stay up until three, scrawling away at our homework over the kitchen table.

We're both exhausted, and she starts to drop the word 'unsustainable' a lot, but some things are bigger than school. After years of my ball-and-chaining, she's thrilled that I've finally started to act like a young person, alive.

We become regulars. The bouncer knows us, offers us cigarettes between set breaks. The bartender, cool at first, eyeing me and my obviously fake ID through the bottom of a pint glass, has become my new best friend. On nights that there is live music, Caro and I are the ones in the front, throbbing with the strobes, setting the pace for the sweaty and communal pulse. Increasingly, here, people seem to smile at me. Me, the girl with the lithe and winding waist, with the shell-green eyes and the dusting of freckles. They're smiling at the girl who comes early and stays late, who dances to every song with a friend, or with strangers, or by herself, the inexplicable hole in her middle floating out across the dance floor like a memory of some eclipsing moon.

7

After a few weeks, Caro begins to flag. She gets wan and circle-eyed. First it's, 'But our rough draft is due in history next week.' Then:

'Are you going out again?' she asks.

I look up from the shirt I'm hunched over on the floor, a shirt I've cropped and painted to look like the Raleigh skyline, lit up at night. I'm gluing on tiny amber sequins to make the windows on the BB&T building glow. My gallery portfolio is half-forgotten under the bed; I'm flooding my life with a new kind of colour.

'Of course,' I say. She just kind of sighs.

'What,' I say at last.

'I'm happy for you,' she says, 'I really—'

'Caroline,' I say. 'Enough with the happy disclaimers.'

'I just worry you're going to wear yourself out,' she says.

But I'm the opposite of worn out. I am more myself than I have ever been. I am just beginning to know how to wear this skin.

*

I'm hungover as hell when my phone goes off the next morning. TAKA, the screen says. I moan, hit IGNORE.

8 MISSED CALLS, the phone says.

MOTHER, the phone says.

Jesus.

Caro sticks her head in on her way out – ponytailed and makeup-free, which means she's working at Java Jane today. She likes to smudge on glitter eyeliner and dark lipstick for Walgreens, a look she calls 'corporate whore'. I don't know why Caro needs two jobs – our rent is dirt cheap, and we've got the whole gap year ahead to save up for college – but arguing with her is like arguing with a motivational poster: SUCCESS: A JOURNEY NOT A DESTINATION! (In other words, frustrating, and full of kitten photos.)

'How was the rest of your night?' she asks.

'Good,' I tell her, blearily. 'I met a very handsome doughnut maker. He wants me to move in with him and be his doughnut inspiration.'

'I'm so happy for you,' she says. 'Can you leave the blender when you move out? I like it.'

'He will give me one million blenders,' I say to my pillow.

'Sounds like a keeper,' she says. 'I've got to go. Don't be late to the doctor.'

'Don't *you* be late to the doctor,' I say, pointing a finger gun in her general direction. She winks at me and vanishes down the stairs.

On my way into Takahashi's office, I listen to my voicemail.

'Morgan, I've got something important to discuss with you,' my mother's voice announces drily. In the background, I hear a timid voice asking her for the final time to turn off her cellular device and fasten her safety belt, and Mother sighs. 'Christ on a stick. Just clear some time this afternoon for a call,' she says. 'Take care of yourself.' Even from here, 7,300 miles away and eight hours later, I can hear the echo of the implied threat: *or else I will.*

I slump cotton-mouthed into Dr Takahashi's waiting room, thankful for once for the dim fluorescent lighting. I try flipping through *Better Homes and Gardens*, but the pictures of food make me feel nauseated, as do the teeth of happy magazine people pretending to joyfully eat salad.

Dr Takahashi seems even more distant than usual at my appointment today, distracted. I've always found it easy to tell him things, maybe because he never seems to want to hear them. But when I ask him about my health, the weather, his family, and receive nothing but vague, one-word answers, I start to lose patience. At last I blurt, 'I finally started having fun like a real young person.'

'So I hear,' Taka says.

I blink down at the part in his hair. 'Excuse me?'

His hands, probing the edges of the Hole with sterile gloved fingers, go still for a moment before fluttering back to life, pushing and patting.

He says, not looking up, 'You said were out late. I assumed that's why you're tired.'

'You assumed I was out having fun? Do you remember who you're talking to?'

He looks up at me, eyebrow raised, his nose inches from the Hole.

'Okay, fine,' I say, still feeling a little dubious. 'Yeah. I am going out. I found a really great club in town.'

He pulls out a small ruler, takes measurements. 'A club, huh?' he says. 'Aren't you a little young?'

'It's all-ages.'

Taka frowns at his ruler. 'I hope you're being careful.'

'Actually,' I hedge. He is so intent on his examination, I feel like I can test the words out, without the consequences of having someone listen. 'I might have let some people see the Hole.'

He frowns at my stomach, then turns away, checking something on my chart. 'Straighten up,' he instructs me. Disappointment curls deep in my chest.

'A lot of people, actually,' I say, defiantly. 'I'm not even sure how many. Hundreds, probably.'

'That's good,' he says. But he's fading out again, entering something on the computer. I bounce my heels against the edge of the table like a child. At the computer, Taka pauses and clicks. Then clicks again. His frown deepens.

'Have you noticed any changes in the Hole lately?' he asks.

'Like what?' I ask.

'Just changes. Pain, a change in sensation, in size—'

'Change in size?' I ask. 'What, like getting bigger?'

He glances up, sharply. 'Do you feel like it's any bigger?'

'No,' I say, startled by his sudden intensity. 'I mean. Did you notice something in your measurements?'

'Oh,' he says. 'Of course not.' But there is something studied in this blankness. I wonder if this is something they teach in medical school: How to Avoid Your Patient's Gaze When You Suspect They Might Be Dying. He doesn't look at me as he moves around the room, snapping off his gloves and throwing them away.

'Is your mother in town?' he asks. I shake my head. Something around his eyes relaxes slightly. He washes his hands. 'Have her call me when she gets back, please.'

I look out the window. 'Okay,' I say, even though it isn't. I want to ask, *what are you hiding from me, and why are you telling my mother about it.* I want to tell him, *something so big has happened to me. People have seen me for who I really am, and the world didn't end like I always thought it would.*

I'm checking out when Amanda, the nurse, pokes her head into reception. She and the receptionist confer quickly, in low tones. The receptionist keeps glancing up at me with wide, purple-lined eyes. Amanda vanishes back into the offices on the silent swish of nurse shoes, and the receptionist rolls her chair back to the window.

'Dr Takahashi would like you to come back on eleventh October,' the receptionist says, circling something illegible on a calendar. 'That's in two weeks. A Sunday.'

46

'Why?' I ask. 'He literally just saw me. Should I just run back there for a minute?'

'That won't be necessary,' the receptionist says. 'He'd just like to see you for a routine check-up.'

I don't know this receptionist. She has frosted blonde hair and a wispy little voice, artificially high, and I suddenly feel like everything about her is a lie.

'He didn't mention anything to me,' I say. 'Is the office even open on Sundays?'

She purses her little lips. 'Dr Takahashi is very busy,' she says. 'Come back in two weeks, please. He has a *lot* of appointments today.'

I tug at the hem of my shirt, feeling suddenly exposed, and initial on the line, turn to go. The empty space in my middle burns as I step out of the office and into the bright, velvet light of a southern September, wondering what it is that I'm not being told.

8

Texts I write and do not send to my best friend who isn't home when I get there:

hey I need to talk to y—

hey this kind of weird thing happened at Taka's today, I feel like he is hiding something from me and I need you here to tell me that I'm paranoid or else I'll go full-scale conspiracy theorist and start posting in chatrooms about the Illuminati's involvement in 9/11

hey I know you're sick of it but can we go out tonight? I really need to get my mind off this thing Taka sai—

hey are you at Todd's

is he talking about how much he likes string cheese again
because that was really scintillat—

Pull it together, M-Sto.

The cardigan I've picked out for tonight is saffron with
tiny magenta flowers. I feel a tinge of self-consciousness as
Steve, the bouncer, waves me inside, but it dulls to a simmer
as I step over the threshold, shouldering my way to the bar
through crowds that part when they see who I am, or what.
A few people call out to me and I ignore them, and we are all
more comfortable this way: they in their fiction that they are
friends with the Hole Girl, and me in mine, in which I am
noir as shit – so stoic, and so focused on a drink, that I can't
be bothered to look up.

(Because in reality, what would we say? Them: *You have a
Hole in your middle!* Me: *Yeah. Do you?* Them: *Nah.* Me: *Dope.*
It's easier just to head for the bar.)

The bartender's name is Frank, and I like him because he
is an asshole. He isn't nice to anyone and he isn't nice to me,
either, and I feel a kind of love in the way that he doesn't make
me feel special.

'Hey, Em,' the bartender says. Emma Lapis: the obviously
fake name on my obviously fake ID about which Frank obviously gives zero fucks. He is balding with a hard belly and
hates the world. He usually doesn't talk, but his ex-wife is here
tonight and he's trying to look socially successful, the way girls

49

will start laughing too loudly when their exes walk past them at school. On Fran nights, Frank puts on a grimace, forces small talk with college students getting shitty on vodka Red Bulls and churns out perfectly shaken, garnished drinks that are borderline works of art. Once Fran (yes, her real name – honestly, what are the odds on *that* marriage lasting?) brought another man here, and my Guinness was lined with eight lime wedges, a cloud of pearl onions, and a tiny plastic cowboy that toppled from sight and drowned in the foamy head.

I slip onto my stool, at the opposite end of the bar from where Fran sits under a wash of pink lights, drinking Diet Coke and looking everywhere but at Frank. There's a bevy of bachelorettes in the grinning DJ's booth, and the music is out of date and way, way too loud: a white-noise wall that sounds vaguely like 'Single Ladies' mixed with 'That's the Way (I Like It)'. When Frank slides a pint over to me, I lean across the bar.

'You should ignore her,' I scream to him. At him. In movies, people are always having normal-volume conversations in clubs. Let me tell you, ladies and gentlemen, THIS IS A FICTION.

Frank just shakes his head, not meeting my eye.

'Two sixty-three,' he says.

'That's random,' I shout. 'Why?'

He glowers at me. Frank never shouts but is somehow always audible. I do not know if this is a property of being a bartender, or just of being Frank.

'Because,' he answers flatly, and stabs a lemon wedge onto the rim.

I lean against the bar and sip, letting the musky weight of the stout run down my insides and watch customers watching me drink. When I first started coming to the Mansion I didn't know much about alcohol and I still don't, really. I just order dark beers that I don't like because I know that girls are supposed to like light beer, and I don't want anything about my new, free self to be predictable.

I finish my drink, slowly, feeling a buzz crawl up and through my veins. The music has shifted now, a mix of 'We Found Love' and 'SexyBack' that's weirdly working, and my body is beginning to thrum in that way that makes me feel like wings could sprout from my fingers and lift me into flight. I rise from my stool, pretending not to notice the people pretending not to watch, the girls nearby me lifting their phones like they're texting. For a moment, I hover on the metallic edge of self-consciousness, but then the beat drops, and I grin and drop my sweater and—

'Oh my God, it's her!' a voice shrieks. The sweater hits my ankles, and I turn, and a girl's face is in my face: a prettyish woman in her twenties with silver-rimmed eyes, hands filled with Solo cups. Her breath is juniper and cigarettes. 'My friends said you were, like, an internet hoax, but they're a bunch of dumb sluts,' she screams. (Or maybe it's *hairy, crunchy lug nuts!* See previous: audibility in bars.)

I try to shrug her off, but she clings. 'Can we take a selfie?

We have to take a selfie. Oh my God, am I being super awkward?' She turns to the guy next to her, who's eyeballing us both, nonplussed. 'She's, like, legit famous on Public Scrutiny!'

The girl's drinks slosh as she ogles the Hole, and the buzz slowly dulls in my limbs. People staring at the Hole: yes, familiar, check it off the list. But not with this much recognition.

'Public what?' I ask.

'Public Scrutiny,' she says again. 'Oh my God, you don't know Public *Scrutiny*?' She turns to the guy again, lets her head fall on his denim-clad shoulder. 'She's like super famous on the internet and she doesn't even know what Public *Scrutiny* is.'

The guy grins down at her with wet teeth. The kind of smile that makes me worry, makes me wonder if she's with anyone who can get her safely home. 'Isn't that something.' He flicks his pale eyes up to me, like this is a joke that we are sharing.

'It's basically the whole *internet*,' the girl tells the guy and the guy's shoulder and me.

'Cool,' I say. I look for Frank, wanting to telegraph, *get this chick a cab*, but he either doesn't care or is way ahead of me, leaning on the till and thumbing through his phone. I slip out of her grip and into the crowd, trying to shake the weight of too many invisible eyes on my limbs. I can't dance off a dim sense of dread at the girl's recognition. It makes me awkward, graceless, feeling as though I am made of lip. My whole body becoming a mouth asking again and sweat-soaked again: *who are you, who are you, looking at me?*

Vaguely nauseated, I leave the dance floor and cut out into the night. I risk a glance back at the bar, but my yellow sweater is long gone – either trampled into the beery underworld beneath the bar rail, or clutched tightly to the gin-soaked bosom of my new biggest fan. The night air is unreasonably chilly for September. I wrap my arms around myself and scurry to my car under the soothing cover of dark.

I get home at 1.30 and drop into my desk chair, my heart jumping into my throat as I open my laptop. I check my email, delete Mother's eighteen unread messages (forwards about gallery openings and fad diets and at least three labelled MORGAN I'M SERIOUS: DO NOT DELETE), check my Facebook (nothing), and then, like it's the most casual thing in the world, google 'Public Scrutiny'.

The first few results are dictionary definitions and a .co.uk site about increasing accountability in modern government. But the fifth result makes my stomach leap into my mouth.

The website is garish and eye-searing: white microprint on a black background that makes the words seem to wiggle and jump. PUBLIC SCRUTINY screams a banner in green. NEWS. CULTURE. GOSSIP. And underneath it: YOUR WALLS HAVE EARS YOUR STREETS HAVE EYES.

It's tacky and awful and isn't sure if it wants to be an

anarchist political rag or a gossip site or some hybrid little sister of the two, punked up and decked out in their stolen leather jacket. My first thought is, *what is this?* and my second thought is *does anyone actually read this?* and my third is *oh, my God.*

Because I'm the top story.

The headlining photo is a camera phone shot taken in the Mansion, on the dance floor. I don't know by whom. In the picture I have my arms lifted, twisting belly-dancer sinuous. It looks as though the smoke machine must have been on, wreathing my face in blue haze. Only the Hole is in clear focus. It cuts through my silhouette like a knife.

Beneath, a caption in screaming green: FREAKISH DANCER BARES THE 'HOLE' PACKAGE AT LOCAL CLUB. There's a link to an article with a photo gallery. I check the byline, see that the article is over two weeks old. Numbly, I begin to scroll.

An intrepid tipster (thanks, Sierra89!) sent PUBLIC SCRUTINY this shot from the Mansion's Intergalatic Flash Jam on 19 September. Optical illusion? Photoshop fake? Either way, somebody's taking her Black Hole costume very seriously.

I send Caro a Facebook message with a link: I'M FAMOUS ON THE INTERNET. I'm looking through the site masthead, trying to figure out who these people are, when my phone rings.

'Oh my God,' Caro says.

I step out into the hallway. Her bedroom door yawns open,

dark and vacant, the doorframe freckled with sticky notes: *florid, riparian, polemic.* 'Where are you?' I whisper.

'Work,' she says. Her voice has a damp, echoing quality. 'Graveyard shift.'

'Is your new job in a dungeon? It sounds like you're in a dungeon.'

'One: basically, yes. The bathroom at Walgreens. And two: lots of places echo; don't be place-ist.'

'Are you sitting on a toilet right now?'

'No,' she says reverberantly. 'I mean, I could, for verisimilitude. I told Tricia I had the runs when I saw your message; she's covering for me. Anyway, Morgan: holy shit, are you all right?'

I look around my room. Same windows, same walls. Same deep blue shadows thrown into the same corners from my desk lamp, just like they were last night, and the night before.

'Yeah,' I say.

'This is a big deal. This is a really big fucking deal.' There is a muffling, a wash of static. 'Just a minute!' Caro shouts to someone else, and then her breath is there again in my ear. 'Is there anything I can do?' she asks.

'I don't think so,' I say, scrolling absently. I spot a link below the article, in red: Comments: 57.

'Just a *minute*,' Caro shouts again to somebody else, 'I'm shitting my *brains* out in here.' She sighs, turns back to the receiver. 'Jesus. Some people don't have any respect.'

'You're telling me,' I say, automatically. I click to expand the comments, and the page triples in length. There are comments, and comments within comments. They spill heavily to the bottom, punctuated by more links. Comments <1, 2, 3>

'You should probably get back to work before you get in trouble,' I tell Caroline.

'I'll get off at five a.m.,' she says. 'Are you going to stay up? Want to go to Waffle House?'

'I'm fine,' I say, distantly. 'I think I'm going to go to bed, actually. Thanks for pretending to have diarrhoea for me.'

'Hey, anytime,' she says. 'Seriously. We'll talk about this in the morning.'

'Yep,' I say. 'Wash your hands.'

'Love you,' she says, and then her voice is gone, leaving me with the sudden awareness of the warmth of the phone against my ear. I hold it there for a few seconds before replacing it on the desk. Then I begin to read.

It's a borderline rabid discussion about whether or not the picture is Photoshopped. About whether it's a trick of mirrors. About makeup artists people know who could totally do that, just watch this video, isn't that amazing. There are people accusing each other of being Nazis, of being gay, of being gay Nazis; spammers offering to EARN $$$ FROM HOME START TODAY. It's basically internet business as usual. But now, surreally, it's *my* business on the internet. It's like seeing a teacher in the grocery store: the shock of an uprooted face among the same old apples and oranges, the sense that these

familiar things should have nothing in common, but somehow, you are realising for the first time, they do.

I click onto the second page, and my stomach drops.

jpnfile: I CAN TELL U WAT TO DO WITH THE EXTRA HOLE

atlasunplugged: LOL

jpnfile: B==D~~ 2X

B====D~~

yaya13: SHES ASKING FOR IT SHOWING OFF LIKE THAT I
BET SHE LUVS IT IN EVERY HOLE WHATTA SLUT FREAK

I turn away from the computer, a sickening roar in my ears.
I get it, I do. Of all of the extremely obvious metaphors my
body invites, GIANT WALKING VAGINA is in the top
five; my artist's self-portrait for AP art last year was done in
the style of Georgia O'Keefe for a *reason*. But this feels more
personal than a few douchey guys at Mansion air-humping
the Hole while their girlfriends frown nearby. More vitriolic.
Behind the safe anonymity of the screen, there's an unleashing
of lust and scorn and hate that I've never felt in real life. I wrap
my left arm around my middle, as though these strangers are
in my room now, shouting *slut slut slut* in mechanical voices,
grinding the air to a pulp.

I shut down the computer and lock my bedroom door. I crawl into bed, not undressing, the blank eyes of the darkened windows heavy on my back. I hold the Hole to myself in the dark, curled up tightly around this nothing that is mine.

My secret's out.

And now the whole ugly, frightening world thinks it has the right to come in.

9

I revealed myself to the world exactly once before this, on a riverboat tour in France with Mother when I was a toddler. That day is painted for me in fuzzy, Impressionist strokes: the heat of the afternoon, the stink of river water, the sweat rolling down my neck. The relief of the breeze on my bare skin as I shed my little yellow smock. Then uproar: a scream, the sudden roiling of adult-sized limbs, the crashing cascade of international voices flooding my ears. Mother swept me into her arms, shielding me with her body, and the world was dark, then, the solidity and muscle of my mother, an eclipse of breast and bone and orange blossoms. She kept me in onesies and overalls and corduroy dresses after that, the toddler equivalent of straitjackets, until I was old enough to understand: shirts can come off at the doctor's. Shirts do not come off outside.

Mother spent the rest of my life making sure that the Hole was a secret. 'You don't know what you're getting into,' she said tersely, when I saw a circus on TV at six and begged to be allowed to join. I had an entire plan, a magic act: THE AMAZING HOLE GIRL! I would 'swallow' things on stage, make a toy rabbit disappear, dollar bills, a key. I would throw in a few cartwheels. I would be the most famous girl in the world.

'Exactly,' Mother said. 'Don't.'

I always thought it was to keep me out of the clutches of the mad scientists I saw in movies and cartoons, with their beakers and lab coats and static-shocked hair. But I am beginning to understand, now, something my mother learned years ago, when *Fit or Die* blew up and people started calling her 'Captain' and 'Lockjaw' and other, less kind things: how the world turns you into what it wants you to be – a villain, a symbol, a toy. A character that deserves whatever fate they've predetermined for you; a thousand invisible hands shaping you before you can form the word *no*.

'Fuck those guys,' Caro announces definitively at school the next week. 'You've got to quit looking at that stuff. It's not even about you, they're just idiots being idiots on the internet.'

'But it is about me,' I say. We're sitting on the lawn outside the art room at lunch, watching the bright clouds scuttle across the sky. It's Thursday, and the number of sexually harassing comments online has nearly doubled since last weekend. Everything in the cafeteria looked phallic. *Everything.* Carrots. Fish sticks. I couldn't even bring myself to look at the bananas.

'But it's not *you*,' Caro says. She leans back, savouring the crisp September air. Three weeks into the school year, the North Carolina summer is finally beginning to fade to sweater weather, the sun thinning over the sidewalks and trees. 'It's just the concept: girl with hole in middle. They don't know you.'

'They might,' I say. 'They might go to the Mansion.'

'Those people don't know you either,' she says. 'You're just another weirdo they see when they're drunk. Like the Viking girl. Or that guy with the face tattoo.'

'Thanks,' I mumble, shredding a blade of grass.

A group of sophomore guys shuffle by, bouncing off of each other and laughing. Caro lifts her feet to let them pass.

'You know what I mean,' she says. 'People who actually know you think you're a smart, cool, person who's probably not in the market for an anatomically unlikely threesome.' She waggles her eyebrows at me. 'Or are you?'

The sophomore guys slow. I become aware of a sudden stillness, the weight of attention bent toward me. It's a horror movie moment – *don't look up!* But I do.

There are good and bad kinds of staring. For example, the *you're so gorgeous I can't look away* stare. Or its second-cousin, the *you've got something on your face and it is kind of gross*. But this stare these boys are giving me is the worst kind: the kind you start to get from older men when you're a girl and you're thirteen or fourteen. As though they know a dark, dirty secret about you, and by meeting their eyes, you are somehow conceding that it is true.

One of the boys glances back and mutters something to his friends, and they all laugh. He turns to me and opens his mouth.

'I have to go to the bathroom,' I blurt to Caro, leaping to my feet. 'Are you coming?'

She closes her eyes, tilts her face to the sky. 'I'm good.'

'*Caro.*'

'What?' she asks, oblivious. 'I'll be right here.'

I go and stand in front of the mirror, forcing myself to breathe. Since when can sophomores freak me out? I splash cold water on my face like girls do to calm down in the movies, but because it's public school the water is lukewarm, and I don't feel any calmer, just wetter.

I emerge, blinking into the sunlight. Caro's alone on the grass, daisy-chaining small white clover blossoms absent-mindedly. The boys are gone.

'What's up?' she asks, squinting up at me.

'I think those guys were staring at me,' I say in a low voice.

She looks around. 'Which boys?'

'Those underclassmen.' She looks blank, and I say, 'The ones who were here before. You moved your feet.'

'Them?' she asks, hazily.

'Yes,' I say, urgently. 'Caro, I think they know who I am.'

'Yeah,' she says. 'It's a small school.'

'No,' I say. I gesture to my stomach. 'I mean, *who I am.*'

She lifts herself on her elbows and peers across the quad. People are scattered in clumps across picnic tables and benches, talking and eating and checking their phones. Couples are making out. The stoner kids are playing hacky sack, tie-dyed T-shirts flapping in the breeze of their bodies. Virtually all that's missing from the scene are Bambi and some cartoon bluebirds.

'Morgs,' Caro says patiently. 'You're getting paranoid. Which is a marker of narcissistic personality disorder, which is, ironically, *unlike* Narcissus, super unattractive. Kindly desist.'

'But—'

There's an eruption of laughter and squeals across the lawn, and I jump. But it's just the popular kids going about popular kid business: Ron Brickman lifting Gina Martinez over his head as she shrieks with giggles. Several lunchtime monitors are already Dementor-gliding over.

'I love you,' Caro says. 'You're *fine*. Can we run to the senior lot real quick? I want to grab something from my car.'

She rises and I follow her through the front lawn. Faces turn away from the spectacle and up at us as we pass, but fade away again, casually. It's just an ordinary day; people are just laughing and having ordinary conversations and living their ordinary lives in which they are the main characters, consumed by their own drama. Almost none of them are thinking about me. It's a kind of sad but mostly comforting realisation. Caro's right, I think, as we step out onto the heat-shimmering asphalt. I'm becoming an egomaniac—

Caro gasps, sharply. I stop short.

My car is covered in doughnuts. Plain, frosted, chocolate: marching like sugared ants across the hood, the roof. Sliding lazily down the windshield, leaving viscous trails of icing.

With whiteboard marker, someone's written an 'H' in front of each one.

HO. HO. HO.

Hole, hole, hole.

In the office, while Caro's filing the vandalism report (Mr Crowell: *Why doughnuts?* Caro: *Somebody is clearly making fun of Morgan because she is gluten-intolerant*), I text Mother's assistant to get an excused absence. Then I go home sick for the rest of the week.

I finish all of my homework on Friday morning and spend the rest of the time painting obsessively to keep myself off the internet. It's rough going at first, the weight of the brush awkward and unnatural in my hands. After a long summer of working in charcoal, paint feels like a foreign language, super *parlay voos Fran-says, donde está el baño?* But every time I close my eyes, I see the liquid lights of the Mansion bouncing over the crowd, splashing the world in magenta and violet and cyan, and I want more than anything to flood everything with colour. To make my canvases into tiny doors into that world.

I perk up when Caro drops in the door that evening, looking frazzled in her Walgreens uniform and aquamarine eyeshadow. 'Hi,' I say from the living room floor, where I'm crouching like Gollum in front of the easel. 'Hi, hi, hi.'

'Hi, castaway,' she says. She holds out an azure bottle. 'This came, from your mom. It's supposed to be lotus and white tea, but I think it smells like feet, kind of?'

I glance at the label – ALANNA STONE VENUS RISING SPA FRAGRANCE. PRE-MARKET. NOT FOR RESALE – and set it to the side. Caro takes in my rainbow-smeared arms, the variously terrible paintings leaning up against the skirting boards of the room, drying. 'So,' she says, carefully. 'How's solitary confinement?'

I fling myself backwards onto the warped hardwood. 'So *boring*. But now you're home! Let's hang out! Let's watch vintage horror movies and make every flavour of popcorn!'

She collapses into the ratty rose-printed wingback chair we got at a yard sale. 'I'm going to a show with Todd tonight.'

'Noooooooo,' I moan.

'You're welcome to come.'

'Noooooooo.'

She studies my painting. 'Are those doughnuts?'

I sit up protectively, Secret Security-blocking the canvas with my body. 'Maybe,' I say. 'The Loblolly lady told me to make art from experience. This is me. Arting from experience.' I add, dramatically, 'Arting from *trauma*.'

'Morgs, I don't want to diminish your trauma—'

'Thank you. Kindly do not.'

Caro sighs. 'Are you coming back to school tomorrow?'

I mix up bright pink and start adding sprinkles to a doughnut, spelling *slut*.

'You've got to come back sometime.'

'They know,' I say. 'Somebody at school recognised me. Soon everyone's going to know.' I sprinkle the doughnut harder, and harder. 'I won't be able to get away from it.'

'And what if they do recognise you?' Caro asks. 'You've been going out for weeks. Raleigh's not big. The internet's even smaller. It's not surprising people know who you are. Or if not, that they'll find out pretty soon. You must have known this would happen eventually.'

The top of the doughnut has gone entirely pink. I set down the brush.

'It's not that they know,' I say at last. 'It's just. I came out because I wanted to be who I am and not hide it. I want to have that be okay. I want to walk into a room and feel the way normal people do when they walk into a room. Like, *hey, Kevin's here, awesome! Now we can all keep doing exactly what we were doing but it will be way better!* That's what the Mansion is for me. Or at least, it was. Now it's all *get your camera, I'm gonna hurl, two holes one girl lols!*'

Caro crosses the room and sits behind me. She begins smoothing my hair.

'Morgs, your body is weird,' she says. 'People are going to be weird about it. You either have to be okay with that, or you have to hide.'

'But that's messed up,' I say. 'It's like guys who say that rape victims were "asking for it" by wearing short skirts. Nobody *asks* to be raped. I'm not *asking* to be stalked and fetishised by internet weirdos and pastry vandals.' I turn to her. 'What

66

about you, Miss Body Revolution? When you wear short dresses and fitted clothing, are you *asking* people to call you fat?'

She leans back from me, chewing thoughtfully on the end of her braid.

'No,' she says, at last. 'But until the world gets better, I think I have to expect it.'

Boring Todd appears a few minutes later, bearing a small bouquet of daffodils. We sit in uncomfortable silence while Caro goes upstairs to get ready for the show.

Here's the thing: Todd is the most boring person alive, but he's actually a supremely decent human. He even knows about the Hole. Caro didn't tell – he saw it for himself once, popping upstairs while we were getting dressed to go out. Caro took him aside, spoke quietly for a few minutes. Of everyone I know, he's taken to it the most easily. He doesn't stammer on the word 'whole', or awkwardly avoid looking at my stomach, the way strangers do at the Mansion. I wish he did. It'd be nice to have an excuse to legitimately dislike him. He just has a way of making me disappear when he's around, or making Caro disappear – somehow, the two of us don't exist for each other in the same way any more. I hate it.

'How's it going, Morgan?' he asks.

'Fine,' I say, my shoulders tensing up around my ears.

He sits down on the couch, amiably, as if happy for my company. 'I'm trying to write a song,' he says. 'I think I've got the melody figured out. I just need the lyrics.'

'Cool,' I say.

We sit. He hums.

'I had some really good yogurt today,' he pipes up, hopefully. 'It was Greek.'

'That sounds great.' I turn and shout up the stairs, '*Caro.*'

She bounces down in a shell-coloured 1950s housewife dress, tied in the back with a bow. Todd looks up at her, and his breath catches. God, they're gross.

'Morgs, you sure you don't want to come?' Caro asks, beaming as Todd hands her the daffodils.

'I think I'm good,' I say. I don't really want to be alone, but there's nothing worse than a pity invite: a night of smiling and laughing to show how grateful you are to be there, and meanwhile everyone's wishing you would just leave so they can make out.

They leave, a bundle of noise and smiles and last-minute invitations. I stare at the painting a while longer, then run my fingers through the paint, streaking and marbling and digging thick rivulets until the whole thing is a muddy, swirling moonscape, pocked with canyons and craters. The house is bloated with silence.

I take the quick, shameful body shower of the Failed Human Being and lie on my bed, marinating in the chaos of detail that fills my room: art prints on the ceiling by Dalí and Escher, Shaun Tan and Jenn Hales; the bookshelves along the wall overflowing with unopened self-improvement books from Mother. On my bedside table, a fringe-haired

Barbie with a hole Caro carved into her plastic stomach with scissors for my tenth birthday leans against an X-ray of my ribs: a ghostly black-and-white ladder interrupted by a great Hole-shaped chasm.

When I moved into this room, I wanted to make it the most *me* space imaginable. But lying here now, itchy and unhappy as beads of water prickle dry on my skin, I can't help but feel my world is elsewhere.

The comments left on the Public Scrutiny photo gallery have more than doubled. I glaze past anything written in all caps or GIFs or emojis. There are still plenty of stomach-curlingly detailed sexual comments about what guys would like to do with the Hole, but they feel less shocking now. Exposure therapy, I guess. Like Mother says[1]: 'Whatever doesn't kill you will shred those abs like a Vitamix.'[2]

blrrdlinez: that hole tho

GASHer: You wouldn't even have to take turns? She could make a very profitable business out of this . . .

anayama: this is NASTEE whys she showin ppl this?? nobody wants 2 see that!!

---

1 said
2 In *Ab Destroyers: Plank Fit*

I breathe long and slow through my nose. I think about Caro, unafraid to go out in her cute dress. No, not unafraid: just loving herself too fiercely to give a shit what anyone says or thinks.

olgagarchy: I'm just saying, given that this is actually a genetic condition, and not body modification or a hoax: is it our place to classify her as 'freak'? While the stigma of being born with a differently abled body certainly hasn't gone away in the 21st century, it's less pervasive than it was in the days of Chang & Eng-style 'circus freaks'. We wouldn't classify Iraq veterans who are missing limbs as 'freaks'.

I sit up, starting to smile.

amerika2012: Yeah, but she's missing a liver not a limb

benderlvr: if she's missing a liver she shouldn't be at a bar. :D

amerika2012: lol

janeyz: Why is it any of our business what she's missing? She's not asking for our permission. She's just out dancing with her friends.

olgagarchy: I'm just saying, who are we to freak out about the differently bodied? It shouldn't be our place to tell her to hide her body if she doesn't want to hide it. If she thinks her body is beautiful enough to bring it out in public, more power to her.

slingshot87: Amen olga, that's pretty fucking brave.

The thread goes on a few comments further (spanky-mod66: POWER TO THE FREAKS!), and I read to the end, feeling a blush of warmth that curls down to my toes. The comments fill me the way hot cocoa does when you come in from the snow – the low and quiet, yellow-kitchen warmth of being safe and loved. I click on their screen names, hoping to pair them with faces, but the profiles reveal nothing significant: olgagarchy posts often, slingshot87 mostly comments on music-related stories, janeyz has been a member since October 2013. I doodle the names onto a sheet of paper, wondering who these people are who have said these true, generous things; who have taken me seriously and said, *yes, just being who you are is a brave thing.*

I bookmark the page, then pull out the Sea World T-shirt.

The world feels new as I leave the apartment. I step out like a foal, trembling past earlier terrors, the potential in my canvas humming behind me as I head out into a night rich with kindness.

10

I shed my sweater (oversized, navy blue, covered in little country geese) and slip onto the dance floor, fending off the usuals: the endless spin cycle of college students and hipsters and lonely adults looking for a thing they can't name and not finding it here, either. My skin hums with self-consciousness. It's strange being here and knowing that I'm being watched, and recorded – that tomorrow, a dozen new photos of me will go up on a website I have no control over. It makes me want to be careful, at first – to never get caught in a sneeze or a yawn or a moment where one of my eyes is half-open – but I feel cradled by the knowledge that at least some of the Public Scrutineers will treat me kindly, generously. I smile into the music, and feel my body melt away.

But a tap on my shoulder pulls me back to earth. I shrug it off at first, but there it is again, a gentle *knock-knock-knock*. As if to say, *I-know-you*. I turn.

The guy is cute, cuter than I usually pay attention to or trust. He's older, too, probably in college. He shouts something that I can't hear, and I ignore him. But he leans down and tries again, directly in my ear.

'Buy you a drink?'

I shake my head. I try to keep dancing, but the guy's chest is in my face. He leans over me, and I clip his throat with my shoulder.

'Water?' he shouts.

I blink up at him. 'What?' I shout.

His breath is hot on my ear, steam in a room full of steam.

'Do you want a water?' he shouts. 'Or, like, a Coke or something.'

'No,' I shout.

'What?' he shouts.

'Don't buy me anything,' I shout.

'Why?' he shouts.

'I can buy my own drinks,' I shout.

'That's boring,' he shouts.

I shrug, exaggerated. It is a shout-shrug. 'I guess I'm boring,' I shout.

His eyes flicker to the Hole. My eyes flicker away: to the wall, to the stage, to the ceiling – to some other space, where a cute college guy is not looking at this part of my body I can't change and thinking that it tells him anything about who I am.

I feel a rush of warmth on my right ear and glance up, too late, to see his jaw at my cheek. *Too sexy to be boring*, uncurls in a breath, like a kiss. And then he's gone.

73

I feel a hiss around my ankles as I stand there, dumbly, the rest of the dance floor bouncing on without me. It's such an obvious line, obviously meaningless. But nobody but Caro has ever called me sexy before.

The smoke machine fog curls up around my waist, and my eyes sting with frustration and particulate matter. I try to keep dancing, but my heart's not in it. A glittering girl next to me is trying to get a shot of me on her camera phone while her friends flail like sexy rag dolls to the beat. All of a sudden I know I can't do it any more. I'm so tired of being the Girl with the Hole.

I turn to go and smack right into the cute boy. He's holding two cups. He bows, extends one with a flourish.

'A boring drink,' he shouts in my ear, 'for a boring girl.'

This is the number one rule of being a Vulnerable Young Woman Alone at a Party, or a Club, or In Public Anywhere At Any Time: *do not drink a drink handed to you by a strange man*.

But I'm tired of being a vulnerable young woman. I'm tired of saying no to life.

I take a sip. It tastes like Coke.

'Did you put drugs in it?' I shout.

'What?' he shouts.

'Drugs,' I shout.

'Nope,' he shouts. 'Drugging chicks is shitty.'

I flash him a smile. The Coke simmers acidic around my molars.

'Thanks,' I shout.

He grins at me. 'It's cool,' he shouts. He reaches out with his free hand, squeezes my shoulder. Dance floors are all about skin on skin, being jostled and stepped on and grabbed. But this touch is intentional, his hand strong and soft. Warmth roils my stomach.

'Hey,' I shout. 'Did you say I was sexy? Before, I mean?'

He grins. It is a beautiful thing, ruler-straight and dimpled. I always thought the concept of dimples was fundamentally weird. Little pock-marks in people's faces, attractive? But now I understand: these are places where surprise tenderness lies. Dimples you could curl up and go to sleep in.

'I call it like I see it,' he shouts. Then he waves to somebody over my head, and says, 'Hold on.'

I try to keep dancing, but it's difficult with the Coke sloshing around in the cup, and I feel irritated and flattered and dumb. I wander off the dance floor, stash the cup on a table. I wonder if the cute guy is watching from somewhere, or if Public Scrutiny is, or nobody. I wait a while and then wander towards my car, the memory of that word, *sexy*, wrapped around me like the sweater that I'll realise I forgot later.

Safely at home, I creep past Caro's room, close and lock my bedroom door, check and double-check the shades.

Then I approach the mirror, which hangs, dusty, inside my closet door, where it dutifully spends its days reflecting my winter coats back into the dark. I don't spend much time with mirrors. I'm not afraid of the self-esteem damage that inevitably comes of staring into a two-dimensional pane of glass and wishing you were somebody three-dimensionally different. It's just kind of boring. (I tried covering them all last week, while I was working on a self-portrait in black and white and wanted to see if I'd start unconsciously picturing my face in greyscale, but Caro came home and delivered an hour-long lecture titled *This Had Better Be Because You're Sitting Shiva and Not Because You Have a Fucked-Up Self Image, Because You're Gorgeous, You Idiot.*)

Alone, now, I study my reflection: yep, still stick skinny.

Yep, still dusted with freckles that Caroline calls 'adorable' and I call 'sun damage'.

But I feel the bright joy of that word racing beneath my skin. I stare at my face, my body, the Hole, wondering where the *sexy* is that he saw. I've never felt capital-s Sexy, that tidal wave of power and invulnerability and infinite cleavage. Sexy was, as defined by my childhood viewings of *Grease* – a thing to grow into, to do a dance number about; a thing that all teen girls could access if they had the right lip gloss and Victoria's Secret PINK cheekies and convertibles driven by the right boys. A thing that happens to girls who aren't cripplingly unhappy in their own skins. A thing that never happened for me.

But then, for a moment, there was tonight.

11

The next few nights I haunt the edges of the crowd at Mansion, trying to look for the Coke guy without seeming like I'm looking for him. But when the next weekend rolls around and he hasn't reappeared, I begin to lose all hope.

'I am going to be alone for ever,' I announce to Caro at Java Jane that Saturday afternoon. The coffee shop is on the NC State campus but is popular with my classmates, and I crept into the warm, brightly lit front room only after verifying that the coast was clear. I've been trying to keep a low profile at school all week. It honestly hasn't been too bad – some whispers and stares, sure, and a new security officer patrolling the parking lot – but I still feel twitchy in public, invisible eyes tickling the back of my neck.

Caro laughs, looking up from her watch. 'You're not going to be alone for ever,' she says.

'I'm going to be alone, and I'm going to die a virgin.'

Caro sighs, tucks a slim pile of flashcards into her apron pocket. 'Morgs, you're beautiful. I know it. You know it. Cute boys at clubs know it.'

'One boy.'

'A stunningly handsome boy.'

I groan and drop my head to the counter, knocking a few points off Java Jane's sanitation rating. 'He doesn't really like me.'

'He bought you a Coke. It's very charming.'

'I don't trust charming.'

'Dear Morgan: how did I end up with a best friend who was such a cynic?'

I stare into the space between us, casting about for some truth to fling into it. *Because I'm a freak. Because guys are always after something. Because I'm seventeen, and I've always thought I was going to die alone, and it is too intoxicating and painful and wonderful to believe that after a lifetime of hiding who I am, somebody might like me for exactly that.*

'Must be my dazzling good looks,' I say at last.

'Precisely,' she says. 'Hey, do you have a quarter? I want Skittles.'

'Take one from the tip jar.'

'I am,' she says. 'It's called "the tip jar of our friendship".'

'You're the worst,' I say, fishing in my pocket. 'I'm a starving artist, did you know that?'

'Yeah,' she says. 'My tax dollars support people like you. Twist the handle extra hard, it'll give you more candy.'

'My mother supports people like me,' I say, cranking the dial. A small, bright cascade of candy pours into my palm like rain. Caro leans forward, begins picking the reds and purples out of my palm, leaving me the greens, yellows and oranges.

'Well, she's a taxing woman,' she says. 'So, hey, I was thinking—'

The bell chimes and she dumps the candy in my hand, putting on a customer-service face as she wipes her palms. I scoot further down the counter while Caro takes a sandwich order, asks about somebody's divorce. She takes a genuine interest in people. It's adorable and annoying.

I sigh and settle in as the guy at the counter talks about who's going to get the dog, and I begin rearranging the to-go cups in order of aesthetic pleasingness. I lift the bottom one and uncover a small stack of flash cards: *neophyte. Rococo. Vexation.*

The customer goes and Caro washes her hand at the sink. She turns and I wave *ignominious* at her. She turns off the water.

'So, yeah,' she says, as though continuing a conversation we'd both been a part of. 'I've been looking at applying to college.'

'Yeah, I know,' I say. 'In two years.'

'Next year,' she says.

There's a pang in my chest, a quick fizzle of anxiety.

'Oh,' I say. 'Wow. That's awesome.'

'I've been reading up on financial aid,' she says, drying her hands. 'And if I get my SATs up, I qualify for merit-based aid at Northeastern.'

'In Boston,' I say, stupidly.

She nods, face glowing.

'Like, seven hundred-miles-away-Boston.'

'Yeah,' she says, like it's obvious. 'They have one of the best sociology programmes in the country.'

'But we had a plan,' I say. 'Our gap year.' The year we were meant to spend together between high school and college, hitchhiking and doing guerrilla art projects and – I don't know. Being Morgan and Caro, I guess, for one last little piece of forever, before the real thing came and swept us away.

'I know,' she says. 'But I've just been thinking. Why wait to get started on living our lives? I mean, look at you. Your world has expanded by a factor of ten in the last month alone. And all you did was change your shirt.'

'Yeah,' I say. 'You can, too. None of that necessitates going away to college.'

'I want that,' she says. She beams down at the counter as she runs a cloth over it. 'I want to grow. To be something. I can either spend the next two years making people coffee and punching in coupon codes for Oreos and scraping together enough change to go to the two-dollar movie on weekends, or I can knuckle down this year and then go do something bigger. Meet people who are making things they're excited about and doing things that might change the world a little so that maybe someday I can too, instead of spending the rest of my life working part-time jobs that make me want to jump off a bridge.' She pulls a quarter out of the tip jar, rolls it across her knuckles. 'I've been reading all of these articles by these amazing, super-smart women about being more than society gives you permission to be,' she says. 'And then we changed Jane today, and it made me think, you know? It kind of seemed like a sign.'

I follow her gaze to the mannequin, Java Jane, sitting in the front window. The employees change its (her?) outfit once a month, in accordance with holidays, or the seasons, or a game against NC State's arch-rivals, UNC and Duke. Today, Java Jane is sporting a Catholic schoolgirl's uniform and a back-pack, wearing a bright yellow button that says NUMBER #1 TEACHER.

'Java Jane's slutty back-to-school outfit made you want to go to college?'

'Yeah, kind of.' She turns to me, a challenging eyebrow lifted. 'Plus, all day long I hear the State students talking about classes, and registration, and what dorm they're in, and I feel like I'm missing out, you know? Most of Todd's friends have already graduated. Everyone I know is starting to talk about college visits and SATs.'

'Not everybody.'

'*Almost* everybody,' she says. 'Don't you ever feel weird about that?'

I stack and restack the cups. I don't say, *only my entire life.*

Because the thing is, I have thought about it.

Of course I have.

As last summer stretched on, the conversations at the YYS shows turned to majors and mini fridges. One by one I watched the healthy, happy, sun-kissed people around us turn to the future. I know it's long past time to start thinking about joining the real world.

I just can't ever imagine the world feeling ready for *me*.

'You should come with me, Morgs,' Caro says. 'It'll be great. We can sign up for feminist film theory courses and learn Russian and ironically rush a sorority together.'

I open my mouth to reply, but somebody comes up to the counter for a refill, and Caro ducks to fill it. Then the bell chimes, and there's a bright burst of customers through the door. Then another. The line stretches on and on. I unstack all of the cup sleeves and pretend they are bubbles underwater, and I am drowning. I wait for Caro to be free so I can breathe again.

When the line of customers becomes so deep that Johnny the Androgynously Sexy Tattooed Dishwasher has to emerge from the back to help take orders, I blow Caro a kiss and drop the rest of the Skittles into the tip jar with the pennies and dollar bills. I cycle slowly home, away from the university. The sun is hot, but the air is just beginning to crisp again, summer shaking its wet dog hide and creeping, remorsefully, under the porch to make way for autumn. I try to imagine my life without Caroline in it as I coast towards home.

What do I have without my best friend? Some internet stalkers, a guy who bought me a soda, a doctor who won't come clean with me and a wreck of a fledgling art career that my mom's more interested in than I am. And it's all okay right now, knowing that I can come home to affirmative sticky notes and sprawling vegetarian chili dinners, to someone who will try optimistically to weave braids in my too-short hair and tell me that of course I won't be alone for ever. But without Caro there to hold it together, my life is just a collection of disparate pieces, incidental and sad. Like that poem we read last year in English, when we did *Things Fall Apart*: the centre cannot hold.

These are the things I'm thinking when a guy jumps in front of my bike.

12

I scream and jerk the handlebars hard to the right, bumping up over the kerb. I spill onto the concrete, knees and elbows stinging.

'Oh my God,' says a voice, rushing over. A boy's hand is in my face, reaching for my arm, helping me up. 'Are you okay?'

'Yeah,' I say, groggily. I extricate myself from my bike, which clangs to the sidewalk in a protest of clicking spokes. I take in everything slowly, mechanically: the wheels don't seem bent, which is good. My elbow is bleeding a little, which is bad. I turn my attention to the guy in front of me. He's about my age, pale, with thin features and a yellow T-shirt, baggy and oversized.

'What were you doing in the bike lane?' I ask. I feel thick-tongued, stupid with gratitude to be alive. Thanks heaps, adrenalin. 'You should be more careful.'

'Yeah,' he says, running a hand over the back of his neck. 'I know. I'm sorry. I just wanted to get your attention.'

My focus sharpens. He looks up at me through his eyebrows, gaze guiltily flickering to my stomach.

'You're Morgan Stone, right?' he asks.

Oh, my God.

'Oh my God,' I say out loud. 'Are you kidding me?'

He flinches a little. 'I know; it was a stupid way to try to get your attention—'

'*Stupid*?' My voice is rising. 'Stupid. You nearly got me *killed*.'

'I know,' he says. 'I'm sorry. Just – look. I found your picture online, and I needed to—'

A trickle of blood runs down my elbow and spatters on the sidewalk.

'Needed to what?' My tone is deadly calm now. 'Needed to get a look for yourself? Needed to tell me in person how I can fuck myself? Needed to come get a photo, so your friends, if you even have any, will believe you met the freak in real life?'

The jerk looks completely stunned. Whatever he expected – a cringing girl, a cooing flirt – I am not it.

'I just,' he sputters.

'You don't *need* to do anything,' I tell him. 'You *need* to let me live my own life in my own body and respect that it has nothing to do with you.'

I fling my leg over my bike and turn back to him as I push away. 'Tell all your little friends. I'm over this.'

*

My elbow stings the whole way home, and I can feel a bruise forming on my solar plexus where it knocked into the handlebars, and I have school on Monday and tomorrow my doctor will tell me that I'm probably dying, but right now, lord almighty, I feel like a queen.

At home, I log into Public Scrutiny. I create a new user: MissAbyss. Enough sitting on the sidelines while other people control my narrative. I am queen of the night. I am do-not-stare-too-long-into-me-because-I-will-stare-back-into-you.

I sweep through the board. I correct. I excoriate. I do not use emojis. When some idiot proposes omg she could totally do 138, get it, double 69??, I smack him down so hard with anatomical logic that I can practically see his head spin on the other side of the internet.

I push back from the computer, cracking my neck, and get dressed to go out. Behind me, my laptop chimes, and chimes again, and favourites and notifications and upvotes come flooding into my account. I don't even care. I own this night.

I breeze past the bouncer and step into the Mansion, and a roar goes up. I lift my arms and grin, letting the blue and silver lights wash over me. I drink them in. I am filled, and alive. I pull my sweater off and fling it into the crowd, and then a searing light blinds my vision.

I look up through the dazzling dark just in time to see them charging in: an android-faced young reporter, immaculately coiffed and lipsticked, flanked by a cameraman and two tech guys in black. People are pointing at me, and trying to jostle into the view of the camera. One girl shouts to no one in particular, 'Leave her alone! Leave her alone!'

The anchorwoman gets in my face. 'Morgan Stone,' she shouts over the music. I think. Even this close, it's mostly just lip-reading. 'Your mother, Alanna, has made a career from pushing the perfect body. How does she feel about yours?'

I freeze, knocked totally off balance.

I know the press. I get the press. Mother mostly kept me out of the spotlight, but I'm used to seeing a parade of cameras and microphones trotted through our huge, freezing house. Mother was even a cover girl, briefly, when I was eight and *Fit or Die* blew up. 'They will take everything you say out of context,' she told me one night, five vodka martinis in over an unflattering story in *Cosmo*. 'And no matter what you do, they will make you look the way they want you to look. You can be a *saint*, Morgan. A saint. And they'll turn you into Charles Manson.'

I blink, panicked, into the camera's spotlight for a second, and I suddenly understand the phrase *deer in the headlights*. Then I dive into the writhing crowd.

It was one thing to yell at a kid on the street. To anonymously rage at a bunch of trolls on the internet. But this is way too big. This, I don't know how to control.

Also, Mother is going to kill me.

I crawl to the centre of the dance floor and huddle beneath the central disco ball in a half-crouch. I can see the camera's spotlight bobbing around. I feel like an insect: voiceless, cowering, wanting nothing more than to skitter from the light.

The people around me are mostly too drunk to call attention to me. A large woman in an aqua bodysuit stares, and I worry for a second that she'll out me. But then the rational voice in my head whispers, *she's staring because you're squatting on a dance floor like a total weirdo*, and I straighten up and push away, heading towards the empty stage at the back of the room.

A hand on my shoulder stops me in my tracks. I jerk away, and turn. It's the cute guy.

He is taller than I remembered; his eyes, in the strobe light, something beyond blue. I have never tasted anything that colour.

He smiles, bends down to my ear. 'Looks like you've got an audience,' he says.

'Yeah,' I say. A sudden howl of feedback erases my voice from the room, but he must be able to see the panic in my face. He puts his hand on my elbow. Despite myself, I feel a rushing warmth, my whole universe coalescing into the pads of four fingers, of skin on skin.

The camera crew are circling the dance floor like sharks. I want this man to be the sweet, confident hero who knows me better than either of us is willing to admit, the one who will claim me, fold me up in his arms and take me away, the one who will save me from myself.

But he doesn't.

He just stands there.

And because I've been waiting for seventeen years and my patience has worn thin and the back door beckons like a metaphor, I'm the one who says, 'Want to get out of here?'

'Okay,' he says. An easy smile, but eyes jumping from the Hole to my face and back to the Hole again. 'Yeah, I do.'

There is a shout behind me. A bevy of college students surges toward us, phones extended and flashing.

'Hurry,' I tell the Coke guy. He laughs and pulls me forward, and the crowd's protests flutter to the ground like paper as the door slides shut and we plunge together into the night.

We creep past the darkened news vans out front, skirting streetlights. Once off the block, I begin to giggle. I try to smother it, but the laughter crawls up out of my throat, hysterical. The Coke guy starts to laugh, too, but his laughter is a question mark. He gestures back towards the Mansion.

'So,' he says.

I shake my head. 'Can we just not talk about it?'

'Sure,' he says. 'Not talking. I am excellent at not talking.'

I laugh, and he laughs, and I look at him in the streetlight. He jerks his head over his shoulder, like this is a language that we speak now, and begins to walk. Brimming with hope and fear and wishing, I follow.

We trace the veins of the city with our feet and come to rest in a small park. We lie beneath the swings, staring up at the sky. The stars are dim through the sweaty haze of light pollution and the collective body heat of the city. We listen to the soft creak of the chains in the breeze, bits of mulch slowly gluing themselves to my back and thighs.

His name is Chad. Of course it is.

'What does that mean?' he laughs when I tell him this.

'I don't know,' I lie. I know exactly. 'You look like a Chad. Or a Brent. Or a ... I don't know. Masculine Monosyllabic White Dude Name.'

He laughs again, a flash of Ken-doll teeth. His laugh is a little uncomfortable. I regret making the joke. I regret not just saying, *you look like this friend/cousin of mine who is also named Chad! Ha ha, small world!* But then there's the risk of his saying, *um, I remind you of your cousin?* and then I would stammer and flush and explain that I am not actually incestuous, that that is just a stereotype about Girls With Holes In Their Torsos that is not actually true, and then he would say, *wait, that's a stereotype?* and at that point I realise that even my fantasy version of him is pretty dense, and start to question my own lack of self-respect, at which point my brain might actually begin to melt.

'Okay, I guess,' he says. He pokes me in the arm. 'Well, you look like a ... Holly.'

I tingle a little bit, touched by the attention. *Somebody thinks I look like a something! Somebody has been paying enough attention to me to think he knows something about me!* I laugh, poke him back. 'Why Holly?'

'You know?' he says. 'Like Holey?'

I try to pretend my world isn't shattering inside. 'Ugh,' I groan.

He chuckles. 'Come on,' he says. 'I thought it was pretty funny.'

I'm not sure which is worse: that he identifies me as Holey, or that he thinks this is a good joke.

'Hey,' he says, suddenly. He takes my hand. It is an impulsive gesture, sweet. 'I'm sorry,' he says. 'I didn't mean to offend you. It's just. I don't know.' He looks me up and down in the orange streetlight, taking me in. 'You're different from anyone else I've ever met.'

I say, 'Most girls don't have a tunnel through their torsos.'

His eyes flick to the Hole again. It's something he can't help, a hiccup. 'That's not what I mean,' he says.

I laugh, but my heart feels bruised. 'Sure it is,' I say. 'I mean, let's be honest.'

He runs his knuckles up and down my bare arm. My skin prickles all over, twelve hundred sparks of electricity.

'It's okay,' I say. I am having a little trouble focusing. His fingers trace my shoulder, my collarbone. 'I guess I am kind of –' my voice catches, '– a freak.'

'Hey, don't say that,' he says, softly. His voice drops, becoming low and husky, and because it seems a little ungainly, a little awkward and uncalculated, I like it. His fingers trace my cheek. 'You know,' he says, 'you're pretty cool.'

And then his lips are on mine, and the softness is coming in waves. Beyond us, the world is night; above us, an orange streetlamp singing hallelujah. I'm out in the warm velvet night on the earth in the open air in the arms of a handsome stranger who is the first boy to kiss me after having seen me for everything that I am. I feel the earth digging into my shoulder blades and drink in his kisses like a seed finally cracking its hard outer shell and beginning to reach for the light.

Something begins to build in me, to thrill deep in my belly. A heat. He has thrown one leg over mine, and is pressing into me. Hand circling lightly up my stomach, and I am fighting the urge to remove it, or to guide it closer, when there is a startling flash of light, and a shout.

The cameras have found us.

I lose Chad in the explosion of flashes that scatter starbursts in my eyes as I cover my face with my hands, scramble to my feet, and run. The shouts and lights fade as I stumble through alleys and into places girls shouldn't be alone at night, or ever, slowing only when my legs threaten to give out. Mother's voice snaps in the back of my mind, *Morgan, for heaven's sakes, get an Uber*, but I scuttle from the thought on terrified crab legs. Everything feels enormous and threatening now, except the safe pools of streetlight that I count like blessings until I am home.

I knock on the door to my apartment long after midnight – my keys probably spilled out somewhere in the dark and humid playground mulch. I lean my head against the door frame, exhausted. My knocks are intermittent, the coded flashing of a lighthouse out into the dark. I am signalling safe harbours, I am signalling coral shoals to submarine blades. When I'm this tired, everything seems too flat, too hard, too real. Over my head, the stairwell fluorescents mercilessly illuminate everything with the unsentimental detailing of hospital lights: my dishevelled hair; my red and blistered little toes curling like shrimp in my ill-chosen shoes.

Caroline opens the door after minutes or seconds, face rumpled and unwashed. She makes a sound when she sees me. I am gratified to see the flood of worry in her sleep-small eyes.

'Are you okay?' she asks.

I shake my head.

'Do you want to talk about it?'

I kind of nod, and kind of shake, and without a word, she opens her arms. I fall into them.

She sets me on the couch with a soft flannel blanket, switches on warm yellow lamps. She disappears and returns in a moment with a box of tissues.

'Do I need to call 911?' she asks.

I shake my head.

'Are you sure?'

I nod. I cup the tissue box in my lap like a fallen egg. Caro says, 'So what happened?'

I look up at her and force a smile. 'The press found out about me.'

It sounds ridiculous the second the words leave my mouth. But Caro doesn't say, *that's why you're knocking on our door at three a.m.?* Instead she pulls my head into her lap, smooths my hair. The apartment is warm with the murmurs of domesticity: the scent of vanilla, the comforting echoes of silverware clinking, cabinets opening and shutting. Even the quiet is so much fuller when Caro is here.

Then I feel the weight of the air shift, and sit up. Todd's here. Of course he is. It's not like Caro's life pauses when I'm not there. Just the other way around.

'Hey Morgan,' Todd says, without affect. He looks sleepy, loose-limbed in a white T-shirt and cotton drawstring pyjama pants, balancing three mugs of cocoa. 'How's it going?'

I just nod. Caro reaches up to relieve him of the mugs. I reach for one instinctively, like a child.

'I'm sorry to bother you guys,' I say.

'You're not bothering us,' Todd says, and Caro just says, 'Shh.'

I sit between them and we sip our cocoa, Caro leaning against my shoulder, Todd awkward but close, his arm thrown across the back of the sofa. I can feel myself growing warm and sleepy. This is what it means, I think dimly, feeling Caro lift the mug from my hands from somewhere far away. This is what it means to have people who will never leave you. A blanket, a cocoa, and two warm shoulders to fall asleep on when everything else around you is exploding in strange fireworks, altering the starscape above your little world for ever.

13

My car is still marooned by the Mansion, probably fluttering with parking tickets, so Caro drives me to Dr Takahashi's office in the morning. She says little on the ride over, and for this, I am grateful. The radio murmurs softly, and the smell of cooling coffee curls up from an open thermos in the cup holder. I realise too late that it's meant to be for me – Caro's a tea drinker – and let it sit quietly between us, warming the car with its fragrance.

We park for a moment and sit. Then she unclicks her seat-belt and goes to open her door. 'You don't have—' I begin, with a rush of relief.

'Sure I do,' she says, swinging her bag onto her shoulder. I hurry to catch up.

When we turn the corner, flashbulbs explode in our faces. Caro swears magnificently as the microphones descend like locusts.

'Hole Girl!' a man shouts.

'Are you excited—'

'How do you feel?'

I spy at least three different network logos, five cameras, a multicoloured flurry of blazers. Beyond the primped and powdered anchorpersons are a clump of unmistakably ordinary people, holding cameras and iPhones aloft. I cringe, unconsciously hollowing my body around the Hole. For a fleeting moment I think I can turn my whole self inside-out, disappear into it, and never have to feel anyone's eyes on me again. But Caro grips my arm and surges forward through the knot of reporters towards the clinic until we stumble through the front doors, the cameras behind us clicking greedily.

'Jesus,' Caro mutters as we take the elevator up to the third floor. 'You didn't tell me it was this bad.'

'It wasn't.' I slump against the wall. 'I can never go outside again.'

'God, I just want to go out there and punch somebody.'

I try to imagine Caro throwing right hooks in her yellow sundress and daisy-printed flats. Once upon a time, this would have made me laugh, but not today. Today I want to spend the morning riding up and down with my best friend in these few square feet, listening to canned soft jazz and existing in a place between floors. But the doors slide open with a gentle ding, and there, immaculate in an expensive charcoal suit, is my mother.

'I'm dead,' I whisper.

She has her back to us, but it's unmistakably Mother: hip cocked, arms crossed, rapping out words to Dr Takahashi

96

that make him look like he wants to disappear into the floor. She is a tall, handsome woman with a physicality that might be called lanky if she were younger and more boyish. There is something unremittingly severe in the length of her limbs, as though, given the burden of carrying around these few inches of bone, she has no patience left for you and yours. On camera, she smiles with a terrible ferocity, telling unseen housewives through clenched, perfect teeth that they're doing excellent squats.

She turns, and sees me. I resist the urge to mash the Door Close button.

She is not smiling.

'Keep your back straight, Morgan,' she says brusquely, crossing to me. 'You look like a bonobo monkey. Why haven't you returned my calls?'

'Mother – ow.' I shift away from her as she presses her thumbs into the balls of my shoulders, pushing them back. 'Mother, what are you doing here? If this is about the media, then I'm sorry, you were right—'

'The what?' she asks, turning me around. 'Oh. Them. No, that was bound to happen sooner or later.' She brushes a perfunctory hand through my short hair and sighs.

'Then what—' I begin, but she shushes me, her eyes on the doctors. I turn to Caro, who raises her eyebrows in a silent question. Over by the empty reception desk, Dr Takahashi huddles with a red-headed woman in a white lab coat. Small clusters of people in casual dress dot the waiting room, sipping coffee from Styrofoam cups. At first I assume that they are fellow patients, but then realise with a chill that they are all, with varying degrees of subtlety, staring at me. There is a sharpness in their gazes that belies medical training. The cuts of their multitudinous jaws are crisp. Clipboards perch in their hands; there are small mics, visual recording equipment.

My guts tighten like a drawstring. Caro's hand reaches out, and I lace my fingers with hers as the woman in the lab coat steps forward. Her smile looks uncomfortable, straining at the cage of her cheeks. She extends a hand and, reluctantly, I drop Caro's to shake it. The woman's grasp is firm, almost hard. She holds on just a minute too long.

'Morgan Stone,' the woman says. 'It's a pleasure to finally meet you. Parker Morse. I head the genetic abnormality team at the Crestfield Medical Group out of New York.'

I glance at Dr Takahashi in confusion, but as always, his expression is unreadable. The light glints off his glasses.

'What?' I ask, but the woman is already reaching backwards, ushering forwards. She says,

'And this is Howie.'

There's a rustle of motion as a boy about my age rises from his chair and comes over to join us. He's slender-faced with thick, honey-brown curls and a baggy yellow T-shirt. I blink at him, the memory of adrenalin beginning to claw through my veins as it clicks into place: it's the boy who jumped in front of my bike.

My eyes jump from him to the red-haired woman and back again. 'What are you—'

The boy lifts his shirt, and behind me, Caro gasps.

Sitting squat as an egg on the left side of his lower abdomen is a lump. An oblong protrusion of unmistakable smooth skin. I stare at it and know it immediately: it's *exactly* the shape of the Hole.

It's the perfect fit.

14

'I've been working with Howie since his adolescence.' Dr Morse stands too close to me as she speaks, leaning slightly forward, as though to peer through my eyes and see where in my body this information lands. 'His is a unique deformity. We've tried multiple excision procedures, and the lump grows back nearly overnight, to precisely the same size and shape. Core extractions, chemical burns and freezing produce the same effect. As you can see: no scarring. Pristine, smooth flesh.' She reaches out, handling the Lump with a cool professionalism. The boy flinches. But he doesn't move.

'I don't see what this has to do with Morgan,' Caro says, chin set. But I'm beginning, through my shock, to guess what this has to do with me, and I suspect Caro is, too. Dr Morse's smile jumps back onto her face, straining around her teeth.

'And who is this?' she asks.

'Her best friend,' Caro says.

The doctor nods and smiles. 'Ah,' she says, eyes flitting to Mother.

'Caroline is practically family,' Mother says, but something in Morse's face makes her own close like a purse. She turns to Caroline. 'Would you mind giving us a moment?' she asks, low.

For the first time, I become truly frightened. Because Mother never concedes to anyone.

Dr Morse begins walking away, leading us out of the waiting area and towards the heavy door that leads to the exam rooms. I glance back to Caro, but she is standing by the window over the reporter-filled parking lot, looking away from me. The closing door eclipses her as she magnificently flips someone the bird. And then my best friend is gone, and I'm alone with the doctors, the researchers, my mother. And the boy.

'I realise this must come as a bit of a shock,' Dr Morse says smoothly as we glide down the hall. The researchers crowd in after us, filling the space with a hushed cloud of rustling, the sighs of fabric. 'But rest assured, Morgan, the DNA sequence of your genetic material, juxtaposed with Howie's, is rather stunning.'

I shoot the boy a sidelong glance, but he doesn't meet my gaze. His skinny arms stick out of the sleeves of his baggy T-shirt like wings.

Dr Morse continues, 'We've prepared a short presentation on what this extraordinary DNA match might mean, and the subsequent series of treatments we would like to propose for you and Howie. Morgan, I'm confident we can persuade you that your participation in this process would be highly beneficial. Howie's already agreed. Everything hinges on your consent.'

'Consent to what?' I ask.

'Cure you,' Mother breaks in. 'Morgan, they think they can finally fix the Hole.'

The gnat-cloud of research scientists is wafted back to the waiting room by Dr Takahashi under the frigid gaze of my mother. Taka then unlocks an office door, and we file in, sit around a table. He tells us: cure is a hasty word.

Dr Morse says: Okay, *treat*, but we have great optimism.

Dr Takahashi: The methods aren't proven.

Dr Morse: Yet.

Dr Takahashi: We will be 100 per cent certain before we make any moves.

Dr Morse: We will be pioneers.

I grip the edge of the table. My traitorous pulse is pounding *hope, no, hope, no, hope.*

Dr Morse throws charts and graphs up onto the wall, shows us the MRIs. Howie's organs are clustered around his Lump the same way mine are around the Hole, squished up and around, neatly circumnavigating our respective irregularities. I can feel Dr Morse's eyes on my face as she clicks back and forth between the two slides that demonstrate our complementary nature: one torso with its darkened, eggy blob on the left-hand side, the other with a bright, clear bubble on the right.

'The physiological similarity is striking enough,' Dr Morse says, and clicks again. 'But the truly remarkable finding is on the genetic level.'

Taka taps a few keys. The screen goes black, then begins to populate with white letters, piling like bad teeth: A, T, C and G, tumbling over one another in countless iterations, white on black. I recognise the letters from freshman biology: the lettered pairs that make up DNA: A, T, C and G. For every A, a T. For every C, a G. For ever and ever, replicated into eternity within the confines of our everyday breathing bodies.

'What is this?' I ask.

'You're looking at the DNA sequence of a human gene,' Dr Morse says. She speaks less to me and more to the screen. She seems to vibrate with excitement. 'Specifically, the ICF-3 gene, as it appears in a common, non-mutated patient, where "common" indicates the absence of physical deformities such as Morgan's and Howie's.' She leans across Taka and presses a key, and two more lines of letters appear below the first one. They blur together before my eyes. I can't make sense of them.

Taka leans back from the keyboard, letting her have it. 'It's a gene responsible for controlling immune response in the body.'

'Immunomodulatory control factor,' Dr Morse cuts in, punching keys.

'Yes,' Taka says, with what might, on an emotive human, be a hint of a smile. 'Dr Morse has been studying it for the past decade, and she believes she's isolated—'

'If you look here,' Morse cuts in. She taps a few keys, and the screen zooms in to one section of the code. 'In the common – that is, non-mutated – patient, the four hundred and sixty-third base pair is an A. In the two of you, a slight genetic mutation throws each of you off balance, with Morgan expressing a C and Howie expressing a G.'

My head spins. I wish I hadn't spent most of freshman bio drawing comics of anthropomorphic bacteria.

'What Dr Morse means, is,' Taka says, gently, 'we can trace your genetic mutations to the same gene.'

'If we have the same mutation,' I say, 'how come he has a . . . not a Hole? Like me?'

'Because you don't have the same mutation,' Taka says. He looks up at the screen, and I follow his gaze. Two letters are circled there, in two different identical strings of letters.

One C, one G.

'C and G are a complementary pair,' Taka says. 'It's always one or the other.'

'So our mutated DNA—'

'Complements each other. Just as your physical mutations do.'

I stare at the boy across the table. He stares back, something tangled and complicated struggling behind his eyes: want, hope, fear. Recognition.

Both of us are eternal outsiders.

On the deepest, most fundamental level, we're a matched pair of *doesn't belong*.

Taka lets this all settle over our heads. The quiet in the room stretches out into a grey hush, marred only by the ticking of the clock.

Dr Morse clears her throat. 'This mutation is very, very rare. I've been working on the ICF-3 gene for over a decade now, and you are the first human cases I've encountered.'

'This is crazy,' I say, looking to Mother. I want to pass my doubt to her. I want her to take it up and rally for me. But she's looking past me, at the projection. I squeeze the bones of my wrist, feeling alone.

Morse key-taps to another slide.

'I've worked with mice for years,' she says. 'These have been genetically altered so that their ICF-3 gene, like Morgan's, expresses a C. It produces an over-active immunoresponse, causing the body to attack itself.'

In the centre of the screen is a mouse with a hole carved through its abdomen, just to the fore of its hind leg. I gaze, transfixed, as she clicks through the pictures: mice missing paws, missing tails.

She clicks again, and we flash to the image of an infant mouse carcass, pinned, translucent belly painfully exposed. A perfect hole pierces its neck like an exquisite bullet wound. Light shines through in a tiny, bloodless pinprick, a glow in the mouse's hairless pink throat.

Behind me, Mother makes a noise.

'Morgan was very lucky,' Taka says, voice low. 'That the Hole manifested for her in a relatively harmless location.

It seems Dr Morse's test subjects were not always so fortunate.'

'It's the first human case in history,' Morse says, brightly. She clicks again, and I glimpse a mouse in a jar, perfectly preserved, with a hole corkscrewing through the centre of its skull. The room swims a moment, and I focus on the table, on breathing.

'What about the boy?' Mother's voice asks.

Dr Morse smiles at Howie. For the first time, her smile seems fond, unforced.

'Their mutations correspond,' she says. 'Physiologically and genetically. A436C and A436G. C and G. Morgan is, literally, the other half of Howie's complementary base pair.'

My cheeks burn for a reason I can't quite explain. I look up at the boy and find his eyes on me. Our gazes skitter away from each other, singeing.

'It will take many more years of study to even understand your conditions,' Dr Takahashi says.

'We're making rapid strides in gene therapy,' Dr Morse says. She is obviously fighting to contain her excitement, her mouth jumping all over her face as she speaks. 'The sequencing technology alone has come a long way. Every day there are breakthroughs—'

'So you don't know for sure,' I say.

Dr Morse looks up sharply, as though she has forgotten that around the Hole there is a girl.

'The unique features of the ICF-3 gene in particular

suggest a great potential for success,' she says. She looks to Mother. 'Given your consent for treatment, I'd like to try to utilise the genetic material of each patient to positively affect the other.'

'Did it work in the mice?' I ask.

Morse clicks to the next slide. Sleek, healthy mouse.

'Testing has not been done on humans,' Taka says, his voice curt.

'Only for want of subjects,' Dr Morse answers.

Nobody speaks.

'I've prepared a packet of information for each of you to consider before we move further,' Dr Morse says. She slides three fat black binders across the table. Mother's hand closes around my shoulder, and I jump.

'Morgan, I want you to keep an open mind,' she murmurs.

I twist up to see her face, surprised. 'Mother, this is insane,' I say. 'She can't even prove it works in people.'

She bites her lip, and underneath her hard veneer I catch a glimpse of the mother who has wanted nothing more for me my entire life than a cure. Hence the doctors. The skin grafts. The miracle diets. The Tibetan crystal retreats in which my entrepreneurial Full Body Shred™ mother traced my lips with amethysts, humming, her fingers tense with concentration. I want to say, *this is a joke, right? We're both in on this joke?* but all I can see is myself reflected in the orb of her eye, small and warped and whole.

'We'd like to begin as early as next week,' Dr Morse says.

Mother shifts her weight, and suddenly she is solid again, impenetrable.

'There's the matter of the press,' she says. 'Although my daughter has certainly exacerbated the situation by gallivanting topless through nightclubs –' my heart shrivels in my chest, '– someone at your institute must have tipped them off that my daughter would be here today, either without or –' she fixes Dr Morse with a lead-lined gaze, '– *with* your knowledge. My daughter's condition is a sensitive family issue. This can't be allowed to become a media circus.'

Dr Morse's face turns to cement. Dr Takahashi clears his throat, a scattering of pebbles.

'Mrs Stone, we should speak to you about this in the hallway,' he says.

Mother frowns, and tightens her grip on my shoulder for a moment. She and the doctors leave the room and close the door behind them.

I sit in the semi-dark with the Lump boy. He stares at the table as our shared genetic flaws flicker across the far wall. Studying him closely for the first time, I notice details about him in small, intense bursts: a freckle on his nose, his delicately pointed ears. It's too hard to ignore the swell poking at the cotton of his shirt.

'It was you,' I say. 'You jumped in front of my bike.'

His eyes jump up to his brows, meeting my gaze and then falling again, nervously.

'I'm sorry I scared you,' he says. His voice is softer than I remember, with a mellowness that curls up from his tongue and into the air, yellow. Distantly, I realise I could mix that exact shade: cadmium yellow and titanium white, creamy and lilting. 'I wanted to talk to you.'

'You chose a hell of a way to do it.' I'm surprised by how bitter my voice sounds. 'How did you even find me? Did you just jump in front of girls' bikes all morning and hope for the best?'

'No,' he says sheepishly. 'I didn't mean to – you were going faster than I realised. I'm sorry. It was dumb. I should have realised that would freak you out.'

'Yeah, you should have,' I say, folding my arms. 'Shocker, it's scary to have some rando follow you from a coffee shop and then jump in front of your moving vehicle.' I lean back in the chair and stare at the ceiling. 'Do you have any idea what the last few weeks of my life have been like?'

'Yeah,' he says, quietly. 'Yeah. I do.'

I glance up at him. Behind us, the nearly-matched letters of our DNA march off the screen and into oblivion.

'How long have you known?' I ask, more softly.

'About you?'

'About any of it.'

'Dr Morse has been prepping me for it for a while,' he says. 'I found pictures of you online last week. It seemed like a long shot, but.'

He shrugs. I know that shrug. That shrug that means, *but it's only my entire life.*

I want to see some resemblance between us: a symmetrical mole, a shared skin tone or parting of the hair, but there's nothing; his eyes are brown to my green, his hair is a burnt caramel to my black. The only thing we have in common is the caved posture of frightened people: shoulders in, spines curved, to keep our torsos two inches back from the rest of the world.

'This is crazy,' I say.

'It's something,' he says.

'I don't like the idea of somebody fucking around with my genes.'

He lifts his head and meets my gaze, level. 'I'd say they're already pretty fucked, aren't they?'

The door opens, and the bright light of the corridor floods Howie's face with light. The smile I thought I might have seen is washed out and away.

'So, Morgan,' Dr Morse says. Her tone is the kind of casual that is full of teeth. 'What are we thinking?'

I look at Howie. His head is bent to the table, but his gaze jumps up to meet mine. For a second, I think of speckled brown rabbits, leaping through tall grass.

'I need more time,' I say.

Dr Morse's automaton smile snaps back across her face: the expression of someone who has been told too many times in her life, *play nice*. 'Of course,' she says. And then, like she can't help herself, 'The sooner the better.'

I almost miss the *something* that passes between her and Howie as I push past and into the hall.

15

I cross to the window through the bleached, chilly air. I just want to lean my forehead against the cool glass and think, but I catch sight of the crowd below and jolt backwards as a smattering of camera flashes strike the window like popcorn. It's doubled in size since Caroline and I arrived, at least. The air feels tight against my skin, hard to breathe.

Numbly, I slump against the human-sized ruler in the height and weight station and measure myself with my finger. Five foot two: a small, unwavering fact.

There's a low sound behind me, someone clearing their throat. I jump away from the ruler and see Taka.

He cracks a delicate smile. 'Hoping for a growth spurt?'

'Only if tall people don't have to put up with so much bullshit.'

He shrugs. 'I wouldn't know.'

I realise, for maybe the first time, that Taka is almost exactly my height. I'm so often perched up on a table when we interact. I'm not sure we've ever stood face-to-face before.

And though I am shaking and confused and the beginnings of furious, a part of me cannot help but think: *my nose is on level with your nose.*

'How long did you know about this?' I ask.

He puts his hands in his pockets and takes them out again. Like he doesn't know what to do with them without a clipboard.

'The board sent me an article Dr Morse wrote last January on the ICF-3 gene mutation,' he says at last. 'We ran the tests.'

'You knew this cure was out there for nine months,' I say, trying to keep my voice level. I fail. 'Why didn't you tell me?'

The reflected windows flinch in his glasses.

'As you're still a minor, I discussed it with your mother first,' he says. 'She had her assistants look into it. My understanding was that she wanted to tell you herself.'

The 1,900 unheard messages in my phone click into place. In my defence, if she weren't such a drill sergeant to talk to ... but no, really. I have no defence.

'What do you think?' I ask him. He hesitates. 'Honestly.'

Taka picks his words carefully. 'Your physical deformities match Howard's, and your genes express similar mutation, but it guarantees virtually nothing,' he says. 'I haven't seen research specifically disproving what Dr Morse is going after, but that doesn't mean that it works. She's ...' he hesitates, 'ambitious.'

'You still should have said something, Taka.'

His name sounds so small in my voice that I'm frightened.

I want him to reach out to me. I want him to take my hand. But he is not wearing gloves now, and we do not know how to touch each other without them.

He meets my eyes.

He says, 'I didn't want to get your hopes up.'

Mother holds the crowd at bay while Caro steers me to her car. I keep one hand over my face and the other to my stomach, questions pelting off of my exposed skin. I keep my head down as I feel us accelerate onto the street, curl my fingers into the nest of my lap. Beside me, at the wheel, Caro is brimming with energy.

'Oh my God,' she finally explodes. 'Lump Boy? Morgs! Multiple exclamation points!'

I say nothing. Her enthusiasm hovers a moment in the silent interior of the car, then slowly dissipates, the smile fading from her face. I stare at the skin forming on the top of the cold cup of coffee between us. It shivers when we slow for a red light.

'Taka doesn't think it'll work,' I say at last.

She nods carefully, keeping her eyes on the traffic, feeling me out. Mother must have filled her in in the waiting room. She didn't like that Caro knew my secret when we were children, but she must be grateful now to have someone to talk to, even if it's her teenaged daughter's best friend. I imagine the two of them waiting among the benches and magazines, their heads bent together, clashing smells nestling in their collarbones: dollar store lemon shampoo and Mother's latest tester, *Dusk* or *Gibbous* or *Provoke*, hundreds of dollars and mere centimetres apart. Somehow, this makes everything scarier.

'What do you think?' Caro asks.

'Do I think it'll work, or do I think I want to do it?'

'Both. Either.'

'I don't know.'

Caro glances up at the rear-view mirror. I instinctively mimic her. If we are being followed by the press, I can't tell. Every car looks like an ordinary car, an anonymity that felt safe until this moment. Now I want to hide from everything.

Caro catches my eye, reaches out and squeezes my hand. 'It'll be fine, Morgs,' she says, and I want to ask, *what will?* But I don't want to know the answer, either.

She turns up the radio to cover our silence, and I relax back in the comfortable sleeve of noise. I try to imagine my life without the Hole: all of those giant sweaters tossed in the trash, along with my insecurities. All of those belly shirts stripped of their magic, baring an ordinary belly. Whole, I would be stronger, bolder. I would laugh with my mouth wide open. I would take lovers, five hundred lovers. I would wake early and paint masterpieces until dawn, until the five hundred lovers rose from bed to stroke my bare shoulder with their five hundred hands, and feed me five hundred grapes. 'I knew all along that the only thing holding me back was the Hole in my middle,' I would throatily tell the editors of

Esquire. I would take their hands. 'No,' I would say. 'It's okay. I'm touched by your concern, but don't worry about me. I am all better now. Now, I am cured.'

The world outside comes to a stop, and I blink up at the mossy mortar of our apartment building. The five hundred lovers come crashing down into the chalk-crumbling brick. I want to laugh at myself, but don't. The movement of my chest might shudder into crying.

'Do you need me to call in sick?' Caro asks. 'My shift manager's been a total dick lately anyway. We can skip town, maybe head to the beach. Or stay in. Anything you want. We could eat ice cream in the dark and watch cartoons. You know, whatever.'

'Your boss already hates you,' I say.

Caro shrugs. 'It's just sublimated self-loathing,' she says. 'She'll be extra passive-aggressive for a few weeks, no big deal.'

I lean back in the seat, feeling the weight of the whole world beneath me.

'That's okay,' I say.

'You're sure?'

'Really.'

Caro tilts her head back and forth.

'All right,' she says at last.

She opens the door. I don't move, cradle myself in the seat.

'You know I'll need to kick you out of the car in five minutes if I'm going to work,' she says.

I nod against the headrest, staring straight ahead. Caro

lingers a moment longer, clearly about to say something, but then thinks better of it. She walks up to our building in a flash of sun. I linger in the car a few precious minutes more, wondering about the Lump, and the Hole, and all of the places the cooling tyres beneath my feet could take me if only I knew which direction to point the car.

16

I sleep uneasily that night, bobbing in and out of the silty air of dreaming. The Lump boy makes an uncomfortable shape in my subconscious. I can't stop thinking about his hope, struggling against the shy bent of his head.

My alarm jolts me awake at 7 a.m., my cotton nightshirt a second sweaty skin. Caro sticks her head from her door as I stumble toward the bathroom. She looks worried.

'Um, Morgs?' she says. 'You should probably see this.'

I follow her in, squinting against the sun creeping cheerily through her windows. I lean over her shoulder to peer at her computer screen and moan.

'No way,' I mutter into her clavicle. It shifts, apologetically, *yes*.

We're on the news.

This is no small local story. I'm on Buzzfeed, the Daily Beast, the AOL homepage. I open the tabs quickly, scattering them across Caro's screen like a little kid dumping Halloween candy onto the bedroom floor. MATCH MADE IN HEAVEN – OR

SCIENCE? the first headline chirps cheerfully. Subtitle: Pair united for genetic study.

I feel the floor fall out from under me. My body is certainly no longer in the room. It is out there, on the internet, replicated something-point-four million times. Caro right-clicks on headlines, scattering a spray of new tabs across the screen: THE MISSING PIECE OF HER and A PERFECT FIT! and TWO HALVES MAKE A WHOLE - OR CURE A HOLE? There are no photos of Howie and me together, but the resourceful media has made do, favouring a mash-up: on one side, Howie standing bare-chested and emotionless against a clinical white background. On the other, a Public Scrutiny photo of my faceless silhouette, punctured irrevocably by Hole.

Caro opens PUZZLE PIECE PAIR TOGETHER AT LAST.

Science or fiction? This is the question on the lips of medical professionals around the country after the discovery of a young couple whose compatibility stretches way beyond chemistry - and straight into biology.

'They share a complementary genetic mutation,' said researcher Dr Parker Morse in an interview on Sunday. 'Compounded with their mirrored physiology, it's really quite remarkable.'

Morgan Stone, 17, and Howard Garrison, 18, are marked by matching deformities that make them literal human puzzle pieces: a four-inch long lump of flesh on his lower abdomen matches a hole that punctures Stone's torso.

These deformities baffled doctors for years.

'Morgan's in particular is really quite eye-catching,' said Morse. 'It's my understanding she uses it as a gimmick in the local club scene. On the other hand, Howie is very shy about his body, which is ... why it took them so long to get together.'

'That she-devil,' Caro gasps.

'I am going to kill her,' I announce matter-of-factly.

We keep reading. The piece guides the reader through an infographic about the ICF-3 gene, teases us with sidebar links to Public Scrutiny and to a list of Fifteen Famous Freaks You Won't Believe! Halfway down the page we encounter a photo of Howie. His eyes are lifted to the camera, and bright.

'I would say I'm cautiously excited about [Stone],' Garrison commented. 'I mean, it's wild to think about, but what if this is it? What if I was put on this earth to meet this person?'

The medical field is divided.

'Fifty per cent of human DNA is shared with a banana,' said geneticist Dr Amy Olvides of the Brooks Institute. 'There's almost no chance that this is more than an accident of physiology.'

But outside of the scientific community, people see the sweeter side.

'I think it's beautiful,' said Jennifer Carson, 24, who waited outside the doctor's office Sunday to see the pair united. 'It's kind of like solid proof that there's one person out there for you ... I'm really happy that they found each other.'

This happiness is echoed by Morse, Garrison's personal doctor.

'It's been a long, hard road for Howie,' she revealed. 'We have a great deal of hope for the possibilities of this union.'

Ms Stone could not be reached for comment.

Caro pushes back from the computer. 'Just for the record, I do not like this woman.'

I sink slowly onto Caro's bed, remembering Dr Morse's tense smile, the undercurrent of anger lacing her voice when I told her I needed time to think. Taka's word: *ambitious*.

'She's mad,' I say, slowly.

'Why?'

'I'm not sure. Maybe because I didn't fall at her feet and proclaim her my saviour.' I flop over, pull Caro's stuffed unicorn to my chest. 'But that's crazy, right? I mean, this is a totally bananas medical procedure. I'd be insane not to think it over.'

Caro snorts. 'No wonder she let you get out without talking to the press yesterday. She was probably afraid you'd go off of her message.'

'Damn right I would've,' I say.

Caro bats her eyes at me. 'Who, you?' she asks, and despite myself, I laugh. 'Todd's giving me a ride to school today,' she says, closing the laptop. 'Want a lift?'

'What about the press?' I ask, automatically. 'You aren't worried they'll jump the car?'

'Screw the press,' she says. 'Just brush your teeth and get ready. You smell like eight different dead things.'

I blow into her face. 'This is the breath of fame,' I say. 'Get used to it.'

But my head feels light and disconnected as I wander into the hall, the enormity of my altered life following me from Caro's bedroom into the bathroom. I focus on concrete, mundane things. *Hello, same sink. Hello, same towel.* I brush, spit and rinse. The toothpaste spit of fame looks no different from the toothpaste spit of yester-me. For some reason I find this hilarious. I start laughing and can't stop. I laugh until my gut seizes and I dry heave over the toilet, tears stinging my eyes, sides still convulsing. *Ha ha! My life is in shambles!*

'Hey Morgs,' Caro calls, clattering by with her backpack. 'Your ancient phone wants something.'

I dry my eyes, scoop my phone off the bed. There are thirty-four new missed calls. Thirty-three are from numbers I don't recognise. The other one is from Mother.

It takes her a long time to pick up. When she does, she sounds rushed.

'I want you to come over right away,' she says.

For the first time in recent memory, I don't want to argue with my mother. I am really, really ready for some responsible adult to pick me up out of the mess my life has become.

I'm texting Mother's assistant to call in an excused absence for me when my phone buzzes again.

'Morgan?' my mother says. 'Wear something nice.'

*

The outside world seems bright and strange, aggressively three-dimensional. I find myself peeking at people in passing cars, studying them at traffic lights. *Have you read the news? Have you?*

Mother lives in the far north part of town, where the sound drops away and the earth unfurls into a hushed green expanse in which dazzling white estates are set like pearls. The street lamps are hand lit by a man in a taupe uniform at dusk, extinguished at dawn. I know she wishes I would spend more time here while she travels, but the house and all it stands for rubs me like a poorly tailored shirt. I chafe. At this moment, though, her mini-estate with its gates and codes and impermeable walls of wealth and class promises refuge. I know we live in a democracy. I know this isn't supposed to be the way it works. But the truth is: with a certain amount of money, nobody can touch you.

Maybe this is why I reject my mother's lifestyle. Maybe I'm dying to be touched.

I punch in the gate code and pull up the long circular driveway. There's an unfamiliar Lexus parked in front of the house, and my hands stiffen on the wheel. Who has she got in there? A reporter? Ira Glass? Oprah? For a long moment, I sit in the ticking car, ruing my decision not to just crash on the way over and die a quick and easy death. My phone rattles in the cup holder. A text from Caro:

are you coming to school today?

I glance up at the house, type back, I dunno. depends on what Mother's got in store for me.

A pause, and then she responds: okay.

The blinking ellipsis appears below her words, indicating that she's typing something else. I watch it, waiting, but it disappears again. Nothing.

I drop my phone into my bag, trying to shake the unsettled feeling as I force myself up and across the lawn. It's peaceful here: the air is laden with the breath of roses, so quiet that it's hard to believe there's a world outside, let alone a city.

I lean into the doorbell and the door swings inward almost immediately, revealing not the latest maid, but my mother. Exhaustion clings to her face in the small lines that she is having difficulty shaking lately: scraps of tiredness around the lips, creeping into the eyes. She's wearing yesterday's suit.

'Morgan,' she says too loudly, with a trademark *five-more-push-ups* smile. 'How are you?'

Mother does not smile off-camera. My sense of alarm sharpens.

'Who's here?' I ask. 'I need to talk to you.'

'What a fan*tas*tic sweater,' she proclaims, and her voice drops. 'For once. Come in, I have somebody for you to meet.' She ushers me across a black-slate foyer the size of a five-car garage. Above the slightly sour smell of sleeplessness, a new perfume rolls off her skin: ambergris and neroli and faint hints of jasmine. *Celestia*, or maybe *Electra Complex*.

'What's going on?' I ask. 'What did the doctors say? Mother? *Mother*. Can we at least take a minute to talk about how I'm on *all* of the internet?'

'In a moment,' Mother says. 'First, we need to discuss the gallery I bought you.'

'The *what*?'

She buffets me into the living room, a high-ceilinged dream in glass and steel. The furniture is sleek, spare, a closer modern to cutting-edge than mid-century, all accents of charcoal and cream. Floor-to-ceiling windows drink in the crisp October light, casting a glow on the only bit of colour in the room: an emerald-hued oil portrait I did of Mother, hanging in an alcove. It looks grossly out of place in this Shrine to Monochrome.

'Marcel, this is my daughter. Morgan, this is your manager, Marcel Jasper-Banff.'

The man rises and extends a hand. Feeling like I'm underwater, I take it.

He is small, immaculate, his palm soft. He moves precisely through the space, constantly framing himself: *The Manager at Work. The Reluctant Handshake. Thinker, Refusing Açai Juice.*

'I've asked Marcel to produce your first show,' Mother says. 'It's not that I don't think you couldn't break out on your own. Eventually. Probably. If you ever put in the focus. But the early application deadlines for RISD and the Pratt Institute are about to pass us by, and given the attention you've been receiving in the press, we think you can spin this—'

'Mother, stop. *Stop.* I need to talk to you about what Doct—'
I pause, glancing sidelong at Marcel, who studies the window.
Small Man Wonders What He's Doing Here.

'Marcel's up to speed on your media debacle and health
situation,' Mother announces. 'That's why he's here.'

I close my eyes and breathe the ionised air and accept the
fact that my mother is an insane person.

'Okay,' I say. 'Great. Let's just step off the crazy train for a
second.' I turn to Marcel. *Caught in the Crossfire, #3.* 'I'm sorry,
Marcel,' I say. 'I'm sure you're a decent human, and I'm sure
my mother is paying you an obscene amount of money to be
here, but I'm having a lot of feelings right now, and there are
a few things I need to talk with my mom about that aren't my
professional development opportunities.'

'Morgan,' Mother says. Her voice is cold. 'This is a prime
opportunity.'

'It's not an opportunity. It's my life fucking exploding.'

'Morgan, language.'

'Mother, completely inappropriate response to an emotional crisis.'

'I understand that it seems like a radical connection,'
Marcel speaks up. His voice is high and light, velveting the
room. 'But your mother's right. This would be an – actually,
the – most effective way for you to spin the attention you've
been receiving into a springboard for your art career.'

I glare at the side of Mother's face.

'Please,' Marcel says. 'This will just be a minute.'

He crosses to a glossy binder, flips it open with a finger. The pages open to a double spread of works I recognise as mine from early last year, when I was just beginning to play with abstract expressionism: an unsteady blue circle hovering in a field of green, an angry slash of yellow vivisecting the remaining white.

'You're a ... developing talent,' he says. 'If we had the time, I'd want to send you to an intensive programme to refine your technique a bit before—'

'But we don't,' Mother says, pointedly.

'No,' Marcel agrees with a small, compact sigh. 'As it is, you have a number of solid pieces. Possibly sellable in smaller galleries.'

Despite myself, and my annoyance with Mother, my heart leaps. *I do? I am?* Like: you can spend every day of your life thinking of yourself as an artist. But it is nothing, nothing like hearing it from somebody else.

Marcel goes on. 'But your portfolio isn't ... ' he gestures, shaping the air into something I strain to see before he drops his hands again, leaving the space between us formless, 'cohesive.'

'So cohere it,' Mother says.

Marcel frowns. 'This is your debut in the art world,' he says, speaking to me directly. Despite myself, this makes me like him. 'We'll need to shape this exhibition,' he continues. 'Is there a common theme your work speaks to? What do you want to say? What's important to you?'

126

Not dying alone. Being able to step outside without starting a riot. Setting Dr Morse's hair on fire.

I open my mouth, and Marcel looks at me expectantly, all soft hands and expensive suit. I feel paralyzed, close my mouth again. Mother sighs through her nose.

'Think it through,' Marcel says. 'Let's meet later this week with a list. Look through your catalogue – it would be ideal to develop a show from pre-existing pieces. We *could* put up some new work, but your mother doesn't want the opening any later than Black Friday—'

'The day after Thanksgiving?' I say, distantly.

'That's the one.'

'That's, like, a month from now.'

'Seven weeks,' Mother says. 'Really, though, it'd be best to meet that November 1 deadline ...'

Marcel tips his head back and forth, weighing, with a slightly pained expression. 'Not if we want to generate buzz. Either way, it would be risky. Get me a list based on the pieces you have, and we'll go from there.'

Seven weeks. God knows where I could be in seven weeks. Cured. Dead. Touring with Ripley's Believe It or Not. I want to laugh. But not, like, funny-laugh. Like, the-inmates-have-taken-over-the-asylum laugh.

'What about school?' I ask.

Mother waves a hand dismissively. 'Oh, you're *absolutely* not going to school. Not until this blows over. We'll take a medical leave. *Not,*' she says, as if I'm about to jump up and down like a little kid on a snow day, 'a vacation. You have to keep your grades up. I'll have someone deliver your assignments to you.'

'Mother,' I say again, softly. 'Slow down. Every single piece of my life is exploding. I'm not ready to jump into Having a Career. And I – I don't even know if I want to go to college next year.'

I don't even know if I want: the padding cowards use to cushion their hearts' desires.

'Of course you do,' Mother says. Her voice is firm, but she's not looking at me. I follow her gaze to that little green portrait I did of her last Christmas, and can't help but see myself there: an out-of-place splotch marring Mother's otherwise perfect world. That she displays proudly, even when it clashes with everything else she's worked so hard to create.

I'm suddenly grateful she won't look at me. My mother and I have spent my whole life building up emotional ramparts to weather each other's storms. If she knows I saw this tenderness in her face, it would rip us both wide open.

I pull in a heavy breath and turn to Marcel. It's just a list. It doesn't mean anything. 'I'll work on it,' I tell him.

In my periphery, I see Mother's shoulders straighten, settle.

'Perfect,' Marcel says. 'We'll talk in a week. Good luck with the press. Try to keep your head down.'

He shakes my hand once more, and I think I see a quick frown of disapproval – *Spoiled Rich Girl, Destroying Integrity of the Art World* – before he turns and lets Mother show him

128

out, leaving me alone with the incoherent catalogue of my life's work.

Mother returns while I'm flipping through the pages. The month I did nothing but still lives of porcelain foxes. That spring of woodblock prints. She's catalogued them all and kept them, stockpiling my work as though collecting a body of evidence. For what, I am not sure.

I keep my head down as she stands in the doorway a long moment, observing me. I wonder when our relationship became nothing more than my problems and the heaps of money she threw at them. I wait for her to ask how I'm doing, to tell me that it'll be okay, that she's suing Dr Morse, and that she can fix the Hole in my stomach with the strength of motherly love. But when I look up, she's disappeared into the frozen bowels of the great house, and I am alone, holding the pages of the life she's saved for me, trying to find some story in it.

Back at home I try to paint, but I'm not feeling up to it. My life feels too dramatic; anything I paint too likely to be over-wrought. I put in some effort trying to write Marcel a list of artistic-sounding things I could care about: *Interplay of Colour. Ephemerata. Art as a Product of* _____ . The more adult I try to be, the more I feel like a kid playing Very Pretentious Dress-Up. Because I'm nothing if not committed, I spend the rest of the afternoon hiding under the bed, watching the minutes leak past while my classmates are elsewhere, shouting and bumping each other in the corridors, chewing on pencils, watching other clocks.

My boss from the co-op, Zeke, calls just as school is finishing. I groan, groping in the dusty dark for the phone. I've missed more shifts than should be allowed by law. I probably owe them money at this point, just on the pure employee-shittiness scale.

'Morgan,' Zeke says. 'It's probably best if you don't come in tonight.'

'Zeke—'

'Look,' he says, sounding harried. 'I don't know what's going on, you know, with this whole medical thing. That's your family's business. I just think you'd be better off not coming in again until this whole thing dies down.'

His voice subsides into a fuzz of noise. And then I hear a voice, male and distinct, shout, 'Hey, is the Hole Girl here?'

'Oh my God,' I say.

Zeke drops his voice. 'I won't lie,' he says. 'It's not bad for business. The pre-made deli wraps are pretty much wiped out. Some of these people have been waiting around all morning.' He clears his voice and says to someone else, 'No, we're cash only. Cash *only*. There's an ATM around the corner.' To me, he says, 'Sorry, Morgan.'

'Yeah,' I say. 'Thanks.'

I lie beneath the bed in the semi-dark, feeling like a little kid. There are calls I need to make, the calculations of being an adult. But instead I just stare up at the bedsprings, watching them spiral up, and my life spiral out of control. My phone beeps shrilly as I set it down. VOICEMAIL FULL, the screen alerts me.

I sigh, punch in the code.

'*You have FIFTY new messages,*' the automated voice announces. '*First new message . . .*'

'This is Alex Ramirez from the Daily—'

'John Marcus from H. R. Abrams Med—'

'Miss Stone, I'm Belinda Johnson, features columnist from—'

131

'We were wondering if you could come in—'

I press DELETE until I'm tired of the feeling of my finger on the button, and drop the phone on the floor. It immediately lights up again, a new incoming call from another area code I don't recognise. I leave it there, glowing, to ring itself out silently into the shadows.

Public Scrutiny has posted a dancing *Doctor Who* gif with a server maintenance message, its meagre servers overwhelmed by the sudden attention of the world. My Facebook is inundated with messages and friend requests from people I've never heard of – reporters and researchers and freak-finders and fans. I don't even bother checking my email.

I chop vegetables for dinner, the Lump Boy's quote from the article dancing around my ears: *what if I were put on earth to meet this person.* How epic it sounds. How *Twilight.* As if a simple fact about my body – something about me that I didn't even choose – could give a stranger the right to insert himself into my destiny.

I chop faster, annoyed at him, and the gleeful media, and the swooning public for creating this narrative and placing me unwillingly at its centre. This isn't how destiny happens in the movies. There's girl-meets-boy-and-he's-perfect. There's also girl-meets-boy-and-they-hate-each-other-at-first-but-their-hatred-is-sublimated-sexual-attaction-and-then-they-get-together-and-it's-awesome-and-hot. (Also, girl-meets-girl, because lesbians, holla!) But there's not girl-meets-boy-and-he's-okay-she-guesses-but-they-have-nothing-in-common-and-she-feels-lukewarm-towards-his-skinny-arms.

'Whoa,' Caro says, entering the kitchen with Todd. There are vegetables heaped on every surface: onions, tomatoes, okra, peppers, squash. One lone shallot teeters on the edge of the stove, then plummets to the 1970s gold-and-rust linoleum below.

'Hi, honey,' I say cheerily. 'How was your day?'

'Positively scholastic,' she answers. Behind my back, I feel her and Todd exchange a look. 'What's for dinner?'

'I dunno,' I say. 'But it needed lots of chopping.'

'It smells great,' Todd says, dutifully.

Caro just nods, goes to the pantry and begins measuring out brown rice. There is something eggshell-fragile in the way she crosses the room, like she's afraid to touch my body. She rummages among the dry goods for a while, then asks, too casually, 'You're ... not planning on coming back to school tomorrow, are you?'

'Mother doesn't want me to,' I say. 'So, probably.'

Caro pours the rice into a sieve and begins to rinse it. 'You know, she may have a point.'

My radar goes off and I set down the yam I'm mutilating. 'Caro, why are you agreeing with my mother?'

'Let's have a contest,' she says. 'Who can come up with the most outlandish excuse. Like: Morgan's been selected to appear on *American Gladiators* and she has to go train.'

'Caro.'

'Or: tomorrow is a super obscure Jewish holiday honouring beekeepers. Okay, your turn.'

'It's baseball season,' Todd suggests.

I reach over and turn off the tap. Caro blinks up at me, guiltily. The water scatters from her skin like diamonds.

'Guys.' I turn to face them both. 'What's going on?'

Caro sighs, rustles in her back pocket for her phone, then holds up a picture: Principal Crowell standing at the edge of school property, hands on hips, glaring down a man with a giant-lensed camera.

'They're not allowed on school property,' she says, before I can speak. 'But still. People are talking. A lot.'

'People like who?'

Todd looks up from the log cabin he's building with carrot sticks. 'Everyone,' he says.

Caro's shoulders slump.

'Everyone,' she echoes. 'Even the teachers. You can tell, in the way they shut down the conversations. Apparently there was some huge faculty meeting about it.'

'So?' I ask. 'You said yourself, everyone would find out eventually. And the press isn't allowed on campus, so I'm pretty safe there.'

'But . . . ' She hesitates.

'What?'

'They've been getting in touch with everyone. Someone must have gotten hold of the student email directory . . . I mean, some people are refusing to talk to them, but almost everyone else is going crazy about it. It's pretty bad.' She tries to force a laugh, but anger shines through. 'Randos kept stopping me in the halls, asking when you were coming back, and if they could get your phone number for like –' she draws mincing air quotes, '– "You know, studying, no reason." And Stacia Torres and her queen bee flunkies waited for me outside a bathroom stall to ambush me with an "invitation" to sit at their table at lunch.'

She shakes her head. 'I'm not trying to complain, Morgs. I know this is three million times worse for you. I just wanted you to know. It's nuts out there.'

I realise I am gripping the handle of my knife very, very hard.

'Morgan?' Caro asks. 'Are you okay?'

I carefully lay the knife down in a bunch of kale. 'It's fine,' I say, mechanically. 'Like you said. They had to find out eventually.'

Unless they didn't. Unless I'd just kept my shirt on and my mouth shut.

'Lots of people would kill to get this kind of attention,' Todd points out helpfully. 'What?' he asks, when we both glare at him. 'Hashtag PuzzlePieces was trending on Twitter this morning. YYS has never gotten more than, like, four hundred views on YouTube.'

Caro squeezes my arm. 'Next week, Beyoncé will get pregnant, or Emma Watson will wear a bikini, or something, and everyone will forget about you. But the world is falling for you right now.' Todd pauses in his carrot stick construction and looks up at her, thoughtfully. 'Maybe just ... wait for it to blow over. Get out of town, or go to your mom's place for a little bit. You know?'

'Yeah,' I say. 'Sure.' I don't look at either of them as I leave the kitchen.

Alone in my room, I numbly pull my phone out of my pocket and, feeling like the vainest person in the entire world, google my name.

EPITOME OF MILLENNIAL GENERATION: THE UNWHOLE CHILD

STONE BIRTH DEFECT DUE TO ALANNA'S DIET PILL ADDICTION!!

PUZZLE PIECES PROOF OF TRUE LOVE. CAN YOU FIND YOURS?

The headlines are no worse than this morning, but now my old yearbook photos are everywhere. So is everything I've ever posted on Facebook. So much for privacy settings. I wonder, briefly, which of my 239 'friends' shared my information with a reporter. If the articles are anything to go by, anyone I've ever known is a suspect: quotes from classmates whose names I only vaguely recognise pepper the stories. Tanisha Taylor, a girl I haven't talked to since third grade, has an 'exclusive interview' about my troubled emotional past with *E! Online*:

CLASSMATE REVEALS STONE'S OBSESSION WITH WITCHCRAFT;
HOLE CREATED BY BLACK MAGIC.

There's a pressure building, a low buzz that presses against the windows: the weight of the story the world is creating about me while I sit helplessly inside.

Fuck them all. I drop my pyjama bottoms to the floor, reach for a shiny skirt. On the bed, I see the phone light up again, and again. I turn it off, slip it into my bag.

I pass by the kitchen on my way out. A few notes from a guitar waft out on a wave of simmering sesame oil and soy sauce. It would smell delicious in another life, but in this one, I've lost my appetite.

'Where are you going?' Caro asks, sticking her head through the doorway.

'Out,' I say.

Her eyes flicker over me, filled with a blue concern. 'Are you sure?'

'I can't just stay in here for ever,' I say. 'I can't let the terrorists win.'

She leans against the doorframe and sighs. 'Whatever happened to my introverted loner friend who could watch *Adventure Time* for sixteen hours in a row without blinking, and whine about having to walk all ten feet to the bathroom?'

I lean forward and kiss her on the forehead. 'She learned about being brave and loving herself from her very special best friend. And she's had a very long couple of days, and would like to go have a drink and pretend to be normal for a little while.'

Caro hesitates, clearly struggling between the desire to stay home and the need to offer to come with me. I smile, covering my disappointment.

'It's okay,' I say. 'I need a little time to myself anyway.'

'You sure?' she asks.

'Yeah.'

As I'm lifting my keys from the cracked ceramic dish by the door, she calls, 'I'm sorry I freaked you out. I'm sure everything's going to be fine.' But a line has appeared between her brows, a little comma of worry that injects doubt into her optimism: *it's going to be fine, comma, I hope.*

I roll up to the Mansion with a scarf over my hair, my jacket zipped to the neck. There's a crowd of people hanging around the front gate, but I keep my head down and slip quickly past Steve, the mulleted bouncer. He pats me on the shoulder as I pass, and I stiffen. I don't know that he's ever touched me before. I wonder if being in the news makes your body public property. Or if that's just another property of being *other*.

Inside, the multicoloured lights swirl over a mostly empty dance floor, occasionally throwing the odd college student into rainbow relief. It's a Monday night, after all, and early. I let out a breath and head for the bar. Frank spends an unreasonable amount of time getting to me, lingering over the three other patrons before reluctantly pausing before my stool. He doesn't meet my eyes.

'Can't accept that fake ID, "Emma",' he says.

'Like you cared to begin with,' I say.

The bass beats between us like a heart.

'Saw you on the news,' he says at last.

'You and the rest of the world,' I say. 'Come on, Frank, just give me something. Anything. Surprise me.'

'You're fifteen,' he says.

'Seventeen.'

'Wouldn't have mattered in the seventies,' he says. 'Now, it'll cost me my license.'

He fades away, leaving me alone to choke down my frustration. I scratch at the empty air around my shoulders, look around at the slowly filling club. The cherubs in the rafters choking on dust and house music. The faint stickiness of the floor that crackles beneath my shoes as I shift my weight. Eventually he returns with something in a martini glass that's magenta and choking with bright pink cherries. The rim is furred with sugar crystals, a frilly pink umbrella. It looks, at some point, like it may have been on fire.

I look at him. 'Really?'

Frank pushes his lips out, a lazy man's shrug. 'I thought, now that you were all famous, you'd want something fancy.'

'Fuck you,' I say. The music picks that moment to die, and the words come out too loud. The other customers stir, looking my way. I think I see a ghost of a smile on Frank's face.

He twists away languidly, returns momentarily with a pint of something gut-black and humourless. I lift it to my lips, let the bitterness soak into my gumline.

Frank raises the pink cocktail and takes a sip, grimacing. His face is all squint lines and teeth. 'Better?' he asks. I nod, and he lifts the pink drink again, a toast to me. 'This one's on me. Morgan.'

'It'd better be,' I mutter. He snorts into his umbrella.

Frank nurses the syrupy cherrytini over the next several hours, slipping me a steady succession of dark, bitter beers. People murmur, eye me. I can feel, between the beats, the information passing around like a pulse: *that girl's on the news.*

'So I'm like a VIP now, huh?' I shout to Frank, several drinks in. Mouth ahead of brain.

He looks me dead in the eye. 'You're a regular,' he says. 'Even if you are a shitty tipper.'

Handsome Chad materialises after midnight. I'm cloudy with alcohol, and have somehow made it onto the dance floor. A group of girls wants a picture with me, and I don't care any more. A vague, global magnanimity suffuses my veins. I'm famous now, after all. I keep my jacket zipped, wave for photos.

'Hey,' a voice shouts in my ear. 'Haven't seen you in a while.'

I am unbelievably happy to see him: a handsome pillar of familiarity in a sea of sweaty strangers.

'Hey,' I say. 'Hey. Did you miss me?' I dance up to him, goofily, throwing my hands into the air like this moment is a thing I can grab and keep.

He laughs. 'Of course.' He grabs my hips and dances with me, his teeth flashing cherry and blue in the club's siren-lights. His thumbs lightly trace the curves of my hip bones through my skirt, a secret conversation taking place beneath our words. It is thrilling and delicious. I let my head loll, dropping against his chest.

'You're wasted,' he says.

'*You're* wasted,' I say. This is so witty that I laugh out loud. Chad laughs again, looking around the room in that quick, flashing way that beautiful people have. He squeezes my left hip, and I thrill again.

'Hey, so, did you get home all right the other night? I was worried about you.' I stare up at him and he says, 'At the, uh, playground? Those camera guys started chasing you—'

'Oh, God,' I say. 'Oh, *that*. Yeah. Of course! I was totally fine. It was nothing.'

He laughs again, uneasily. 'Okay. Because I was kind of worried, you know. We got separated, and it was pretty late and stuff, and then I couldn't find you anywhere.'

'You looked for me?'

'Well, yeah,' he says. 'I mean, I don't know the proper protocol or whatever, for what happens when you're making out with someone and a news crew shows up, but I was always taught to walk a girl home.'

'You weren't freaked out?'

'By the press?' he asks. He is a painfully handsome blur.

I blurt, 'Or by me.'

'You?'

'The Hole.'

He lifts his head to the ceiling, his laughter swept away in the music and lights and furry air.

'I was making out with you, wasn't I?' he asks. He reaches down and tweaks the end of my nose. 'No,' he says, firmly. 'You're cool. Seriously, quit worrying about it.'

Warmth and misgiving clash in my stomach. Or maybe it's the beer. 'You didn't talk to them, did you?'

'The camera guys?' He laughs. 'Yeah, I'm selling them my life story. "I Kissed the Hole Girl".'

I slap his arm. It is a little harder than I meant. 'I'm serious. It's ruining my life.'

'Hey,' he says. 'Calm down. I didn't come here to get yelled at.' He catches my hand, and rubs it with his, warming it. 'I didn't talk to the press, okay? I don't kiss and tell.'

'I'm sorry,' I say, feeling stupid. 'It's just – you're the only guy who isn't totally freaked out by the Hole, and then everything—'

He smiles down at me. 'Quit worrying, Holey-Holly. I'm not freaked out. In fact . . . ' He pulls a pen from his pocket, reaches for my hand.

'What are you doing?'

'Making sure I don't lose you again.' He writes a phone number on my palm, folds my fingers tight around it, and kisses them, briefly. The warmth of his breath rushes through them, filling my fist like a heart. 'Hold on to that, okay?' The beat picks up, and his long fingers pull my hips in close, and I melt. The paparazzi is nowhere in sight. I could be any girl on any dance floor: a short, shaggy-haired girl leaning into a gorgeous boy, the happiness in her face nothing if not normal. Just another teenager with a crush. I lift my head, peek at Chad. He's looking down at me with an expression that makes me dizzy.

'So, I guess that's not your boyfriend, huh?' he asks, casually.

I feel like a television abruptly unplugged: the picture shrinking to a small bright speck and dying.

'The *Lump* guy?' I ask. '*No.*' I try to laugh, but I feel wrecked with dismay.

Chad leans down and brushes his lips against my ear, and a thrill goes through me.

'Good,' he murmurs.

I turn my chin toward his, and a flash of light slaps me in the face.

A girl's voice to our left shouts, 'Morgan, hi! Can you unzip your jacket?'

I blink up through the sunspots at a blonde girl waving a clunky black SLR camera in her left hand. She pantomimes unzipping with her right. 'Will you pose with him? With – what's your name?'

I turn my face away, a groan rising in my throat. I can see it now: *Hole Girl Cheating on Epic Puzzle Romance! Millennials These Days, They're Never Satisfied, Am I Right?* Light splashes across our bodies again, and again, and I try, for one last, lingering moment, to hold on to normalcy. But everything is crumbling too fast. Even here, in the arms of a boy who knows exactly what I am and isn't afraid, my otherness catches up. This is it: no matter how much I dance. No matter how spangled my shirts, or professional my art portfolio. I am going to spend the rest of my life getting ambushed by amateur photographers and being followed by strangers who hope to sell the crumbs in my wake to the press in exchange for fifteen minutes of fame. Maybe betrayed by friends. Always second-guessing the words before they come out of my mouth. Never able to get out of the public eye. Chad starts to speak, but I break away. He follows me a few steps, and I can hear him shouting, *it's okay* and *let's get out of here* and *just some dumb girl*. But it isn't.

He catches up to me at the edge of the dance floor.

'Call me,' he shouts.

'I will.'

'Promise,' he says. He looks so uncertain in the strobe lights, blinking between light and dark like *yes* and *no*, back to back to back.

I reach up on tiptoe and kiss his cheek, then step out onto the back porch, into the cigarette and neon haze. Beyond the porch, the October air is soft and dense, the streetlights stippling the sleeping city skyline like fireflies.

I want this world. I wish there were another way to be part of it.

144

I dial Dr Morse. It is late, one in the morning, but she picks up in an instant.

'Yes?' she says.

'I'm ready,' I say. 'Let's do it.'

18

I make the trip to the doctor's office alone on Sunday morning. Some part of me had hoped Caro would come with me again: the two of us hand in hand, battling the flash bulbs and microphones like a sexy phalanx of sisterhood. But she and Todd were already gone when I woke up, and so I drive in in silence. At the edge of the parking lot I grip the black binder of forms to my lonely chest, take a breath, and wade through the sea of reporters, oglers and fans.

'Morgan, over here!'

'Hole Girl, how do you feel?'

'Tell us about your relationship with the Missing Piece!'

Lumpy McLumpface, I want to correct. But I don't want to give the reporters a decent sound bite. They shout and wave, their words knocking against me like pebbles in the surf, tumbling over and over my toes. How do they know when my appointments are: is someone slipping them the schedule, or do they show up every day at dawn on the off-chance I'll be there?

Doctors Morse and Takahashi are standing in the waiting room when I arrive. The team of researchers has been pared down now to a small cluster of people in beige and a pair of brightly scrubbed nurses.

'Good morning,' Dr Morse says. Her red hair is clipped back into a low ponytail. There is a brightness to her today. A sparkle where before there was only spark. 'Sorry about the press.'

'Are you?' I ask. 'I thought you called them off.'

'I'm sorry you find them an inconvenience,' she corrects. 'The more attention we get, the better our funding.'

She smiles at me, entitlement and teeth in a white lab coat.

'This is about funding?' I ask, aghast. 'My best friend is getting harassed at school. There are strangers talking about my vagina on the internet. I lost my job.'

'Let your mother take care of you. The publicity's not hurting her career a bit,' she says, turning back to her clipboard. 'Howie's already in the back. Let's go ahead and get started.'

I go to change, feeling like I've been slapped in the mouth. The new nurse leads me in my poufy, Oompa Loompa-style medical shorts and filmy paper gown to a large, well-lit family medicine room, with twin examination tables and posters of apples and kittens. Howie is there, similarly attired in ridiculous shorts and blue gown, Lump tenting beneath the fabric. He looks up at me when I come in, but when I say nothing he slumps, paper sighing against the table.

Our first appointment is dedicated to physical examination:

the familiarizing of both doctors with our bodies to prepare themselves, and us, for the battery of tests they intend to begin later in the week. We give blood samples, urine samples, faecal samples, cheek swabs. The nurses fuss around us with small and comforting sleights of hand: taking height, weight, temperature, blood pressure. My usual nurse, Amanda, jokes with me about her kindergartener and removes the blood pressure cuff with cool, steady hands, and I wonder if the banality of this routine is meant in part to calm my nerves. I glance up and lock eyes with a blonde researcher, who scratches her ear and looks away again nervously. Even though my forms are signed and the doors are locked, there's something in me that makes these people look at me like a panther pacing in a cage.

I like it.

The nurses fuss with our paper gowns, trying to reveal our torsos without revealing my breasts. Eventually, they work out a system: rigging the gowns so that the material is gathered and tied behind us like giant blue ponytails. I flinch as the paper lifts away and cold air hits my skin. Despite themselves, the researchers murmur. Dr Morse leans in eagerly, gripping the sides of my waist like a latex-fingered lover.

'Incredible,' she breathes.

Her breath rushes hot through the Hole and trickles up my back, rustling the paper gathered there. I take a step back, bumping the examination table. Morse steps with me, oblivious, and gestures for the research team to look.

'Look at the collapse of the intercostal space between ribs

nine and ten,' she says. She lays her hand flat on my midriff as the group crowds in, her spread fingers pulling at the lip of the Hole. I force myself to breathe steadily, avoiding looking at anyone in the face. *She's a professional*, I tell myself. *She's just trying to help. She's going to make me better.* But I flinch as she casually places a hand on my lower breast, pushing it out of the way as she examines my torso. I turn my head and see Howie staring.

There's a sharp pinch inside the Hole, and I slap Dr Morse's latexed wrist away.

'Don't,' I snap. My stomach skitters beneath the skin, all my nerves jangling.

Dr Morse looks up at me, gaze slowly focusing, as though she'd forgotten I was there. She flexes her wrist experimentally.

'I'm just trying to get a measurement,' she says.

'No one touches me there,' I say.

'Surely your physician touches you—'

'I've known Taka since I was ten.'

Dr Morse turns to Dr Takahashi.

'Hiro,' she says. 'Please deal with your patient.'

Taka rises and regards the two of us a long moment. Then he crosses to Dr Morse, speaking quietly in her ear. She goes still, listening, her gloved fingers loosening on my hips. At last, her body folds in a sigh. Taka stands.

'You have full access to her records and information,' he reminds her.

Amanda comes to hover nearby.

'We'll be happy to get you anything you need,' she tells

Morse. Her voice is all sweet tea, but her smile is a hard wedge of lemon. Morse looks up at her and exhales long through her nose.

'Fine,' she says at last. But when she takes her hands away, the imprints of her fingers remain: stark red ellipses promising *future*.

As the team of doctors pokes and prods at me, I peek over at the other table, where Dr Takahashi and another small group of the researchers are studying Howie. He looks ganglier than ever beneath his pouf of crumpled paper, but his awkwardness has melted away. He has none of my discomfort with intense medical scrutiny – he seems as relaxed in Dr Takahashi's gloved hands as an infant in a bath.

Despite his qualms about Dr Morse, my doctor is clearly as fascinated by Howie's body as Howie's doctor is by mine. He moves carefully, asking permission, but a fascination shines behind his glasses. 'Does this hurt?' he asks. 'How does it feel?' Howie: *No, nothing, like a touch, like cold, like hot.* The Lump sticks stiffly out from his side, a smooth oblong knot of fat and blood vessel, cartilage and nerve, downed with the same fine blond hair that shines on his pale stomach. Takahashi runs a finger along its tip, and Howie laughs, the bright, happy sound shattering the tense concentration of the group shining a blue light through my Hole. 'It tickles,' he sheepishly tells the room. A blush creeps up to his ears. Dr Morse, barred from prodding my insides, contents herself with drawing gallons of my blood for testing. She readies the butterfly stick herself, waving Amanda away. 'Not that I doubt this clinic's methods,' she says, in a tone that implies otherwise. 'We just prefer a clean data set.'

Behind her back, Amanda shoots Taka a look. I don't know if I'm supposed to see it, but I laugh aloud. The needle jumps in my arm. 'Ow,' I say.

'This will be easier if you keep still,' Dr Morse raps out.

'I'm sorry,' I say, straight-faced. 'I didn't mean to disrupt your method.'

She sighs, patient and long-suffering. I sneak a peek at Taka. From behind his glasses, he winks.

The clock reads almost noon when my stomach rumbles audibly, and the researchers share a low ripple of laughter. Dr Morse stands, looking exhausted but happy. A glow suffuses her face, and despite her best efforts, one tendril of hair has escaped her silver clip, falling down into her face.

'All right,' she says. 'Almost done.'

Someone groans, and everybody laughs again. The atmosphere has grown convivial in the last hours. The serious business of our bodies has been sampled and charted and captured in photos and scans. The mystery seems more manageable now that it's down on paper.

Dr Takahashi talks us through the next few weeks: their teams have prepped samples of modified genetic material to treat us with. Dr Morse would like to get us started on them as early as next week.

'We're looking at a promising new method from Switzerland that performs gene transfer on a sample of patient cells under controlled conditions in a lab setting and returns the modified cells to the patient,' he tells us. 'We'll be doing so through a series of localised injections over the next several months.' He pauses. 'Do you have questions?' We do not. Taka talks. Everyone nods and nods and nods. Even I feel a strange surge of optimism. The air is like summer camp, and our bodies are sites of camp-wide Colour Wars battles: Lump vs. Hole; the team captains smeared in war paint and calamine lotion. Even when Taka explains the drawbacks, the side effects, it is hard to shake the feeling that at the end of the day, our parents will come to pick us up, and there will be ice creams for all.

'This is a highly experimental procedure,' Taka warns us. 'The altered genetic material could be rejected by your bodies out of hand. That's a best-case scenario. Worst case, cells start proliferating where they aren't supposed to. Or the inverse: if your immune response targets cells in the body other than the desired ones, it could result in any number of side effects.'

'Like ... my ears could close up? Or ...?'

'Cancer,' Taka says flatly. 'Cancer or extreme immuno-deficiency. Things we can't begin to predict.'

People are gathering things, ready to go. I close my eyes, letting the words wash over me. I know I should be more scared. But I feel like I'm on board a boat that's already left the harbour. A boat I boarded because, more than anything, I want to take back control of my life. Even if it means great risk.

'I think we've done enough for the day,' Dr Morse announces. 'Morgan, Howie, thank you. We'll meet again next Saturday, after the results come back from the lab. You can get changed.'

I expect people to ask me questions, but they turn to each other, chatting, stretching, asking about spouses and children. Howie and I stand alone, the air around us empty of hands and eyes for the first time in hours.

'That wasn't so bad,' Howie says to me. I blink, clearing my head of the strange dream of the last few hours, and am surprised to find myself smiling. The Lump is still weird and revolting, and Howie's doctor is a maniac, but his eyes are kind. Maybe he's right. Maybe this isn't so bad.

We follow Amanda down the hall to the dressing rooms where our empty clothes sit huddled in cool, dark cubicles, waiting for us to return and restore them to life. I'm tugging at my bra when there's a knock on the door. It swings open before I can answer. 'Someone's in here,' I blurt as Dr Morse slips into the small room. She leans against the door, arms crossed.

I hastily tug my shirt over my head.

'I was hoping we could chat,' she says.

I can't look at her without remembering the feeling of her latex finger, hot and intrusive, worming into my private space.

'I'm getting dressed,' I say.

She waves a hand dismissively. 'I'm a doctor,' she says. 'I've seen it all.' She fixes me with an intense gaze as I awkwardly pull on my jeans.

'I wanted to talk with you about the Hole,' she says. 'We're going to have to do an internal physical examination eventually.' I extend my hand for a sneaker, and she passes it to me. 'I know it's uncomfortable. But it's for the best.'

'Why?' I ask.

'We have to know exactly what we're working with,' she says.

'Taka already knows,' I say. I step into my other sneaker, mashing the heel. 'You have all of his files.'

Dr Morse blinks several times, a thin and rapid flutter of lashes, as if she is trying to wipe the lack of cooperation from my face.

'You know this will be easier if we trust each other,' she says.

Her voice is cool and condescending: a tone I've heard hundreds of times before from teachers and adults. *Be reasonable. This hurts me more than it hurts you.* A tone that isn't used to being questioned. It probably works great on sweet kids like Howie. But the fire burning in my core? That's a lifetime of being my mother's daughter.

'It'd be easier for me to trust you if you quit treating me like a child,' I say.

'Maybe you should quit acting like one,' she says tightly.

I reach down and free the heel of my sneaker. 'Look. You prepped me for a major medical decision by ambushing me with a camera crew. You've been saying shit things about me in the press – the same press that you fed that tacky story

154

about soulmates to – so now everyone's obsessed with me, *and* convinced that I'm a flaky party girl. So no matter what I do, or what I say about this crazy experiment, no one will take me seriously.'

Morse's jaw tenses. That last part had been an educated guess, but it seems like it landed close to home.

'I'm not a child,' I say. 'There's just something about being strong-armed by someone who seems to have a weirdly personal interest in seeing my insides that makes me go a little Genghis Khan.' I pick up my bag. 'I'm done being your media monkey. Call off the circus. No more Puzzle Pieces. If we do this, we do it quietly.'

'The more attention we get, the better the fundin—'

'I'd bet cash money that if my mom's lawyers looked into how the press got wind of my medical history, your funding would suddenly find itself at risk.' I fold my arms. 'Care to take that bet?'

The air thrums between us, hot. Dr Morse takes a deep breath and closes her eyes, rubbing the eyelids with her thumbs. It is a long count of five.

'We're just trying to help you,' she says.

'Really?' I say. 'Because it seems to me like you're trying to help *you*.'

I step toward her and she moves aside, letting me pass. Her hand closes over my wrist as I turn the knob.

'It's too late, Morgan. Even if I wanted to. Your story is out there in the world, now. Try to at least smile for the cameras.'

I yank my arm from her grip and leave her alone in the tiny room.

Howie is waiting for me in the lobby downstairs, a gangly silhouette against the bright streak of day. Beyond the frosted windows, the black shapes of bodies loom. Anxiety climbs the back of my throat.

'How'd it go?' he asks.

'Fine,' I say, sizing him up. He's back in his baggy clothes, the pale yellow shirt and flop of his hair reminding me of a yellow Labrador puppy. He seems so innocent. But he's been working with Morse for years.

'Howie,' I begin, tentatively. 'I saw your quote in the paper. This whole "Puzzle Piece" thing . . .'

He drops his head, a blush climbing to his ears. 'Oh God, I'm sorry. It's so embarrassing, isn't it?'

'So you don't really think that?' I ask, relieved. 'I mean, that I was put on earth to meet you, or whatever.'

He hesitates.

'Oh my God, you *do*?' I ask, recoiling.

Which is when I trip backward over the doormat.

Which triggers the sliding doors.

Which is when all the mics swing down, and the shiny eyes of the cameras blink open, just in time to capture in high definition the look of disgust on my face.

19

The press descends, thick as black flies.

'Morgan, over here!'

'What did your doctors say about the cure?'

'Puzzle pieces, closer together and smile!'

Howie stands frozen, lone and slump-shouldered in the surging sea of shouts. The cameras eat it all up: the Lump, the Hole. They eat up the clear line of light between our separate bodies.

'Can we talk about this later?' Howie asks in a low voice.

My voice grows louder. 'Why wait? This is what you and your doctor want, right, for me to talk to the press? Pump up the media circus, let them know the freaks are in town?'

Howie ducks his head, as though that will lower the volume of my voice. 'I don't like the press either,' he says softly.

'Tell it to your boss.'

'She's not ... ' he says, then stops, frustrated.

'She's not what?' I ask. 'No, wait. Say it loud enough for the mics. Unlike me, they're super excited to buy your bullshit.'

Howie's face crumples inwards. I know that look. I felt that way every time some Yum Yum Situation groupie teased me about my bulky sweaters. Or when I was always picked last for gym. Or when everyone else at every school paired off happily, two by normal two, and I was left in the cold with my paints, and with a far-away and slowly disappearing best friend, and a Hole sitting boring and empty and useless in my stomach as an ashtray in an airplane lavatory.

I'm sorry sits on the tip of my tongue, an egg waiting to hatch. But with the cameras closing in like that, how can you say anything real?

'I'm just here to get cured,' I say at last. Then I ford the crowd, head down, muscles clenching and knotting secretly beneath my shirt, a sailor's delight: a tie that would never loosen at sea. Half of the cameras follow me, watch me fumble for my car keys with half-camera hearts. But the real story is behind us, standing small and lumpy and stoop-shouldered on the side-walk: *Howie Garrison takes his Lumps. Hole Girl plays with Matches.*

As I drive away, I glance at my face in the rear-view mirror: the girl who looks back is defiant and burning and not sorry at all.

I paint in a frenzy for the rest of the day, trying to chase all thoughts of Howie from my mind, but everything comes out an angry scrawl: yellow shot through with red, shot through furiously with black. I'm furious with Howie for being so stu-pidly vulnerable, and myself for being the One True Asshole who crushed his dreams, and with Dr Morse for planting those barbed wire dreams in the first place.

The crowd of reporters outside the window waxes and wanes, finally thinning when night falls. I turn on the TV to ward away the dark outside, and am sketching in charcoal when the story airs on the local news.

I have been half-expecting it, but my heart still drops when I see my own face on the television, screwed up and silently shouting. I set down my sketch, and turn up the volume just in time to hear my voice shout, false and too tinny:

'The freaks are in town!'

The image of my twisted face freezes over a graphic of two puzzle pieces breaking apart and bursting into flames. The caption reads: MATCH MADE IN HELL.

'So-called Hole Girl Morgan Stone shocked fans today by turning on the boy doctors agree may be the cure for her curious ailment,' a blonde anchorwoman calmly announces before the dripping flames.

I switch networks. And find myself again. And again. *'The freaks!'* I shout on ABC, NBC, WRAL. *'The freaks are in town!'*

'The young 'puzzle pair' at the centre of a controversial genetics study are turning out not *to be such a matched pair after all,'* states a parsnip-nosed anchorman.

'I'm just here to be cured,' I announce on-screen. Cut to Howie's delicate face, collapsing like wet paper in the long-gone sunlight.

'That's not fair,' I say, sitting up on the couch. 'That's not how it happened.' But the cameras stay with Howie's broken eyes as I flip the channels, jumping to a powdered Asian newscaster, then black, then red-headed weighing in on my life in immaculate Midwestern accents. They seem relaxed, even faintly amused. This is a fluff piece, a break from Syria and discretionary budget cuts. They are almost smiling as they smear my life across the nation.

'Morgan Stone and Howie Garrison captured the nation's imaginations – and hearts – earlier this week,' a voiceover reports. *'But now, America's breaking up – with the Hole Girl.'*

'She's just really awful,' an old Southern woman says, squinting into the camera.

'I don't know if they had, like, a fight or something,' a smoky-eyed girl chirps. *'He looked pretty messed up. I mean, they're supposed to be, like, this perfect match, right? But that don't look really perfect.'*

'It seems the biggest Hole here today – is in this young man's heart,' the coiffed anchor concludes, cutting back to a still of Howie's frozen eyes. *'I'm Maya Lang with—'*

I switch off the TV, and let all the sound in the room go with it.

Outside, the last of the light is being wrung from the sky. I blink at the sketch in my lap: one small shape in the centre of a converging mass, the locus twisting off the page like an irrelevant and lifeless galaxy, spiral-armed. I lower my finger and smear into the solitary figure, scribbling faster and faster

160

until my fingers are black and aching and the page is nothing but a grey haze with a pale shadow in the middle: a ghost that won't quite be erased.

I tear the page from the sketchbook with a paper whisper, and stick it to the still-wet oil painting. Then I switch on a lamp and take up the paints once more, painting over and onto the edges of the sketch, moulding the two pieces into one. *I'm not the villain*, I tell myself, and the girls on the news, and Howie's broken face. My muscles stiffen and ache and then fall away, forgotten. At some point I fall into sleep, colours streaking my dreams.

I wake on the couch to a room flooded with too much sun and the rich smell of black coffee. My brushes have been rinsed and are shining in their mason jar. Caro's curled in the armchair nearby, frowning at a floppy workbook. She's dressed for her day off: barefoot and braless, all slouching lines and obtuse angles, a green ceramic mug balanced against her thigh.

'Light reading?' I croak.

She looks up and beams. 'Hey, sleepyhead,' she says, letting the book fall back against her chest. *SAT Test Prep 5000*. There's another on the coffee table, a *Princeton Review* stacked neatly on top of the back issues of *Cosmo* and *The Joy of Cooking*. Multicoloured bookmarks flag its pages.

'Want to know about pi?' she asks. 'I can tell you so much about pi right now.'

I rub my eyes. My fingernails are caked in the crimson of yesterday's catharsis. 'Yeah?'

'Actually, no.' She scoots around in the chair, curling like a shrimp. Slowly she begins to invert her body, wriggling her head towards the floor. 'It turns out I need to re-learn, like, all of geometry. It's pretty depressing.'

I lean forward and rescue her mug, putting it on the floor. I feel like pieces of my brain are strewn across the room. 'I thought you were applying for sociology programs,' I say, foggily, reaching for the *Princeton Review*. 'Do they care about math?'

'They might,' she says cheerfully. 'Anyway, it's kind of empowering, right? It's like reclaiming lost intellectual territory.'

'You are literally the only person in the world who thinks things like that,' I say, flipping through the book and trying not to think about how Caro will move on and up and into some brilliant future while I spend the rest of my life in our apartment, arranging the instant ramen noodles in the pantry by colour and making voodoo dolls of Dr Morse.

'I started working on my personal statement yesterday,' she says. '"Caroline is super goddamned special. Please admit her to your revered institution." What do you think?'

'Sounds like a winner,' I say. I lift her mug and tip a bead of cold tea onto my tongue. I lick my lips and say, uber-casually, 'So, you're serious about school in New England? It's cold up there. They say the word "car" funny.'

'It's whatever. I'll get a coat. And so many adorable mitten sets.' She twists her arms up above her head, begins to pick out strands of hair, to plait a tiny braid. 'Todd said he'd apply for a transfer with me. So I won't be starting totally over.'

'Oh.' I try to think of something to say. 'What about Yum Yum Situation?'

She laughs. 'I think the local music scene will survive without them.'

I study her in her chair and am struck by the impression that her body is a balloon, waiting to float away: the tiny braid in her hair the string. I want to reach out and hold it with equally tiny hands: each finger the perfect word, each nail the one small, shining syllable, that would convince her to stay.

'He could start a solo band,' I say, but my heart's not really in it. 'It could be called "Yum".'

She laughs. 'I'll suggest it. He finished his song, by the way.' She gestures to a stack of CD cases on the table. 'He left a bunch of demos for me to take to Java Jane. You should give it a listen. It's inspired by your press coverage. You'd like it.'

'Yeah,' I say, disinterested, as with all things Todd. A silence stretches between us.

'Morgs, why don't you come with me?' she asks.

'To Java Jane?'

'Doofus. To college.'

Hope leaps up in me, a bright, hard band.

'But I don't know sociology,' I say, like it's a language I can learn. Like it is French.

'You can do an art programme. Or whatever. Don't be obtuse.' Upside-down, she winks. 'See that? SAT word, right there.'

I fall back on the couch, dissipated. 'Yeah,' I say. 'Art programmes.'

'I saw the new painting,' she says, gesturing to the easel. 'How's the gallery thing coming together?'

'You saw the painting,' I say. 'Not great.'

'Everyone has off-days,' she says.

I run my hands through my hair, tossing it like salad. 'I don't know,' I say. 'It was just something I had to get out of my system.'

'Because of the news?' she asks, delicately.

'They made it look worse than it was,' I say at last.

'It looked pretty bad.'

'It was pretty bad.' I stare at the ceiling. 'You think I was a raging bitch, don't you.'

The silence in the room stretches far, far too long.

'You could have been a little nicer,' Caro tries, diplomatically.

'Never mind,' I say. 'Just forget it. Let's talk about not-me for a while.'

'Sure,' Caro says. 'Sorry.' She opens her mouth, and then closes it, and then says, 'But you're going to have to spend a lot of time together, and you have so much in common—'

I slap the study book closed. It's louder than I meant. Caro jumps.

164

'Just what, exactly, do we have in common?' I snap. 'I have a hole in my middle. He has a fatty tumour. All right?'

'All right,' Caro says. 'Sorry.'

'It's like we're two weird endangered sea creatures or something. And if we don't mate, then half the housewives of America are going to call me an asshole on national television.'

Everything is coming out wrong. I want to tell her about Dr Morse's breath in my stomach, her finger in my Hole. The smug purse of her lips when she said, *the more attention we get, the better our funding*, as though the equation is so simple: more money for science while I'm hounded from car to building and back again, while strangers weep over Howie's and my doomed love, and leave doughnuts on my car, and post detailed internet critiques about whether or not my body is punishment for some sin.

'I understand,' Caro says with care. 'But I just worry that maybe you're lonely. In a way that I can't fix,' she adds. 'Or other people can't fix.'

We've been through a lot in the last ten years, but I have never, ever hated Caro until this moment.

'You mean other *normal* people,' I say, flatly. 'You think I need the company of my own kind.'

She scrambles upright. 'What? No. Of course not.' Her words are the right words now, oriented the right way, but deep in their root, I can still hear the tiniest seed of pity.

'No, it's fine.' I bite off each word like it burns. 'The world is full of freaks for me to be friends with. Don't worry about it. You go off to college and make some normal friends for once.'

'Stop,' she says. 'That's not what I meant.'

'Or just hang out with Boring Todd all day. And talk about tyre pressure, or lanyards, or really neat rocks.'

'Will you not call him that?'

I place the *Princeton Review* carefully back on the table and stand. 'Look, I appreciate your *concern*. But you don't need to worry about me being lonely. If spending two years dating a guy who thinks wearing mismatched socks is hilarious isn't lonely, then I don't know what is.'

Caro collects her books. Her blonde hair stands out against the angry red of her face, a thick halo.

'I have to study,' she says.

'Great,' I say. 'Good luck getting into school for normal people. I'm sure you'll be a great success.'

I stalk out of the apartment and hop on my bike, dodging a lone cameraman as I dive down a side alley. I am filled with rage and hurt and an all-consuming hunger. I fly past restaurants and shops, past buildings in which strangers are loving and hating and sitting down to meals together. Someone shouts *Hole Girl* at me from a car window, and I bare my teeth to the empty air, swallowing it all down. I swallow the oaks and the sky and the sun and the clouds. But no matter how fast I go, I will never be full.

*

That night I dream that the Hole heals around a knife. The skin is just tight enough that the blade dimples my skin. I cannot move without cutting myself.

I lie on the floor.

'Help, help!' I say.

Caroline stands over me, watching.

'Caroline, help,' I say.

'Call a doctor,' she says.

'I can't,' I say. 'I can't move. I'll cut myself.'

'You're smart,' she says. 'Figure it out.'

She goes away and leaves me there, frozen, afraid even to breathe.

20

Caro and I step around each other the next few days, a tacit dance of almost-avoidance. She's in the shower while I'm in the kitchen; I'm in my room while she gathers her work things, ties her shoes. I definitely take my meals to my bedroom because I want the quiet time to think about my art. She's definitely spending more nights at Todd's because it's closer to Java Jane, or because the feng shui is better, or because they're staying up long past midnight, plotting their new life without me.

On the fifth day, I listen to Todd's demo to kill the silence. From the opening note it's clear that this is better than typical YYS fare, with an instant catchiness and an urgency that are usually lacking in their light power pop numbers.

Arquette usually does vocals, but instead Todd's voice pours through the speaker. It's light with a rasp I wouldn't have expected. He sings: *'She says you want the whole girl, but I'm just a Hole girl . . .'*

I grab the demo sleeve. HOLE GIRL it reads, in plain black

font. YUM YUM SITUATION. I listen in disbelief as the band swings into the chorus.

'Reach on down and fall right through,
She'll reach for you and she'll fall too,
Hole Girl, Hole Girl,
I'm falling for you.'

My heart does the same choking skip of the ailing coffee machine downstairs. I flip over the sleeve, looking for liner notes, but nothing.

I hope Todd makes a lot of money on it. Maybe I can make up my rent by suing his ass off.

I poke colours at my canvases, watch movies on Caro's Netflix account. The RECENTLY VIEWED window acts like a conversation between us:

Me: *Breaking Bad*
She: *As Good As It Gets*
Me: *Friends*
She: *Once Upon a Time*

This week I've clicked my way through every episode of *My Little Pony: Friendship Is Magic*, hoping to provoke a remonstration – Caro's voice scolding, then breaking into a laugh, and then the two of us able to make this fight into a joke, something stupid we roll our eyes about, *remember that time I yelled at you about Boring Todd because I was secretly afraid you'd leave me for ever? Pass the popcorn* – but I got nothing except colour-burned retinas and the theme song stuck in my head for days, and afterwards she and Todd embarked on a Bill Murray marathon.

Public Scrutiny has churned back to life, with new flashy banner ads showcasing LOCAL SINGLES and HIT THE TARGET TO WIN A FREE CAR! The Hole Girl thread has been revamped and given its own message board, with individual discussion boards for photos, discussion and FAQs. There's a thread with a ReverbNation link to the 'Hole Girl' single, and even a forum dedicated to fan art: pictures strangers drew of me with my Hole, or, anyway, of someone vaguely young and white and female with a Hole. Most of the pictures feature my silhouette only, or make me way prettier than I am in real life. Bustier, too. Occasionally, with cat ears. The Hole is usually in the wrong place, in the middle of my stomach rather than to the lower right, and perfectly round. I look down at the real Hole, sitting innocent and imperfect just above my waistline. I shift to the side, feeling the squish of organs, and the skin around it dimples softly. It seems to me as mundane as flossing.

I skip, grimacing, past the few pieces labelled NSFW. There's a Hole Girl dancing, or posing like a fashion model, or looking longingly out of a window. One woman posts a picture her five-year-old drew after seeing me on the news: a stick-armed girl with a triangle nose and doughnut stomach, smiling in front of a house with a chimney and sun. I open one last image and freeze.

It's a pencil drawing of two girls, hands entwined. One is clearly me – the short dark hair, the trademark crop top and an artistic dusting of freckles. The other is a taller girl with long, straight hair. Both figures stare out at the viewer with the same soft, blank sadness. Both have Holes punched out of their guts.

The piece is titled 'We All Have Holes'.

I suck in my breath, study the drawing more closely. The artist has depicted the Hole fairly accurately – the size, shape and location echo my Hole pretty closely. The other figure's Hole is a perfect mirror image to mine.

I tug at my fingernails. The artist's screen name is mindthegap.

It couldn't be. There couldn't be another one of me.

Could there?

I open a private message to mindthegap. I write, What kind of hole are we talking? Click 'send'. And wait, with a trembling that begins somewhere deep in me and won't stop.

Hit refresh.

Refresh.

Refresh.

A heart-leaping message blinks to life:

mindthegap: I don't have a literal hole! ha ha. I'm not Hole Girl. But I feel like her sometimes.

I should have known. Of course I'm the only one. If I wasn't, I would have met someone else like me by now. Deflated, I feel irritated by the artistic appropriation, by being made metaphor. We all have pain. We all have a sad story. But we don't all have a flesh tunnel carved out of our middles, narrowly missing the spine and scrambling our menstrual cycles.

I navigate back to the original 'We All Have Holes' drawing. Beneath it, I realise that mindthegap posted a message:

Since a few of you asked: I don't have a hole like Hole Girl. But that doesn't mean I'm not full of holes. I can't seem to connect with anyone, I'm like a human sieve. I walk through the halls at school and everyone else seems to pass right through me. There's so much noise. People laugh all the time. What are they even laughing at? Nothing, it's just so that other people will notice them. My mom says I'm depressed, but I think I'm right. I wish I had a real Hole that I could crawl into and disappear.

The thread stretches on:

piranhanna: I know just how you feel. Sometimes I feel like I'm the only real person on the planet.

chippedshoulder: It hurts so much . . .

rickz3: My Hole is that I'm in love with my best friend . . .

janeyz: My Hole is that my uncle molested me from the time I was four until I was thirteen. I've never told anyone until now.

My scorn begins to burn off as I read two pages, three, four. None of these people have literal Holes. But some do have other physical deformities, and other sadnesses separate but great. There is something fragile and touching in their honesty, lonely strangers pouring their woes out into the ether, and to each other, and trusting they'll find kindness.

I pop open a new message to mindthegap.

I get what you mean.

And she, almost immediately:

So, what would be your Hole?

It would be so easy just to tell her. It might even be a relief. But, studying the original picture, I feel helplessly shallow. It's impossible to ignore that this piece of weird fan art buried on the internet is doing what I've failed to do in my own work: bringing people together. Changing the world.

This whole girl is better than I am at articulating what it means to live life with a Hole. How disappointed would she be to discover the actual me?

I write: Artist's block, I guess.

And also, that I somehow manage to hurt everyone around me, and I'm afraid I'll never stop.

And that no matter what I do, I am going to be alone for ever.

Then I pull on an overlarge hoodie and slink from the house, the silent sound of failure echoing in my ears.

I bike through the NC State campus, wishing I could afford to go to a movie and escape myself. The wind glides down my narrow chest and whispers around the Hole, the day threading through me.

I want more than ever to talk to Caro. To say, *is that song about me?* To ask, *what's so wrong with me that you have to leave?* That my dad left. That my mom had to start leaving when I was thirteen. I blink away tears, because tears don't do anything except make you look more pathetic when the fact is just that you want to change your life, and you can't.

I pedal harder, the fibres of my thigh muscles burning. Someone shouts to my right, and I automatically ignore it. The shout becomes louder, more insistent, and there's something blue in my peripheral vision. Something blue, and tall, and extremely familiar.

I skid to a stop, the adrenalin roar falling silent in my ears.

'Hey,' he says. 'You were really booking it.'

I blink up at Handsome Chad. He's glistening, tan and honey-haired in running shorts and a tank top. I'm used to noticing musculature in a prescribed, artistic way, but the lanky, golden muscles of his arms make something in me seize up. *Woah*, I think.

'You're a runner,' I say, stupidly. Of course he is. Chad grins and shrugs.

'I work out,' he says. 'So what happened to you the other night?'

I unpeel my fingers from the brakes, wishing my body would quit pounding. 'I just got sick of having cameras shoved in my face.'

'You don't like the whole celebrity thing?'

'*No*,' I say, too emphatically. I peer into his eyes, trying to glean some kernel of understanding, but his face is inscrutable.

'Oh,' he says. 'Yeah, I guess it's kind of a drag.' He rumples into a grin and my insides flip. 'I thought you were mad at me or something.'

I remember the secret language of his hands tracing my hipbones and am suddenly aware of the sweat stains beneath my arms, the fact that I look like a mushroom in my bike helmet. 'No,' I say again, more quietly. 'Definitely not.'

He breathes out. 'Whew. That's a relief.' He reaches down, traces my forearm with a finger. My skin explodes into points of light.

He says, 'You've got to quit disappearing on me like that, Cinderella.'

'I'm working on it,' I say.

'Yeah?' he says. 'You coming out tonight?'

His eyes are the whole sky's worth of blue. I look up into them, and try to remember feeling like I was going to die alone, and suddenly it seems like a made-up thing, a story that happened to somebody else. I look at this boy who knew about the Hole and kissed me anyway, and kissing him was like the idea of champagne: warmth and bubbles and golden light.

I say, 'Yes.'

On the way home, I take a detour via the pharmacy. I stand a long time in the personal hygiene aisle, pretending to deliberate between brands of tampons as I slowly, unabashedly reach beneath my jacket and knock a mint green box of condoms into my bag. Cyndi Lauper is singing about how girls just wanna have fun, and because she is right, I wink at the stockroom boy as I saunter toward the lipstick display, a box of shoplifted contraception riding safely along in my purse.

Here are the reasons to not lose my virginity:

1. Lack of interested partner
2. Fear it will hurt
3. Certainty I will do it wrong

Number three is the one that worries me the most. Most of my knowledge of the actual act of sex is vague. Even the romance novels Caroline and I used to read aloud to each other when we were twelve, giggling, gave me nothing to work with: two-dimensional characters with names like Chastity and Randolphe endlessly penetrating each other's throbbing sexes with their throbbing sexes. What was I supposed to do? What if we get them mixed up? What if it turns out that *sex* doesn't mean what I think it does at all?

But I also never thought I could dance. I never thought I could be myself in public and have anyone still be interested. And so maybe I can do this, too.

The second the sun goes down, I lock my bedroom door and get ready for the most important night of my life. I slip into a tiny barely-a-shirt, a navy blue bikini top studded with rhinestone stars. Even for Mansion me, it's pretty slutty, all done up in rhinestones, with perfect little sequined moons adorning the nipples. *Night breasts!* I had proclaimed to Caro when I found it, promenading into her dressing room at Goodwill. She had rolled her eyes. *Morgs, I don't even want to think about where that's been.* Me: *On somebody's boobs, probably.* She'd made me take it to the dry cleaner's.

I lean towards the mirror, drinking in my naked face: the small green eyes, the sharp, pale cheeks, the colourless lips. My breath clouds the glass. I fade away like a magician behind the fog, pull out the eyeliner I filched from Caroline's bathroom drawer, and go to work.

I sketch lightly along the lash line of my right eye with the eye pencil. Step back and survey. It's not really noticeable. I turn my face right and left, telling myself: *pretty side. Boring side. Pretty side. Boring side.*

Fuck it.

I deepen the line, bring it around my lower lid. I blink and the line jumps a little. 'Crap,' I mutter. I try to wipe it down but it just sort of smears. How does Caroline do this? I switch around, try to give my eyes a shape. I hold my mouth open, eyes perfectly still. I think cat. I think Cleopatra.

When I set down the pencil, my eyes are dramatic and bright, dark-fringed sea glass glimmering palely in my face. I pull out the lip gloss, apply it as if I know what I'm doing. It's thick and sticky and vaguely lemonade-scented.

I step back and look at myself. My mouth is a new and shining thing: full and ripe as a peach. My cheeks look kind of washed out, but I didn't steal any blusher, so it will have to do.

Hey baby, I mouth at the mirror. *What's your number?*

I smile coyly. I bite my lower lip. The strange, sexy me in the mirror looks wild. She looks treacherous. She's not the girl you fall in love with. She's the one who leaves you bruised.

'My place or yours?' I ask the mirror, low and throaty. Laugh condescendingly.

I lower my eyelids at the mirror. Let my lips go long and soft. I puff them out, *Playboy*-languid. I wink seductively at the mirror. I am the world's sexiest duck.

'Hey baby,' I say. 'Got a lighter? I'd like to smoke *you* below the belt.'

I'm trying to push my breasts together to make cleavage when my phone rings and I jump.

The phone rings again, screen glowing cool and blue. Caroline. I scoop the makeup under my pillow, my whole body one big heartbeat.

'Hello?'

There's a silence on the other end. Again, I say, 'Hello?'

Cotton wisps of sound filter up to my ear: a muffling of music, a distant, male voice. A pocket dial. She didn't mean to call me at all.

I grip the phone so tightly that my fingers ache. I want to shout, 'Caro, hello! I am going to go have sex now with a gorgeous, normal boy even though you've spent the last decade of our friendship secretly believing no one would ever want me!' I want to whisper, 'I am going to go have sex now for the first time ever and even though we are fighting right now I want you to tell me it will be okay!'

I pull the phone, still glowing, from my ear. I watch the timer count up slowly, second by empty second. Then I hit END.

21

I blast through the door of the Mansion at full stride. I am a girl on a mission. Or maybe a woman. I've never been sure when that transition happens. Maybe it's tonight.

I snake right out into the centre of the dance floor, and like magnets, the two of us come together.

'Hey,' I shout.

'Hey,' Chad shouts. He grins down at me from his great height. Once, this would have melted me down, but tonight, I am elemental. I am fire. I take his hand, place it on my hip.

'You look *smoking* tonight,' he says, with an easy grin. But there's something beneath our ordinary language, a palpable thing, throbbing with the music. His eyes search mine a second too long, questioning.

I pull his face to mine, and let our bodies be the answer.

I have never done this, so I don't know the protocol for getting from the club to his apartment. I don't even know if it should be his apartment or my apartment, but his seems riskier in a way that I am suddenly unafraid of. So when I don't offer, he doesn't ask. He leads me down the sidewalk and unlocks the doors of a low black car. I buckle in, looking at the interior, thinking: *this is the car of the boy I am going to sleep with.* There is the scent of cigarettes and musk, a masculine tang that I understand, with a jolt, is the smell of him that has accumulated in this small space.

'I don't have a condom,' he says, through the silent ringing in our ears.

'I do,' I say.

He flashes me a smile in the dark. 'Well, all righty, then.'

I don't know what to say to him in this space between leaving and arriving, but it turns out not to matter. We make out at red lights, make out when he stops for gas, when he parks the car. His hands graze my thighs, my sides, my breasts – lightly at first, but then hungrily, confidently. He smiles at me, and his smile is the smile of a man who knows where his next meal is coming from.

We fall through the front door tangled, our hands too busy to reach for lights. My sweater is on the floor, his lips on my neck. Everything in me is throbbing with how easy it is not to be alone; I slip my hands under his shirt, not because I think it is something I am supposed to do, but because I want it. I surprise myself with wanting it. He lifts his shirt above his head and throws it away into the dark room. Then he reaches behind me, tugs at the knot of my halter top. It slips to the floor in a hushed cascade of lapis and silver beads, and for a

181

second, I think I might go with it. But then we're kissing, and it's skin against skin, and it feels better than I could have imagined: the blood rushing beneath the muscled coolness, the softness, the yielding. I open my mouth to him, hungry.

He makes a low sound, his hands running up and down my sides, my back. There is a shuffling at the door, and he pulls back suddenly, laughs and swears, *shit*.

'Roommate,' he says, and pulls me by the hand through the dark to more dark. 'I'll be right back,' he says, and ducks back out into the hall.

On the other side of the door, a lamp switches on. I sway a little in the empty space of the dark room, keeping my eyes on the crack of light beneath the door. I am cold. My shirt is still in the front room, and the air that had caressed my bare skin has turned chilly and brusque. I need Chad's hands to come back, and his lips to keep mine busy so that they won't form the question I'm trying not to ask myself: *what am I doing here?*

The room floods with light, and Chad ducks back in. 'Hey,' he says, a laugh in his voice. 'Sorry about that.' He closes the door with his elbow. He has something in his hands. There's a whisper-flick of a switch and then a tiny bead of light suspended in the gloom: a lighter and candles.

'Aren't you romantic,' I say. It is disorienting to hear my voice sounding so much like mine, as though I am not standing half-naked in the room of a stranger – the same voice that orders tacos at the drive-through, and says *bless you* to sneezes. Chad laughs, uncomfortably.

'What can I say.' The flickering light of the candles illuminates the cluttered surface in small breaths. 'Keeping it classy for the ladies.'

'Ladies, plural?' I ask. 'You're pretty popular, huh?'

'Yeah, well, you know,' he says, and laughs again. Then we're kissing before the wave of misgiving can finish washing over me, and he's pulling me to the bed, and it's so easy to be pulled.

We devour each other. Everything in those romance books makes sense – the low moans, the urgency, the sense of plundering and being plundered. He looks down and smiles, candlelight painting the side of his face in flickering gold. I melt inside.

He shifts so that I'm on top of him. We're both shirtless in our jeans, and his hands are on my breasts, and beneath me, the hard lump of his erection. I am both frightened and hungry. Chad runs his hand down my pelvis, dangerously close to the Hole, and I gasp.

'Baby, are you ready for me?' he whispers.

Yes, and no, and I don't know, and it had better be now, or never.

'I think so,' I whisper.

'Have you got a condom?' he asks.

'Oh,' I say in a normal voice. 'Yeah. It's in my back pocket ...'

I start to turn, to fumble for it, but then Chad grins. 'Wait,' he says. 'I got it.' I thought we were supposed to be carried away by passion in this moment, transformed into sexier versions of ourselves, but he sounds surprisingly normal. 'Check this out,' he says.

Then he starts to push his fingers through the Hole.

I feel myself freeze, choke on nothing. His fingers are thick and hard and piling up against my organs. I look into his face, aghast. He laughs again.

'I thought I could reach it from here,' he says. 'I should have lubed up first, huh?'

I look down at the beautiful stranger wadded in strange sheets, still hard beneath me, while his hand struggles against my insides like a worm. I don't know what I am supposed to do now, what the normal, sexy girl would do. Laugh, or playfully slap his wrist. Something cool and unfeeling that would let us both walk out of here tomorrow unbruised: just two more lovely young people who lie back casually against the pillows after sex, lighting each other's cigarettes and saying disaffected things about their parents, or life these days, before sliding golden-eyed back into the seamless world, never to see each other again.

I feel bile rise in my throat, and something else.

I reach down and take the thick stump of his wrist between my thumb and forefinger, and gently remove him from my body. Then I climb from his bed, and stand on numb feet.

'Hey,' he says. 'What's wrong?'

'Nothing,' I say. I am in automatic. I am a robot. 'I've got to go.'

His face twists in the candlelight. 'Hey, come here,' he says. 'What's going on?'

I take my jeans from his limp hands, shimmy them on and step into my shoes, smashing the heels into the floor.

'This isn't working,' I say. I realise distantly that my shirt is somewhere out on the living room floor, and grab something off the dresser to wrap myself in. A sweatshirt.

He's sitting up. 'Come *on*,' he says. 'Are you seriously leaving right now?' There's anger in his voice.

'This was a mistake,' I say, very calmly. I grab my bag with trembling fingers, and let myself out.

He doesn't follow me, and I don't blame him. It's not until I get to the parking lot that I lean into the bushes, and vomit.

22

I leave that small part of myself in shrubbery and walk through the dark toward the lights of Western Boulevard. I can't stop sensing his fingers. They crawl inside me like ghosts.

The street is busy and alive even at this hour, cars slamming through the stop-lit night. I glance into the yellow windows of restaurants and bars as I slide past them. I could go inside, curl into a booth and mop my eyes with paper napkins. But I don't. I don't want to go anywhere, because I don't want what just happened to me to have happened, and I think if I keep moving it will still be *happening*. It will still be a thing I can change. Not: *I was violated and then I ate a cheeseburger with extra pickles*, tucked greasily into my memory like a soiled tissue into a winter pocket.

I dodge the students who trickle by in clumps and the girls who walk by themselves, hurriedly, keys in their fists. I pass in and out of streetlights alone, letting the roars of cars wash over me as they steer toward well-lit homes. I consider, in a clinical, detached way, the force of those thousands of pounds of metal hurtling through the darkness

I'm waiting to cross a street when a car pulls up next to me and stops. The window rolls down. Something traitorous in me thinks, *Chad?* and I feel sick.

'Hey,' the passenger shouts – a woman. Middle-aged, dressed to go out. I step towards the car, and the driver leans across to the window.

'You're the Hole Girl, aren't you?' the driver asks. 'From the news?'

I shake my head, instinctively taking a step backwards. There's a flurry of motion inside the car. I cringe away half a second too late, and something strikes the side of my skull with a thud, sprays half of my face with something wet. I stumble into the gutter, stunned. A plastic Starbucks cup bounces in the road.

'You're a fucking bitch!' the driver spits and guns the engine, shooting ahead through traffic.

The wind picks up and whistles cold as I sit on the kerb, shaking. I want to call Caro, but she's not speaking to me. I want to call my mother and tell her how right she was, what a mistake it's been to show myself to the world and expect to be treated with love. But my phone is on my bed at home, across town, abandoned in a fit of recklessness. I make myself rise on trembling legs, wipe Frappuccino from my nose, and push my tired body towards the only place left that can make it halfway right. My feet fall into a rhythm on the sidewalk: I *want* to be *fixed*. I *want* to be *fixed*. Right *left* right *left*.

Deep inside me, the ghost fingers writhe like worms.

My back and legs are aching by the time I emerge into the medical complex parking lot. All I can do is sit here and wait for morning. Lay myself at Morse's mercy, and say, *you were right. I don't want this thing any more.* Try not to look as her gloved hands reach for my stomach.

The flat grey facade is lit at night, granting the building a strange, industrial beauty. The parking lot is empty except for a single crappy old car that probably belongs to a drug dealer or a homeless person. I give it wide berth, swing like a satellite toward the amber pool of light by the door. I'm halfway there when a dark figure emerges from the building. For a moment, my heart snaps up to my throat like a rubber band – then I recognise the stooped, eggshell-frail posture and shoulders and I stop in my tracks, defeated.

Howie doesn't look any happier to see me than I am him.

I ask, 'What are you doing here?'

'Parker – Dr Morse – and I were going over a few things,' he says. The moon is tucked like a bright coin in the sky behind him. I can't imagine what he and his doctor were talking about at 3.30 in the morning, but I assume we're operating on a mutual don't-ask-don't-tell policy. He stares at me a beat too long, and I become painfully aware of my dishevelled appearance: mascara-smeared and on foot, draped in a man's sweatshirt. Irritation struggles with concern in his face, and I can't stand it, can't stand the weight of the Lump Boy's pity, and I begin, 'I'm sorry about the—'

He says, 'Do you need a ride home?'

I think about Caro, and how *home* is so broken, and then I start to cry.

We sit in Howie's car for a long time. He says nothing, doesn't touch me. I wish he would. I want him to remind me that he is here, witnessing my private unhappiness, so that I could hate him for it. But he just looks out the window in silence, letting me be private without making me be alone.

My sobs dry up to a snuffle. Howie passes me a crumpled paper napkin.

'It's the only one I have,' he says, apologetically. I dab economically, blow and wipe.

'I can't go home,' I say.

He doesn't ask. 'Okay,' he says. 'I can take you to my hotel. It's not very nice or anything, but I can sleep on the couch, or in the car—'

'No,' I say.

A breeze stirs the night. The branches above us throw shadows through the windshield.

'Do you want to talk?' he asks.

'No.'

'Do you want to be quiet?'

'Yeah.'

'Okay.'

He lets me sit in his car until I am all right. It is hours, centuries, years. Empires of myself rise and fall as the shadows pass over our strange and separate bodies.

Howie wakes me just before dawn. The interior of the car is sketched in graphite, thick with the hair of morning breath. Down in the footwell, my feet are freezing.

I blink, gluey, and he says, again, 'Morgan.'

'What time is it?'

'Just before five.' He passes this fact to me like a pebble, polished and smooth. I want to rub it with my fingers, tuck it into my pocket.

'Morgan?'

I jolt fully awake. 'Our appointment's at eight,' I say blearily.

'I know,' he says. 'But I figured you wouldn't want the press to see us arrive together, and they should start getting here pretty soon. So . . . '

I study his face, slowly glowing into being through the breath-fogged windshield. I can see precisely how I would paint that not-quite-question in his lips.

'I don't—' I say. He hears the apology before I can make it, and shakes his head.

'I can drop you off at a diner or a coffee shop or wherever if you can't go home,' he says. 'I don't know what's open this early, but if you know a place, I can take you.'

I sit up, rubbing my eyes. An unfamiliar corduroy jacket collapses onto my legs with a long sigh of warmth.

'My car's at the Mansion,' I say. 'If – I mean, if you could take me there. If you don't mind.'

He doesn't meet my gaze. But maybe it's because I'm not meeting his.

We drive through the city in silence, our still-fogged windows rolled down. I'm cold, and want to wrap the jacket around me, but I leave it on my lap. I am afraid of acknowledging the kindness of it.

Light is beginning to fill the sky when we trundle past the Mansion. My car is the only one on the block. Before he pulls away, Howie reaches into the backseat and unearths a black T-shirt, gigantic and soft. 'Take it,' he says.

'I don't—'

'It's cleaner than what you're wearing.'

I pause on the sidewalk.

'Thanks,' I say. 'For the ride, and for not—'

I am still reaching for the word, but he shakes his head before I can get there.

'Don't worry about it,' he says. His gaze is on the seat, on the door handle, on the sky behind my head. 'I'll see you at eight, okay?'

It's my hand that closes the door, but his voice that pushes it shut.

23

I go to Java Jane when it opens at six, hoping and fearing that Caro will be behind the counter. She isn't.

In the bathroom, I shed the Frappuccino-stiff sweatshirt and exchange it for Howie's black tee. It's soft against my bare skin. I don't want to smell it, but I can't help it. It's all cedar and warmth, too clean for the backseat of a car. I wonder about this boy, and then I wonder about Chad, and I shudder over the sink. I wash my hands, and wash and wash, and when that's not enough I wash my face too, cold water and industrial pink pearlescent soap stinging my eyes. I open my mouth wide, running my foamy hands over my tongue and swiping my fingers over and behind my molars, gagging as I hit the back of my throat. I dry my face with paper towels and blink into the mirror. The same old features blink back at me bewildered, as though unsure why this time, like all of the others, didn't work out for the best.

I should check on the Hole, but I can't bring myself to look. I imagine it gaping, disfigured. I want to pull the whole thing from my body, leave it leaking in the restroom's pink trashcan. But instead I buy a coffee and a pumpkin scone and sit by the window. My body feels like a mess of doll parts sacked in skin.

Ordinary people come in for half-caf and skinny and soy, for regular and extra shots. In the window, Java Jane is dressed as a sexy witch in a Mardi Gras mask and miniskirt, a plastic Halloween bucket dangling from her fingers.

On my way out, I spot my toroid silhouette on the cover of the *Indy Week*, and I dump the entire stack of newspapers into the recycling bin.

Howie is, as promised, nowhere to be seen when I arrive fifteen minutes late for our appointment. The crowd outside is bigger and more raucous than usual. I step from the car and am engulfed in a battery of flashes and shouts.

'Are you excited for today's—'

'What can you tell us—'

I squint past the expensive recording equipment, past the vitriolic Hole Girl haters, and peer at the people who wait quietly in the fringes, hugging themselves in the chill morning air. They are as young as twelve, as old as seventy – some men, but mostly women, girls in baggy sweaters, in crop tops, cupping coffee, holding signs. HOLE GIRL, WE LOVE YOU and PUZZLE PIECES FOR EVER and WE ALL HAVE HOLES.

'Have you and the Lump Boy—'

'Miss Stone, people have been—'

Go away, I want to say – not to the press, but to these people

193

silently huddled and waiting behind them, certain that they've found an empowering metaphor for their lives in me. I feel Chad's fingers writhe in my stomach as I turn my face away and head inside.

The nurses have solved the problem of our cumbersome paper gowns by chopping them off at the ribs, leaving Howie and me with floating blue vests. I tug at the edges of mine, intensely aware of my nudity beneath the paper. Amanda told me I could keep my bra on, but I haven't been home, and my moon-and-stars bikini top is abandoned on the floor of Chad's living room.

The research team shuffles to life when I enter, a flurry of paper coffee cups tucking away under chairs.

Dr Morse looks at her watch.

'Kind of you to join us,' she says. Her hair is a deep, rich red, the roots shining crimson in the light.

I'm with Taka today. He makes small talk with me as he feels my back and kidneys. His eyes flicker to my face as he monitors my blood pressure. He frowns, and re-inflates the sleeve.

'How are you feeling?' he asks.

'Peachy.' My voice lurches out of my throat like something half-dead, coated in soap scum. I wonder if there's some sort of Victorian test that doctors can perform to verify that I lost my Hole virginity. I sneak a peek down at the Hole through Taka's busy hands. It sits in my stomach unchanged: same smooth skin, same oblong scoop missing from my midriff.

Relief jolts through me. Taka, hand on my abs, frowns and looks up with a question in his face, but just squeezes my hand with his gloved one before retreating to the computer.

I find Howie, similarly blue-vested, in the corner. Our eyes lock for a brief second, and then he returns his gaze to the middle distance, erasing himself from the room. I remember suddenly the crumpled, snot-smeared paper napkin tucked away in the passenger door of his car. A souvenir of my secret self that I wish more than anything I'd thrown away.

'All right,' Dr Morse says at the end of the hour, smiling as she pulls off her gloves. 'Let's just do one initial merge and then wrap up.'

There's a murmur among the researchers, an unzipping of camera bags. I look from Morse to Takahashi, confused.

'We want to fit you together,' she says. 'To get some initial data regarding the compatibility of your external mutations pre-treatment.'

'How is that medically necessary?' I ask.

Dr Morse faces me full-on.

She says, 'So that we can trace the physiological progress of the treatment. We want to get a sense of whether your deformities degrade at the same rate.'

I swallow. 'Use a ruler.'

She steps closer.

'Miss Stone,' she says, an exasperated kindergarten teacher.

I look to Taka, but he turns to the sink, giving me the blank expanse of his back.

'Howie, are you ready?' Dr Morse asks. There's surgical steel in her voice. Across the room, Howie rises.

It feels as though gravity has collected in a pool around this moment: these events taking on an irresistible weight. The fabric of the universe stretching so that everything in my life slides toward this instant: my birth, my paintings, my dreams. The sandwich I had for lunch yesterday, my mother, the shape of my toenails: everything in service of this moment when our bodies merge.

I look helplessly around the room for sympathetic eyes that will hold mine, but there is nothing. The nurse and aides drift in the background like brightly coloured fish, humming from one machine to the next, checking monitors, quiet and calm. Their gazes dart out at our torsos and flash away again from beneath their smooth-handed tasks. I feel the room waver beneath my feet.

'Wait.'

Everyone's attention snaps up to Howie like a trampoline released.

'Parker,' Howie says, softly. 'I need to talk to Morgan for a minute.'

Dr Morse's voice is clamps and grips. She says, 'Can it wait?'

Howie says, 'No.'

The researchers shift and look awkwardly to the floor, to the note pads, to suddenly interesting things on their phones. The nurses busy themselves with re-stocking tongue depressors. There is nothing but air standing between Howie and his angry doctor.

'One minute,' he says again. Dr Morse closes her eyes and, face pinched, jerks her head towards the door. The weight of everyone's expectations rolls across my shoulder blades as we pass. I follow Howie out into the hushed, low-ceilinged hallway.

He catches my arm outside the changing room doors, and I flinch. He loosens his grip, but doesn't let me go. 'You don't want to do this,' he says. 'Everyone in the room can tell.'

'No,' I say.

'What do you think is going to happen?' he asks.

'I don't know,' I say.

He pushes his floppy fringe out of his eyes, clearly frustrated. 'Morgan, it's just bodies.'

'No,' I say, crossing my arms over my stomach. 'It's *my* body.'

He studies me a long moment. Not like before, eyes leaping shyly up and away. But slow and steady, a subtle shift.

He says, 'What do you want?'

'What do you mean?'

'I mean, if you could do anything right now. Be anywhere. Where would it be?'

'Anywhere but here,' I say, honestly.

He runs a hand over the back of his neck. A small smile tugs at the corner of his mouth.

'You know, that sounds pretty good to me, too.'

I hesitate. I'm still not sure what side he's on. If this is a ploy on his and Morse's part to gain my trust. But I remember the way he didn't touch me last night. Didn't make me explain anything. And despite myself, something small and quiet clicks into place.

I glance back toward the empty bend in the hallway. Just beyond, the room full of researchers waits to fit our bodies together like inhuman puzzle pieces.

'Do you want to get out of here?' I ask Howie.

He grins. 'Grab your clothes,' he says. 'I know a way out.'

We clatter down a back stairwell to a cold cement-slabbed landing lit dimly by a glowing emergency exit sign. Howie draws up short at the door, studying the warning: ALARM WILL SOUND.

He turns back to me, face full of apology. 'I thought—' he begins.

I push past him and slam the red emergency bar with my hip. Sunlight hits me full in the face. An alarm shrieks out into the air behind the building, and for a moment, I'm deaf and blind. Then Howie streaks past, and I follow, giddiness jerking laughter from our bodies as we fly over the landscaping and towards the street where his battered Nissan sits in the sun, waiting.

Howie cranks the engine to life just as people begin to round the corner, zombie hordes bearing high-tech cameras. I catch one last glimpse of the building as we surge away: faces in the windows, blinking out of view as the sun races across the glass alongside us. And then we're past the stop sign, past the on-ramp, out onto the highway and gloriously gone.

Howie steers us easily down lazily curving roads out into the country, open windows letting the autumn air flow giddily through our hair. It's weird to be back in the car again under such different circumstances. I search for the ghost of my morning self, sobbing in the shadow-fingered dark. But everything is mellow autumn sunshine and a distant hint of wood smoke, the kiss of October. It's like last night never happened, like we're two ordinary kids skipping school. Not running from mad scientists and national media. Not with hearts exhausted from a lifetime of breaking.

It happened, I tell myself, fiercely. *It happened, it was true, everything is not okay.*

I sneak a peek at Howie. The wind lifts his floppy fringe and taps it against his forehead, rhythmically, like a little game. He catches my eye and beams.

Everything is not okay.

I look away from him, checking the rear-view mirror. We're all alone. 'How did you lose them so easily?' I ask. 'Have you done this before?'

'Done what?'

'Dodged the paparazzi.'

Howie laughs. It is as bright and startling as the first time I heard it: a child's laugh, purely happy.

'No,' he says. 'I just know the roads. I grew up here.'

I twist in my seat. 'Wait, what? We seriously grew up an hour apart?'

'Hour and a half, two. I moved to New York last year for college.'

I study him, struggling to overlay this new information onto his existing features. The pale skin and skinny arms don't mesh with my idea of brawny, deeply tanned small-town farm boys.

I say, 'You don't sound like you grew up here.'

He grins. 'It's amazing what you learn your first year of school,' he says. 'I done been learned to hitch a stick up my britches and talk like one of them city boys,' he drawls.

The vowels are so spot-on that I laugh, half-amused and half-surprised. Howie beams, unabashed. He bobs his head with a theatrical flourish.

'*Merci, merci,*' he murmurs. '*Mademoiselle est tres belle.*'

'You mean *gentile*, not *belle*.'

'Of course,' he says. 'My mistake.'

I wrinkle my brow. 'Are you flirting with me?'

'What?' he says. 'Never.'

'Look,' I say. 'This Hole–Lump thing—'

'Is science,' he says. 'Is about the cure. Is about Parker's thirst for fame and power. Is nonsense. Doesn't mean we have to be friends. All of the above. Right?' He slows, pulls into the parking lot of a gas station. There is nothing around us but loblolly pine trees, farms and sky.

'Don't get me wrong, but didn't you tell me yesterday that you bought into it?'

'No.' He pulls on the emergency brake, turns to face me. 'You asked me if I believed in it. I had to think about it.'

And then I fell on my own ass jumping to conclusions. Great.

'Well?' I ask.

He tilts his head back against his seat, studying the fields beyond.

'I'm still thinking,' he says, and flushes slightly. 'Not about the epic romance. That's stupid. But, I don't know. I've been given the opportunity to meet someone with the exact equal and opposite problem I've had my entire life. Like I've been Yin this entire time, and then you walk up, and you're like, *hey, I'm Yang. How's it going?*'

'I think you flipped the genders there.'

'This is just a rare opportunity for cultural exchange. We small-town boys have to take what we can get, you know.'

I crack a grin. 'New York is small-town?'

'You know, it's strange,' he says. 'There's actually not culture there? It's a common misconception.'

'Wow,' I say. 'Those poor deluded tourists.'

He nods, seriously. 'They ran out in 1997. All they have now is knock-off culture. People sell it on street corners. You can't tell it from the real thing, if you don't look too closely.'

The car idles in the lot. The SNAPPY MART sign looms over our heads. I know Howie's waiting for me to give him directions: to say turn around, take me home. I study him in glances, little sips of water. His brown eyes quick. His smile comfortable. The Lump a distant memory on the far side of his body.

'Where to?' I ask.

'You tell me,' he says.

'Anywhere?' I ask.

He checks his gas gauge. 'Well, I can't cross oceans.'

'How about time?' I ask.

Conversation with him feels so natural. Words tumbling from our lips like sweaters dropping to so many floors.

'Anywhere but the 1980s,' he says. 'I can't do the big hair thing.'

'When you found me last night,' I say, suddenly.

I can feel his attention focus on me. The lines of my face feel sharp, clear.

'You don't have to talk about it,' he says.

I shake my head. The words come, and I bite them back again. My mind in pieces: mascara, the club, my shirt unstringing on the floor.

'I just really wanted to be normal,' I say. 'But then, once I had it, I realised normal kind of sucks.'

He nods, gazing out at the highway.

'I know,' he says, quietly.

Warm simplicity suffuses my veins. I am suddenly, painfully aware of how precious and fragile this moment is, the first time in my life I've felt perfect understanding.

We sit in silence for a moment. Howie seems to be weighing something.

'How do you feel about wise women?' he asks at last.

'As a cultural construct or in reality?'

'The latter,' he says. 'Well, both. Eventually. But right now, the latter.'

I wonder about that *eventually*. I say, 'Pro.'

'Good,' he says, shifting the car into reverse. 'Then there's someone I think you should meet.'

'Who?'

He pulls us out onto the highway. 'My mom.'

24

The town of Silver Creek nestles in a cupped palm of earth between golden tobacco fields and pine-covered hills. Howie guides the car off of the highway and onto a smaller one, then a smaller one still, the white lines of the road finally falling into forgetfulness and the crumbling red clay shoulder, and he tells me everything.

The Lump manifested before he was born. When he was a baby it was no larger than a knuckle, protruding over the waist of his diaper. Doctors ran scans, did biopsies. His parents thought too much about the word *cancer*. Two days after his first birthday, Howie had his first excision.

'And then they change the bandage the next day, and boom,' he says, gesturing. 'Right back where it started. No blood, no scars, no nothing. The bandage was perfectly clean, with a Lump in the middle. The nurses were certain they'd switched babies – that they'd done surgery on some other kid, and I'd somehow ended up in the recovery room by mistake. But the surgeon swore by it. The charts checked out. Besides, who else could it be? There were no other kids with a Lump.'

They performed a second excision the following week, and the results were the same. The doctors were astounded. They called in specialists. The specialists called specialer specialists.

'And you spent the rest of your life in and out of clinics,' I say.

He smiles. 'Lucky guess.'

'And each new doctor was so optimistic. Like they were the one who was finally going to figure you out.'

Howie nods and nods, watching the road. 'Like when someone else has a Rubik's cube in their hands, and they're fumbling around like a total idiot with it, and you're like, "give it to me, I know I can figure it out in like, ten seconds." And then you get it and fumble around like an idiot.'

I laugh. 'I never spent much time with Rubik's cubes.'

'Pardon me,' he says. 'I didn't realise I was in the presence of someone too cool for the art of the humble Rubik.'

'Mother thinks toys make kids soft,' I say. 'I had books, mainly.'

'Ah,' he says. 'You were the smart kid.'

'Yeah,' I say, rolling my head against the head rest. 'No, actually. Just lonely. I never even went to school until –' *Caro,* '– until we moved to the South. Mother was basically afraid to let me out of her sight when I was little. Like she was convinced that some mad scientists in lab coats with Einstein

205

hair would shove me into a van and do experiments on me if I wasn't with her 24/7.'

'What about your dad?' Howie asks.

'He left when I was four.'

'I'm sorry,' Howie says, quietly.

'It's okay,' I lie.

'I'm sorry,' Howie says again.

The car is nothing but wind and grains of asphalt. I turn to the window in time to see the rail run out, and the river disappear behind us. We're stretching into cotton country now.

'I don't really remember him,' I say.

'I'm sorry,' he says, a third time, and I have no defences left.

Just when I am beginning to think that Howie doesn't have the first clue where we are or where we're heading, we pass a hand-painted sign: WELCOME TO SILVER CREEK, THE FONT OF PROSPERITY.

'Is there actually a silver creek, or is this one of those towns named after the nature they bulldozed to build it? All Whispering Pines or Spring Valley?' I ask.

Howie raises a lecturing finger. 'There is indeed a Silver Creek. Fun local fact. It smells like sulphur, and drinking the water is supposed to make you virile.'

'Did you try it?'

He makes a face. 'No. But the whole high school football team got heavy metal poisoning on prom night, so that tradition's obviously alive and kicking.'

We creep through a minuscule downtown: a gas station and

a Mexican restaurant, an old-fashioned drug store. Starbucks hasn't seemed to have heard of the place, nor has McDonald's. I breathe shallowly, afraid of infecting the town with the microbes from the modern world.

'Are you sure the press won't find us here?' I ask. 'It seems like your house is the first place they'd look.'

Howie shakes his head. 'My family is one of my best-kept secrets,' he says. 'Garrison is a pseudonym.'

'What's your real name?'

He grins. 'That'd be telling.'

'Does that actually work?'

He shrugs. 'It has. The research team all signed nondisclosure agreements. And Parker wants to write the book on ICF-3, so she's not going to tell anyone how to find me. Competition and all.'

'And you put on a big shirt and hide in plain sight,' I murmur. We pass a roadside sign advertising Peach's, Tomatoe's, Ripe Watermellons and pull up to a four-way junction. Long grass grows through the stop sign. 'I'm the opposite. Mother's always been in the public eye, and I'm her Holey little secret.'

'Well, it's not that easy to hide me,' Howie says. We accelerate again, the air plucking at our clothes with undiscerning fingers. 'I stick out, if you'll pardon my saying so.'

'I won't,' I say.

'Fair enough,' he says, and grins ruefully. 'That's why New York is such a dream. Nobody looks at you twice. And even if they did, the Lump isn't anything there. I've got nothing on half the guys who walk down the street. It's this great melting pot – bring me your weirdos, your crazies, your freaks. My parents love that I'm there. Not too many kids make it out of S-Creek.' We slow, signalling, and the sound of the wind drops away outside the windows, leaving nothing behind it but the cicada-rich silence of the country.

'Wait,' I say, suddenly. 'If your family lives so close by, how come they weren't there with you at any of the appointments?'

'They wanted to let me do it on my own.'

I goggle a little. 'What's that like?'

He laughs. 'You'll see.' He turns us past a rooster-shaped mailbox and onto a gravelled driveway. 'Brace yourself,' he adds. 'My family is *extremely* normal.'

The driveway is a long tunnel of pine. We emerge into a clearing with two old cars and a tin-roofed house. A pair of golden retrievers bound up to the car as we draw to a standstill, two excited splashes of fur and barking. Howie laughs as he climbs from the car, leaning down for a face full of doggie kisses. I tentatively follow, and the dogs flood towards me, barking furiously, all tails and slobbery teeth. One jumps up, punching me in the stomach with twin muddy paws.

'Zoe! Max!' Howie shouts, running around to the passenger side. 'I'm sorry. Are you okay with dogs?'

'Yeah,' I gasp. I reach for a dog to prove how okay I am, but only get a glancing grasp of a tail.

Three kids tumble out through the screen door and onto the porch, the medley of their voices circling the syllables of Howie's name as they launch themselves down the stairs. They are followed by a slender woman in jeans and a sweatshirt, who watches as the two youngest wrap themselves gleefully around Howie's legs. An older boy hangs back, trying to be cool until Howie reaches out for a fist-bump, and the boy dimples into a smile, eye teeth piling up like a traffic jam.

Howie wades up to the porch and wraps his mother in an embrace. They hold each other, rocking back and forth. The expression on her face is pure happiness. I fidget by the car, mopping at the paw prints on Howie's T-shirt. I think about my own mother, and realise I'm not even sure where she is right now. LA, maybe, or Paris. I avert my eyes from Howie's Happy Family Time, feeling stupid for thinking I was done being an outsider.

One of the dogs barks sharply at my side, and I jolt. The woman looks up and catches a glimpse of me. Her smile fades. She pulls back, says something to Howie.

A voice by my elbow says, 'You're the one who's mean to my brother on TV.' A little girl in a pink T-shirt is squinting up at me through her fringe, nose wrinkled. The older boy flushes, ears bright red.

'Riley, shut up,' he says in a low voice.

'Why are you here?' the girl asks me.

'Riley, Kevin, Tyler,' Howie says, coming to my rescue. 'This is my friend Morgan.'

The younger boy says, 'If she's your friend then why did Mom call her—'

'The TV people make everything look worse than it actually is, you know that,' Howie says. 'Morgan's really nice. Right, Morgan?'

Riley's eyebrows sit low and fuzzy over her brown eyes.

'Are you his girlfriend?' she asks flatly.

Howie pulls a tick off the dog's ear, face averted.

I tell her, 'The TV people lie about a lot of stuff.'

'I knew it!' the younger boy shouts. 'I knew you weren't his girlfriend! He only likes blondes.'

'Okay, Kevin,' Howie says. 'That's awesome. Hey, I'll bet you can't beat me to the house.'

Wordlessly, Kevin takes off running, and after a second, the older boy, Tyler, follows. Riley hovers by my side as we mount the porch steps, mouth curled down with distrust.

Howie's mother stands at the top of the stairs with her arms crossed. She is tiny in every sense of the word, but no less terrifying for it. Grey streaks through the long brown braid she wears down her back. Her sweatshirt is flecked with house paint.

Finally, she extends a hand.

'Rachel,' she says.

'Morgan.'

'I know,' she says.

'Thanks for having me,' I say.

She expels a long sigh through her nose and releases my hand from her grip.

'Howie tells me that the news took your quotes out of context,' she says.

'Yeah,' I say.

'They must have been pretty far out of context,' she says.

'Mom,' Howie says. She ignores him. I rub at the railing with a thumb. The wood is old and soft, and my thumbnail reveals a line of hard, bright newness.

'They wanted to tell a certain story,' I tell her. 'And I deviated from it.'

Something behind her eyes softens. Not much. But enough.

'Well,' she says at last. 'We do like deviants around here.' She steps back, and reaches for the screen door handle. 'You two must be hungry.'

'We're okay—' I start, and Howie squeezes my arm.

'You're at my mother's house,' he whispers. 'You're definitely hungry.'

Howie's mom makes grilled cheese sandwiches in a cast-iron frying pan, standing on one leg like a stork as she casually butters slices of homemade bread. The boys run in and out, pouring careful glasses of red Kool-Aid before dashing back to the living room. Riley sits in the corner with an armload of Barbies, watching me sideways as she aggressively yanks off their dresses. The lazy sound of video game violence filters through the sunny kitchen.

'They get to play video games during the day now?' Howie asks.

211

'They get an hour on weekends,' Rachel says. 'If their homework is done.'

The pan murmurs to itself, a quiet conversation of heat and grease.

'Is Dad around?' Howie asks.

'He should be in his office,' his mother says. She glances up the stairs, calling, 'Richard!'

'He's probably got his headphones on.' Howie says, rising. 'I'll pop in.'

'Don't be long,' Rachel says. 'Unless you want a congealed cheese sandwich.'

Howie pops a salute. I shoot him a desperate glance, and he smiles, mouths, *it's okay*. He disappears up the stairs, leaving me alone in the kitchen with his mother. I rest my elbows on the table, watching her chop apples and pile them on the plates. My mother has a chef and a nutritionist, maids, gardeners, a driver. She keeps the moons of her nails immaculate.

'So, Morgan,' Rachel says. 'Tell me about yourself.'

I chew my lip. 'Well,' I say. 'I have a hole in my middle.'

'So I hear,' she says, drily.

'I'm not trying to be smart. It's not information I volunteer very often.'

She nods slowly, sits down across from me and passes a plate. Steam breathes from her sandwich, leaving a velvet halo on the blue clay dish.

'We've been following you on the news,' she says quietly. 'Seeing you here was the last thing I expected.'

'I know,' I say. 'I'm sorry.' She's still waiting, and I add, defensively, 'They distorted a lot of things.'

'So you're not just here –' the kitchen, the sandwich, her unreadable face, '– to be cured.'

'No. I mean, yes.' I straighten my spine. 'You don't understand what it's like. They ripped my life away, all so they can have a good story. Or get a Nobel Prize. Or whatever. Nobody actually cares about who I am, or what I want.'

I remember, belatedly, that she knows exactly what it's like: that she spent years raising a child just like me. But she doesn't correct me.

'Um,' I say, hesitating. But I take the plunge. 'Howie said you didn't come with him to the appointment because he wanted to do it on his own.'

Her forehead wrinkles, wary. 'That's right.'

'But you guys seem so ... I don't know ...' *Warm. Nice. Familial.* 'Don't you want to be involved?'

She lifts her eyes to mine. 'Sometimes, stepping back is the best way to be involved.'

I stab my finger into the crust of my sandwich. 'Try telling that to my mother.'

She takes a bite of her sandwich, chews.

'It's not about what your mother wants,' she says, lifting her grey eyes to mine. 'What do you want?'

I look down at my plate, turning it around and around.

'For my life to finally be ordinary,' I say. My voice cracks on the word.

Rachel's hand covers my own, and I look up, surprised. Warmth and pity shine through her exasperation.

'Honey,' she says. 'That's never going to happen. So you should quit worrying about it.'

She squeezes my hand.

'Besides,' she says. 'What fun would that be?'

Howie's grilled cheese has gone cold by the time he returns to the kitchen with his father, who greets me with a hand-shake and a tentative smile. He is a small, slight man, with sunburned ears and nimble hands. He has Howie's drooping slant of the eyes.

'Morgan Stone,' he says. 'You're quite the celebrity in our house.'

'Richard,' his wife says, warningly.

'"Here come the freaks!"' he quotes, chuckling.

A sandwich crust twists in my throat, dry. Richard claps me on the back.

'That's all right,' he says. 'In this house, we're all freaks. Some of us are just more subtle about it than you flashy celebrity types.'

'So,' I say, weakly. 'You're not going to make a Hole big deal about it?'

Laughter bubbles up from Richard's stomach, crinkling his eyes. 'She's great,' he tells his wife. 'Isn't she great?' He turns back to me. 'Howie tells me you're an artist.'

My impulse is to deny it, so I surprise myself by saying, *yes.*

He sits down next to me. 'That's fantastic,' he says, grabbing a bite of Howie's sandwich. 'What is it you do?'

I glance at Howie. He says, 'Actually, I'd like to show Morgan something upstairs real quick.' He looks at me, eyebrow perked like a question mark. I hesitate, then nod.

'You kids behave,' Richard calls up the stairs after us. Howie's mother says something, and both Howie's dad and Riley start laughing, the sounds of their merriment fading as we disappear upwards into the house.

'See?' Howie says. 'I knew my mom would love you.'

'I don't know if I'd go that far,' I say.

'She's a mom,' he says. 'And you're a poor lost chickadee. She can't help herself.'

'My mother completely lacks that maternal instinct,' I say.

'I'm sure she's got one,' he says. We round a landing. 'It's probably just really deep down,' he adds, pushing open a door. '*Et voila*: my secret abode.'

His attic bedroom room is small and pine-walled with twin skylights in the pitched roof. There's a small bed in the corner with a blue quilt. The walls are entirely covered with bookcases. I look around for the typical boy things – band posters, trophies, battered guitars – and find none. Just sky and books, and a small woven rug on the floor in shades of cornflower and sea.

'It's great,' I say.

'My room was off the living room when I was a kid,' he says, flopping on the bed. 'It was more convenient to have me on the ground floor – I was always on some nauseating drug, or recovering from surgery. But for my fourteenth birthday Mom refurbished the attic and gave it to me. I love it up here.'

I drift over to his bookshelves, studying titles. 'I thought you said you never had to recover from surgeries.'

He curls himself into a ball, rocks to a seated position. 'Healing isn't the same as recovering. It takes a lot of energy to regrow a minor body mass in one night.' He lifts his T-shirt and addresses the Lump. 'Especially one as resplendent as this guy here.'

'Ugh,' I say, fighting a mixture of amusement and revulsion. 'You talk to it?'

'You *don't* talk to the Hole?'

A terrible shrill giggle escapes my lips. 'No, I don't talk to the Hole. Why would I talk to the Hole?'

'I can't believe you never – I mean, the poor thing. It's definitely suffering from low self-esteem.' He cranes his neck and looks down at the Lump. 'Have you ever heard anything that awful, Rupert?'

'You call it Rupert?'

'Sometimes,' he says. 'Today it looks like a Rupert. Don't you think?'

'Please put that thing away,' I protest, laughing. I can feel my face going hot.

'What?' he asks. 'It's just a harmless genetic mutation.'

'I'm going to talk about this on Oprah,' I say. 'He invited me up to his room, and then he showed me his Lump!'

He drops his T-shirt, waving his hands in mock surrender. 'My reputation!' he says. 'It will be ruthlessly besmirched. I take it back, I take it all back.' He turns to the shelf over the bed, and pulls out a black plastic three-ring binder. 'Well, since you've killed the mood, I may as well show you this.'

A faded piece of notebook paper taped to the front reads BOOK OF FREAKS in careful, childish writing.

I open the cover. A black and white photo stares up at me, a photocopy of two serious-looking Siamese twins, and beside it a handwritten caption: CHANG AND ENG. Most famous Siamese conjoined twins in history.

'I started this journal when I was ten,' Howie explains. 'I guess I needed to know that I wasn't the only freak in the world. It became sort of an obsession. More than anything, I wanted to find somebody else like me.'

I turn the pages. The Snake Woman. Howler the Monkey Man. Beautiful Regina. The One and Only Human Sawhorse.

'And did you, ever?'

'Find someone like me? No,' he says. 'But even if they weren't different in exactly the same way, it was enough just knowing there were others out there. It made it better somehow.'

Each page features at least one photo, pasted into place, with a name and description, sometimes, birth and death dates. I've just finished reading about Vladimir Ironikov, the Giant of St Petersburg, when I turn the page to find what looks like a screenplay:

Vladimir: What would you like to get for lunch today Howard?

Me: I think some soup and also a cheeseburger, with some juice and a cookie. What about you Vlad?

Vlad: HA HA HA! I WILL EAT FOR LUNCH FIFTY CHEESEBURGERS BECAUSE I AM SO GIANT!

Me: Wow!

'What is this?'

'I used to imagine what I would say to each person in this book if I met them,' he says. He keeps his eyes on the script, speaking steadily, but his ears are have pinked. I can't help but laugh.

'Yeah, okay,' Howie says. 'Again, I was ten.'

'Are they all like this?'

He fiddles with a stray thread. 'It depends on what I needed to hear when I wrote them. You know. Sometimes funny, sometimes wise.' His eyes jump up to my face and away as he speaks. 'I wouldn't look at Svetlana the Snake Empress if I were you. I wrote her when I was thirteen. It's, um, spicy.'

I turn a page to the Lost Angel of Appalachia. She's beautiful in the 1940s style: my age but somehow older, with thin lips and thick kohl around the eyes. A pair of white feathered wings peek out from her gauzy white gown. A Beauteous Angel Fallen from Heaven with Real Wings Growing Out of Her Body! the photocopied advert proclaims. Now in a Limited

Time Engagement with Wiley and Person's World Famous Three-Ring Circus Extravaganza!

There are more than fifty pages: people with flippers, with tails, with fur, scales, extra heads; strong men, damsels, seductresses, children, midgets, giants. I flip through, idly searching for Holes. A familiar expression haunts the faces of the pages: wearied, patient, looking out at the camera with a sort of bored indulgence that I recognise. *Yes, this is my body. Can we move on please?*

I am looking at the faces of my people.

'Did you ever meet any of them?' I ask.

He shakes his head. 'I was always tied up in hospitals. By the time I was old enough and healthy enough to try, I'd kind of outgrown it, I guess. I went to New York and made some actual friends instead.' He shuts the book, running his finger along the edge.

'We should do it.'

'Do what?' he asks.

I gesture to the binder. The book of strange but familiar faces. 'Meet them.'

He laughs. 'When? Between appointments?'

'Yes,' I say. 'Why not? Until I met you, I'd never dreamed that there might be people in the world who would understand what it was like to live my everyday life. And now you show me this?' I stroke the surface of the book with one finger. 'It's just too tempting a thought to ignore.'

Howie tugs at one ear.

219

'It's kind of crazy,' he says.

'What better sane things do you have to do?' I ask.

He starts to reply, then bites his lip, staring down at the binder. When he finally looks up at me, it is with something like wonder.

'All right,' he says.

Rachel's started making dinner by the time we return and insists we stay, so we settle in for the evening. I follow the kids to the backyard and watch them do flips on the trampoline. Six o'clock comes and goes, and nobody suggests that we watch the news. Instead we traipse into the dining room and crowd around the table. Somewhere, between passing the salad and tucking in, I forget to be a stranger. There is a seductive warmth to the noisy, bouncing energy of this family that feels inclusive. I dab pasta sauce off of Riley's chin. The boys stick out food-covered tongues at me, and I shock them by sticking mine out right back.

'Ew!' Tyler shouts.

'Cool!' Kevin shouts.

'Morgan,' Rachel says warningly.

'Sorry,' I say. I do it again the second she looks away. Howie hides his face in his napkin.

After dinner, Howie follows his dad into the kitchen with a stack of plates. Rachel lingers beside me as I gather my things for the drive home. 'It was a pleasure meeting you,' she says.

'I'm glad Howie brought me.'

'That's Howie, always bringing home strays.' Her smile fades a bit. 'Not too many girls, though.' She holds me out at arm's length, looking me up and down. 'Take good care of my son,' she says as Howie emerges from the kitchen. 'No more out-of-context stuff. Okay? Or I'll hang you by your toenails and flay you.' She says it with a smile, but there's steel beneath. I nod.

Rachel kisses Howie and the two of us head for the car, dogs joyfully flanking us. The kids cluster by the porch railing, waving frantically, backlit by the glowing lights of the house. The night has turned chilly, and wood smoke curls distantly in the air.

I close the car door and turn to a tapping on the window. I crack the door, carefully, and little Riley is standing by, a fistful of goldenrod in her hand.

'Bye,' she says. She thrusts the wildflowers into my hand and then leans in, quickly, and gives me an awkward hug, her face smashing into my chest. Then she pounds back to the house, bare feet skipping over the cooling earth.

Howie puts the car into reverse. We back away, waving until the house is out of sight.

'I didn't think she liked me,' I say.

'She's always been in a house full of brothers,' he says. 'I think she feels left out. You're basically her favourite person now, just for being female.'

'She has excellent taste.'

Howie pulls out onto the main road. 'I can't argue with that.'

I pick at the stems of the wildflowers, staining my thumbnail green. 'Sure you could.' He shakes his head and doesn't look at me. We slide by blue-green floodlights in the dark yards of country houses.

I say, 'Howie, you have exactly zero reasons to be nice to me. I've been nothing but a raging bitch to you since the day we met.'

The outline of him shrugs, dusted with dashboard lights. 'Everyone deserves a second chance,' he says.

'God, you're so nice,' I say. 'It's unreal.'

His face, in profile, slides across the night, eating stars.

'I don't see any reason not to be nice,' he says.

'Because people are the worst. Because they're out to hurt you or exploit you and even if they aren't, they're going to disappoint you.'

'Not all of them.'

'Enough of them.'

'But enough of them aren't, so it's worth trying,' he says. He turns towards me in the dark, starlight sliding over his teeth. 'Even a raging bitch can turn out to be pretty okay if you give her three or four tries.'

I quietly shred goldenrod stems in my lap.

I ask, 'How often has that worked out for you?'

He says, 'Often enough.'

The drive back to civilisation seems to take half the time

of the trip out. We talk about desultory things: our families, favourite teachers, bands, food. By the time we pull up beside my car at the now-deserted medical complex, it's close to ten at night.

'Morgan Stone,' Howie says, seriously. 'I want to thank you for taking this opportunity to be my partner in crime. It was an honour to evade News Channel 11 with you for the last nine hours and forty-three minutes.'

He extends a hand. I shake it. Two formal pumps: one, two.

'Do you want – can I get your number?' I ask. 'You know. For our epic Book of Freaks research adventure.'

'Of course,' he says. 'I look forward to furthering our professional relationship.'

I think I catch a smile, but it's hard to tell in the dark.

'Howie,' I say softly, as he enters his number into my crappy old phone. 'Thanks for taking me to meet your family. And for giving me a second chance.'

He beams so brightly I think he'll light up the night.

'Thanks for being worth it,' he says.

I peer into the glowing windows of houses and shops as I drive groggily home, feeling a wave of warmth for the inhabitants in each one. Feeling that I could step through any door in the city and find a story I wasn't expecting: entire lives rich with kindness and drama and strife that I could have missed out on entirely, just walking by.

I am so glad I opened one today.

25

Back at home, I can't shake the image of a quiet little boy, painstakingly running a glue stick over a sheet of notebook paper, capturing the friends he is sure, somewhere, will understand him. It kills me that Howie and I grew up just two hours away from each other, each reaching silently out into the world and missing each other by inches.

I go straight to the closet beneath the stairs and pull out my portfolio. I haven't looked through it since that gallery visit. It was just a month and a half ago, but it seems like another lifetime. The charcoal drawings are more raw and angular than I remember them, but they aren't as terrible as I convinced myself they were. Page after page, the images stare up at me – the incomplete people that I drew so I could surround myself with other broken things: the breastless mother, the lovers with no mouths, the artist with no vision. These lonely, empty images represent my past. What I want to give them, now, is *life*.

I select a drawing – a theatre of eyeless movie-watchers – and smear my fingers across the charcoal. Absently, I lift my finger to my mouth and, blackening my teeth and tongue, suck away the bitter taste of the past. Then I lift the pieces from the portfolio, one by one, and clip them to my easels. When I run out of easels, I pin them to the walls. Once I've begun, I have trouble stopping, pages spilling onto the counter, the floor. A frenetic energy runs electric in my veins.

I ready my palette. I breathe in, and breathe out something a decade old.

Then I lower my brush.

I tentatively pull colour across one page, then another. Vibrant hues explode around the lonely charcoal figures. I pick up speed, the colours brighter, more primal, more elemental and pure; if my old self had built a wall between her and the rest of the world, I am attacking it with dazzling light, with china blue, with clover, with blood, with streetlight, with moss. I scrape at its mortar with night-breast navy, with lamp-lit yellow, with the fawn-coloured brown of a stranger's eyes. Chinks begin to appear in the darkness of my life, light falling through in crumbs.

The sun has fully risen by the time I stop, bent and sore, the nausea of ignored hunger clawing at my insides. I drop the brushes into thinner to clean them and wash my hands quietly in the sink. I survey the damage as I scrub the colours away from my skin with a rough, flour-stiffened towel. My satisfaction is as deep and blue as the sea.

I pull out my phone, ignoring the fourteen missed calls

from unknown numbers, and dial Marcel. The ring falls distantly in my ear. I'm imagining Howie's face when he sees the work: a slow blush. An astonishment. And, behind the shaggy fringe, a recognition.

'Marcel,' I say to his voicemail. 'I've got the theme for my show. We'll call it *What Am I Missing?*'

26

I wake up at three in the afternoon surrounded by half-sketched ideas, blinking like a disoriented wombat. I drag my weary body to the shower. I'm still braless, my skin sticky with the ghost of vanilla Frappuccino. I peel Howie's T-shirt away and stand under the water, letting the last two days swirl around my ankles and toes and away down the drain.

The press is delighted to have spotted Howie and me fleeing our last appointment together. The more salacious gossip blogs speculate about where we disappeared to for the romantic interlude. There's a general scrambling to settle on a tabloid-appropriate name for the pair of us: the Puzzle Pieces, the Perfect Matches, the Soul Mates, Destiny's Children.

HG & LB gave the docs a slip and snuck back late at night – after who knows what, reports gossip blog *Gotcha!* smugly. Nine hours on the run and back to the doctors at dawn – there's only so far these love-birds can fly without circling back to the meds! Whoever spotted us neglected to mention our distinctly unromantic handshake.

Public Scrutiny is still churning merrily away. There's some more art, and a fan video for Yum Yum Situation's 'Hole Girl' song: an eleven-year-old girl dancing around her bedroom with a black paper circle taped to her stomach. Despite myself, I smile.

There's also a brand new section dedicated to fan fiction. I click in, even though it's eight different kinds of mistake. 'Match Made in Heaven'. 'Hidden Desire'. 'A Hole New World: an Aladdin–Hole Girl Crossover'.

'Is it weird that nothing seems weird any more?' I ask myself aloud.

'Is it weird that I talk to myself more now that Caro's ignoring me?

'Is it definitely time to get out of the house?'

I pat my cheek.

'Yes, insane self,' I say. 'Yes it is.'

My phone lights up as I'm digging for my bike helmet. For once, it's someone I know.

Howie: Hello, Lady M. I've been doing some research into the Tour de Freaks and found someone we should meet. Up for a road trip?

Me: Mmm, would, but have an appointment with Science. v. important.

Howie: What! Sounds boring. Blow it off.

I fiddle with the keys for a moment, then pick up the phone and call his number. He picks up at once.

'Wow,' he says, 'Morgan Stone, calling me. I'm honoured. I'm flabbergasted. I don't know what to say.'

'I got tired of typing,' I say. 'Who is it you think we should meet?'

'Helen Rhees Boyle,' he says. 'The Fallen Angel of Appalachia. Apparently she lives in a small mountain town, five hours from here.'

'How in the world did you find her?' I ask.

'She's got to be ancient by now. Late eighties, ninety maybe. It's a long shot. But we could give it a try. We're young. We're foolish. I have a gas card. Want to go tomorrow? We could make it there and back easily, knock this out before our appointment.' His voice skips lightly over the word, as though this were any other appointment. As though it isn't the start of a potentially endless round of injections that could give us cancer, or kill us, or turn us into ordinary people.

'I can't,' I say, neatly evading the pit. 'I've got a meeting with my manager, and then gallery stuff all week.'

'An appointment I don't have?' he says. 'I'm jealous.'

'I'm feeling weirdly good about it,' I say. 'My project kind of came together last night.'

'That's great,' he says. 'What did you end up doing?'

I blink away images of young Howie, bent over his Book of Freaks.

'Do you want to see?' I ask.

There's a pause on the other end of the phone too long and painful to parse.

'Sure,' he says at last. 'I'd love to.'

We hang up, and I sit still for a moment, trying to list all of the reasons my heart could be pounding so hard.

I spend the rest of the waning afternoon trying to draft an essay about masculinity and solitude in *The Red Badge of Courage* for English class, but keep jumping up to drift anxiously around the apartment, adjusting things that don't need adjusting. There's still no sign of Caro. She has ceased to exist except in lingering scents: her perfume in the bathroom in the evenings; fried eggs this morning; each smell evoking a sleepy pang of happiness in me before I open my eyes and remember, again, that we're still not speaking.

Howie arrives at five, his floppy hair still shower-damp. I'm suddenly hyper-aware of the apartment – the dingy corners, the heavy smell of oils and turpentine, the way the light in the kitchen buzzes like something unfairly trapped. It is painfully different from his family's home.

'It's nice,' he says.

'It's a dump,' I say.

'I'm staying at a Motel 6,' he says. 'I'm elated to be in a room without mystery stains on the walls.'

He studies the brand new erasure paintings, some still wet where I've plastered the sketches to the canvas. The final collection is varied, a wild rash of parakeet colours, but there is a sense of cohesion to it: the clash of charcoal with colour, of movement with loneliness. It creates a tension that hums through the room. The figures' shame and fear have been highlighted, but also transformed. They are washing their failings in colour. They seem to hold their chins high. Pride glows from painting after painting.

Howie studies the legless dancer, saying nothing.

'It's like your Book of Freaks,' I tell him, suddenly uncertain. 'The theme is "what am I missing".'

He paces from one to the next. 'They're good,' he says.

'I know that "good",' I say. 'That's the kind of "good" that comes with a "but".'

He grins guiltily, pauses on a painting of a weaver with no hands. The figure's brow is creased in concentration as a tapestry assembles itself on the loom before him.

'What about the extras?' Howie asks.

'What do you mean?'

He gestures to my stomach, and I rankle instinctively. I'm still not used to anyone addressing the Hole so proprietarily. I have to remind myself of his history, that he knows what he's talking about.

'Everyone here is missing something,' he says. 'Like you. That's how they're different. But what about the rest of us? The people with extras? Extra skin, extra heads, extra wings?'

I feel my shoulders caving in.

'I started this project years ago, at school,' I say. 'Besides,

231

that's not ... This is about absence. You know. Loneliness and lacking.'

'There are plenty of things absent from my life,' he says, preoccupied. 'And I'll bet you a million bucks there are things you can access, looking the way you do, that conjoined twins can't. Or even just people with extra flesh. Or extra weight.' He peeks into the kitchen, at a limbless swimmer framed in aqua. 'Everyone you draw is really skinny.'

I open my mouth and then close it again, choking down the wall of resentment building, stone by slow stone, in my chest.

Howie eyes me closely. 'Oh man,' he says. 'You're someone who doesn't take criticism well, aren't you? You're trying so hard not to be mad at me right this minute.'

Something in me breaks. I laugh, a small flood. I want to say, *how do you know me so well* and can't because it feels too big and so instead I just say, 'You are so nosy.'

He shrugs. 'I spend a lot of time watching people,' he says. 'That's what happens when you grow up on the outside of something. You get to know it better than it knows itself.' The front door opens and closes. Caro ducks into the kitchen and deposits her lunch dishes in the sink. She looks up and smiles. She is occupying as little space as possible.

'Hi,' she says.

'I'm Howie,' Howie says, extending his hand.

She laughs, and I look away from the familiar shine of her brow as she takes Howie's hand. 'I know,' she says. 'You're all over the news. I'm Caroline.'

'Pleasure to meet you,' he says. 'We're critiquing Morgan's art. Care to join us?' As though there is no division between Caro and me. As though crossing that divide is the easiest thing in the world.

'I'm okay,' Caro says. She raises her glass of water to Howie – to us? – and ducks behind a curtain of hair. 'I'm going to go unwind a little bit. Nice meeting you.'

'Bye,' Howie says to her retreating back. 'Happy unwinding.' Upstairs, the bathroom door opens and shuts. 'Roommate?'

'Best friend.'

He rocks on the balls of his feet, as though standing is a little game, and he is winning. 'You don't seem too friendly.'

'We had a fight.'

The pipes giggle in the walls.

'About what?' Howie asks, pulling my attention back down to the kitchen.

I fill my cheeks with air and slowly blow it out.

'You, actually,' I say.

He crosses his arms. 'Really?'

'Yeah.'

'What about me?'

I look up at ceiling for a way to tell this story and make it sound good.

'She thought I should give you another chance,' I say at last. 'After the freaks thing. She said we had too much in common to throw away.' I shift my eyes back to his face, challenging

233

him to laugh, or to leave. Instead, he just looks up the stairs, where Caro disappeared.

'She sounds pretty smart,' he says.

We sit in the living room and plot out our trip to see the Angel the following weekend. We brainstorm questions. Me: *Was it hard to grow up looking like she did? How did she live without loneliness?* Howie: *Did she incorporate religion into her personal narrative or is that merely a stage persona? What decision-making went into capitalizing on her wings? Can she fly?*

'She can't fly,' I say, derisively. I am curled in one corner of the couch, Howie slouching in the other; our bodies tingling with nearness, but not touching.

'Who says?' he asks.

'Physics,' I say.

'Physics is boring,' he sighs to the ceiling. Absently, he reaches up and teases the corner of the breastless mother painting. The pads of his fingers come away sticky with daffodil hue. 'Science dictates everything else in our lives. Does it have to dictate my dreams, too?'

We stare at his yellow fingers. He wipes them on his arm: four war stripes.

'Are you nervous?' I ask.

'About getting cancer and dying from a highly experimental treatment?' he asks. He blows on the stripes. 'Sure. Aren't you?'

'I know I should be,' I say. 'But it's hard to take seriously. It doesn't seem real, somehow.'

He blows on his painted arm again. His arm hairs ruffle around the stripes. 'Like, cancer is a thing that only happens to other people?'

'No. I mean, if the treatment kills me immediately, I won't know it. Even if it kills me slowly, in the end, it won't make a difference, right?' I reach out to the paint, draw a slow spiral on my palm. 'In the end, it doesn't matter; we'll all die eventually. None of this will make any difference.'

'People must love you for your optimism.'

'That's not what I mean. I mean, if it's going to happen anyway, then why not risk everything in pursuit of what we want?'

'What do you want?'

'To be whole,' I say, obviously. 'Don't you?'

He nods his head, back and forth.

'The appointment's at five on Saturday, right?' he asks.

'Yeah.'

'We should ride together.'

My hand whisks closed. Invisibly, the spiral smears in my palm.

'What?' he says.

'Nothing,' I say. 'Okay.'

I make minute adjustments on the paintings that night, readying them for Marcel's appraisal. I stand for a long time in front of the painting Howie criticised of the weaver with no hands and think about 'the extras' and the ways in which having too much can add up to an absence.

I stretch a blank canvas and tentatively sketch out a new weaver, this one with extra hands: hands spilling out of his arms and legs and chest, cascading from his sleeves. His weaving becomes more intricate, shining in his many fingers. His extra hands detangling knots. One holds food to feed him when he hungers; another pair, down by his ankle, hold each other. I frown as I shade the intimate interlacing of the fingers, and when eventually I lean back and study this sketch all I feel is a crush of jealousy. I know that Howie's Lump has kept him from a normal life. But the extras don't add up to a lack, for me – they just look like an embarrassing abundance of wealth and possibility.

I usually dash gesso across the canvas the second it's all gone wrong, but I want to keep this a while. It seems like something I can learn to understand.

27

I wake up sweaty from a dream that Howie and I merged and then fused together, face to face. I go into the bathroom, splash water on my face. The clock reads 4.07.

I flip through my phone. I browse idly around Public Scrutiny, and then tap, innocently, because it's four in the morning and what happens at four in the morning doesn't count, into the fan fiction forum.

Morgan stepped into the private pool and sighed with pure pleasure. It was a delight to get away like this, after the long days of medical experiments. She lowered herself into the crystal clear water, gasping slightly as the water poured sensuously through the Hole.

Her mind went back to earlier in the day, when she was leaving the doctor's office. Someone had left her that mysterious note in her locker: 'Meet me by the pool this afternoon. Wear as little as you dare.'

I can't help it: I giggle. I look around my room, half guilty, half wishing there was someone there to laugh with me. I open my private message folder and send a message to mindthegap.

Did you see the fan fiction? This is crazy!

I'm reading 'ripples spread into the water as someone entered the pool behind her' when she answers:

lol, I'm avoiding that stuff with a ten-foot pole. What are you doing up?

I flash back to my dream about Howie.

Insomnia.

Bummerino. Me too.

Have you done any more drawings lately?

Yeah! I'm working on one right now, actually. It's about Public Scrutiny, *nerd* But I started thinking about the comments people gave on my first piece, that I'm totally humbled by and grateful for, and so it's actually a portrait of all of us with our Holes.

Woah, I think. Woah I type. Can I see? There's a pause

before her next reply. I stare at the screen, wondering. Maybe she's in the bathroom. Maybe she's actually a reporter, and she's standing in a late night newsroom with all of the other reporters, trying to figure out how to pull off this lie with grace.

Her next message comes through with a picture attachment.

It's a pencil sketch of a crowd of individuals done with the same clarity and careful detail of mindthegap's first drawing. There are people of all ages and genders, a monochromatic rainbow of skin tones. I peer closely at the Holes. She's put Holes in eyes, in hearts, in brains. There's a woman with a Hole where her uterus should be, and I remember a user named maryanna writing about her third miscarriage:

> I'm crying as I write this. I don't know if we're going to try again. I'm so afraid and so heartbroken but still can't stop wanting.

The woman in the sketch looks like an everyday housewife – heavy hips, nondescript haircut. Someone whose looks don't hint that she's carrying a heartache bigger than herself. I think again of my fragile, scrawled charcoal figures and realise the things I've been missing.

I get a new message from mindthegap: I just sort of tried to picture what everyone looks like based on the things they said.

mindthegap: I mean, it's not done or anything.

I feel bad, suddenly, imagining her nervousness on the other side of the screen, waiting for my response.

It's awesome! I write. I love it. Sorry, I was trying to guess who people are.

Did you find yourself yet? she asks.

My fingers go cold. I click back into the picture, scan frantically. The iconic Hole Girl figure is in the centre of the page, in baggy jeans and a crop top, fingers interlaced with those of the figures on either side.

I have an inkling. My heart thunders into the mattress.

She writes back, Front left

I zoom in on the drawing. By the lower corner of the page, there's a tall, curly haired girl holding her palms out to the viewer. Each one is pierced by a small, perfect Hole.

I swallow, swallow, breathe.

She's written, Found it yet?

Another message blinks to life.

That's probably not what you look like at all. I don't know why, I imagine you really tall. With sort of a brassy voice. Like, Amazonian. lol

I laugh a little, head swimming.

Why my hands? I write.

You wrote me about your artist's block, remember? You said you hadn't been able to draw anything new for months.

A pause, and then: How is that going, by the way?

I write, A lot better.

!! Can I see your stuff?

I rub my eyes, look at the clock. I have my meeting with
Marcel in less than nine hours.

Soon, I say. I'm going to have a gallery show. I'll send you
an invite.

We bid each other good night/morning, and I drop the
laptop onto the duvet, stretching. I glance around the room
once more, out the window at the pinking sky. I should try
to grab a few more hours of sleep if I'm going to be halfway
coherent at this meeting. But instead ... Morgan turned, slowly,
just in time to see a flash of rippling blond hair as Howie dove
beneath the water. She froze as he stroked powerfully to where she
stood. She closed her eyes, feeling a gentle caress on her ankle.

I glance around the room once more, out the window at the
pinking sky. A few more minutes can't hurt.

The doorbell rings at two that afternoon, and I jump to
answer it. I'm dead on my feet, but I've cleaned, bought flowers, replaced two of the dead light bulbs in the kitchen. I feel
100 per cent more like an adult than I have in my entire life.

I even folded the end of the toilet paper into a neat point, the way they do in hotels.

Marcel follows Mother through the doorway of my apartment. Contrasted against their immaculate bodies, everything seems grimier. I am suddenly acutely aware of the soft swell of stuffing leaking out of the sofa. But Marcel goes directly to work, greeting the paintings with cautious delight. 'Nice,' he murmurs. 'These pieces speak to the Hole in a way that – yes. Yes.' He draws his hand through the air in front of the mouthless maid. 'We can work with this. "What Am I Missing?" by the girl with the Hole in her middle. The media will adore it.'

Mother pauses behind me and grips my shoulder, smelling like plumeria and hints of musk – *Kali Girl*, or *Destroyer of Dreams*. 'It's awfully macabre,' she says. 'Couldn't we come up with something a little more – affirmative?'

'I was thinking about incorporating the concept of extras, too, maybe,' I say. I've been carefully rehearsing all morning. 'I conceived this series as a conversation between longing and outsiderness.'

Marcel is nodding, but not listening.

'*What am I missing?*' he says, suddenly, as if reading from a catalogue. '*The piece challenges the viewer to engage with this question as intimately in their own life as the artist has in hers. The progression of images, ailments more and less visible, provoke feelings of discomfort* – no, no, – *provoke* uncomfortable *truths as Stone confronts the* – no, no, – juxtaposes *the hegemonic discourse of the body with the inescapable concept of absence.'* He pulls out an iPad, starts jotting notes as he drifts into the kitchen. 'Something along those lines – I'll have my assistant draw up the copy.'

His art-speak is amazing. Mother looks displeased, squeezes my shoulder again, harder. I lift my torso, straighten my posture.

'I've been imagining it displayed along a hallway – the first few pictures you see are pretty ordinary-looking, but as you go on, the erasures become more and more apparent. Then right at the end, I hang a self-portrait. You know? As if to say: compared to all of these other people, what am I missing, really?' I look at Mother, who's wearing her polite face. 'It's something I've been thinking about a lot in the last few days, and—'

'A mirror,' Marcel says.

'What?' I ask.

'Yes,' Mother says.

He planes the air with his hand. 'You want the show to move beyond you. It should be provocative, challenge your audience. When the viewer comes to the end, they should confront themselves, hence the mirror. It will drive the question home. Not "What am I missing?" but what are *we* missing? What are *you* missing?'

Marcel shakes his head. His black hair catching the light and holding it, effortlessly.

'Trust me,' he says. 'This is the show you want for your debut. Don't make this about you. Make it about them.'

Mother reaches for her phone. 'Perfect,' she says, crisply.

'I'll have someone pick out a mirror by the end of the week. How large are we thinking?'

'A normal, vanity-sized mirror ought to do the trick,' Marcel says. 'No – full length. Subtle lights. I'm thinking an antique frame. You want that nostalgia angle. We'll play up the lost childhood thing.'

'*Stop*,' I say.

Mother crosses her arms.

'Sweetheart,' she says. 'You're a public figure now. We want to spin this to your best advantage. Marcel has years of experience. Maybe once you're established you can have a little more artistic freedom. Trust me,' she says. 'Marketing can make or break a brand.'

'I'm not a brand,' I say.

'Of course you are,' Mother says. 'You want to be successful in the commercial art world, don't you?'

'Do I?' I ask. 'You're the one who bought me a gallery. And a manager-slash-babysitter.'

Mother lowers her chin. I hold my back so straight it aches.

'I finally found something that I really want to say,' I say. 'If you don't want me to say it my own way, fine. Give your gallery to someone else. I can recommend some very talented fan artists on the internet.'

Mother's pale face draws tight. Marcel shifts, ostentatiously checks his watch.

'Not to be a pill,' he says. 'But I've got a meeting at three—'

'Go,' Mother says.

The Stone women face each other, alone. Even the air shrinks away from the outline of Mother's body.

'Morgan,' she says. 'You *will* do this show.'

'Will I?' I ask.

'We've already sent out the press release,' she says.

'Unrelease it,' I say.

She pinches the bridge of her nose and sighs.

'Your father's coming,' she says at last. 'And I'd appreciate it if you'd kindly make it look as though I haven't been a complete failure as a parent for the last seventeen years.'

My heart fumbles on its beating path.

'I'll pick up the mirror by the end of the week,' she tells me. 'You should up your iron intake; you look peaked.'

She leaves before I can read any more of her face.

28

I sit on the couch thinking, *Dad, Dad, Dad*.

I have two memories of my father. The first is the look of terror on his face the day he left. The other is a riddle.

There are two knights racing on horseback. But there's a twist: the man whose horse crosses the finish line last will win.

Yes, I was three. Yes, I was far too young for logic puzzles. But I struggled with it. I turned it over in my mind while waiting at doctors' offices, and stranded alone in front of the television, and in the bath. It seemed impossible. How do you win a race by losing?

I figured it out, years later, stumbling over the answer randomly, while waiting in line at the DMV to take my driver's test. It had bloomed there, or grown there, while I wasn't looking. Just waiting quietly for me to understand.

I remember the riddle, but not the telling. I have to invent my own memory, largely constructed from Mother recounting it to me: the time the nanny got food poisoning and your father had to put you to bed. It's her four-cocktails story about Dad. Five Manhattans gets me the time he left me in the back of a taxi on holiday and Mother called every company in New York in a rage. (I had fallen asleep in the back seat, and was discovered when the cab was flagged down by an austere woman in minks, bleeding from the forehead, who was trying to get to the hospital.) Six Manhattans gets me the day they met. She usually falls asleep in the middle.

(Do you want to know the answer? The knights switch horses and *then* race.)

(... yeah. Try wrapping your mind around that at three.)

When Mother tells this story, it's as evidence that my father never understood children, was never cut out for parenthood. But to me, the story is this: my dad sitting at the edge of my bed in the dark, easy, loose-muscled at the end of a long day of work and meetings, putting me to bed with ice cream kisses, his voice unwinding around the two of us while outside, the remnants of the day drain away.

I slump on the couch after Mother has gone, feeling heavy all over. It is as if I have spent my life with hollow bones and now they are filling up all at once.

I text Howie.

Still up for that road trip?

Half a minute later, my phone lights up. What about your gallery stuff?

I respond:

n/a

There's a pause, and then he calls me. I wonder if we're allowed to just call each other first, or if texting is a necessary protocol. There are so many rules to being friends with boys.

He says, 'What about the gallery?'

I say, 'I'm out.'

'Oh man,' he says. He sounds genuinely wounded for me. 'They cancelled your show? That sucks.'

'No, the show's still happening. The show must go on.' I can't bring myself to talk about my dad. 'I just don't really get to have a lot of say in stuff.'

'Oh. Is that normal?'

'I'm the wrong person to ask about normal.'

He laughs. 'Fair enough.'

There's a long, awkward, phone-pause, the kind where both people are thinking, *maybe I should just say how awkward this is to diffuse the tension!* and then, *ugh, but wouldn't that just make it more awkward?* and then *shit, what was that, five seconds? Now it's even* more *awkward*, and the tension reaches a critical breaking point and there's nothing left to do but pray for a dropped call or the Rapture.

'This is awk—' I start.

'How about going to the fair?' Howie asks at the same time.

'What?' we both ask. 'No, you first,' we both say.

We laugh, harder than is necessary.

'Seriously, go ahead,' I say. *For the love of God, please.*

'What about the State Fair?' he asks. 'This week is the closing weekend. It's so obvious, I can't believe we didn't think of it before. We don't have to go on a big Tour de Freaks road trip at all.'

'The fair?'

'Yeah,' he says, assuming a barker voice. 'Meet the Amazing Lizard Lady! See a two-headed cow! It's Harvey, the world's smallest horse! Et cetera.'

'I thought the fair was rides,' I say. I step out our door and into the building's stairwell, pacing.

'You've never been? Weren't you ever a child?'

'You fatally underestimate how much I hate fun.'

'Forget fun,' he says. 'They have fried Snickers bars. Also, really big pumpkins.'

'Well, shoot, mister,' I say. 'Sign me up.'

I can hear a smile in his voice. 'Great,' he says. 'How about Friday? I'll pick you up.'

Turning to go back inside, I see a note propped up by the key bowl. I pick it up: *Me and Todd are going out tonight for our 2¼ year anniversary, please don't lock the deadbolt. –C.*

Once I would have been irritated – who celebrates two and a quarter of anything? – but not today. I slip the note into my pocket, where it nestles comfortably next to the warm promise of my tomorrow.

*

I wake too early and stare at my closet in dismay, wondering what one wears on a date-that's-not-a-date, or a date-you-kind-of-hope-is-a-date-but-only-if-the-other-person-thinks-it's-a-date-too, and then wondering when in history clothing got so *complicated*, the simple business of covering our nakedness so nuanced and political. When Howie texts that he's here, I'm in jeans and a cowboy shirt with pearl-snap buttons and yesterday's scarf. It'll serve.

I pull my scarf up to hide my face as I hurry across the parking lot, trying to avoid the photographers who lurk in the meagre landscaping. The landlord has taken to leaving notes on the windshields of their cars, pages torn from spiral-bound notebooks and scrawled on in red Sharpie: PaRKING IS 4 RESiDENTS + GUESTS ONLY!!!!! Passive aggression litters the bushes.

'Miss Stone,' Howie says. 'What a pleasure to see you here.'

I am the World's Most Mortified Cowgirl. 'You read that story, too?'

'What story?'

I buckle my seatbelt, feeling warm and overly aware of my face. 'Nothing.'

Behind us, car doors slam – four, possibly five. The entourage for our soon-to-be-public date. I cool my cheeks with my hands. 'I should have snuck out the back.'

Howie checks the rear-view mirror. 'Don't mind them. They've been camping out at the hotel, too. I met one of them last night at the ice machine, Dev. He's not a bad guy. He lost his job in the recession; always loved photography and decided to make a go of it.'

'Can't he photograph something else?'

Howie shrugs. 'Everyone's got to eat,' he says.

I feel depressed, again, by how nice he is. Sometimes I just want a partner in grumpiness. Someone who won't make me feel like a monster for shouting at those damned kids to get off my lawn. Howie's lawn would be full of puppies playing fetch and adorable tots setting up lemonade stands. Caro's, too. How did I end up surrounded by so many obnoxiously well-adjusted people?

As we drive we talk about the fair, the people we might meet there. We delineate our standards: no self-mutilators, feat performers, or survivors of accidents or illnesses. We are interested in natural deformity – people who cannot help the way they are. Animals, too, don't interest us: the world's biggest pig, the six-legged dog.

'I'm honestly not expecting too much,' Howie says. 'We can treat it like a training run for meeting the Angel next weekend. Worst-case scenario, it's all a wash. Then we just eat fried things on sticks and watch duck races.'

'What about the best-case scenario?' I ask.

Howie shrugs.

'We find an answer.'

Howie buys our tickets (*is* this a date?) and we slam headlong into the overstimulating and overstimulated wall of humanity that is the State Fair on its final Friday of the year. We've

251

arrived just as schools are letting out, and although I eye the flood of people anxiously for familiar faces, the October day is bright, and everything seems oversaturated in colour and promise: Fried Mac-N-Cheese! Tilt-A-Whirl! Guess My Age, Win A Prize! Howie's hand hovers on my elbow as we navigate the dusty pathways. I am stunned by everything, bumping into strollers and small children and the waddling extended families who halt in the middle of traffic to point to every shining thing: elephant ears, the sky ride, stuffed Tweety Birds larger than the cranky toddlers whose mouths pucker around their fists. Overhead, in the distance, the Mega Drop and the big Ferris wheel loom polychrome on the skyline.

'What do you want to do?' Howie asks. A group of girls in old-fashioned dresses bump past him toward the Village of Yesteryear, and we are suddenly toe to toe. Everything smells like cake.

Howie grips my arm. 'Stay on mission.'

I nod. 'Right,' I say.

We pick our way through the crowds, finding the freak shows in small, gemlike clusters. We reject the Incredible Mongolian Sword Swallower, decline to see Samson, The World's Largest Horse. Howie pauses outside Lovely Lela, the Living Mermaid.

'A real, live mermaid!' bellows a recorded voice from speakers outside her tent. 'Pearl of the South Pacific!'

There's a painting on the left side of the tent flap depicting a buxom mermaid beckoning from a tank. On the opposite flap is an enlarged photograph of a woman, presumably Lela, posing with a full-body X-ray. It's ordinary from the waist up – human ribs, neck and spine – but extends downwards into an incredible fusion of bone: her spinal column stretching far below the pelvis, which is narrowed and feline. Delicate bones extend from the tip of the tail, needle-like toes suspended in the shadows of fins.

I chew my lip. Beside me, Howie looks similarly dubious. We've both seen our share of strange X-rays.

'Fake,' I say.

'Only a dollar to find out,' Howie says, reaching for his wallet.

'Hey!' a voice shouts behind us. 'It's them!'

I turn to a flashbulb and blink. 'Howie,' I say, warningly. We've attracted a crowd; and a crowd will attract the press. I can already see the headline: *Freaks at the Freak Show.*

'Direct from the South Seas!' the recorded voice booms on a loop. 'Half-woman, half-fish! She talks to you! A real, live mermaid!'

Howie tugs me towards the tent flap. 'Come on,' he says.

The bouncer-slash-ticket-taker crosses his massive arms and scowls at our unwanted entourage. 'No cameras,' he grunts. We shove two dollars into his hand and duck inside while, behind us, photographers scramble with camera bags and excuses.

It takes a moment for our eyes to adjust to the dusky interior of the tent. There's a second flap of canvas, and then a small, dark room. At its centre is a dimly lit aquarium behind a wall of chicken wire. Lovely Lela sits in it on a large concrete boulder, immersed to the waist.

She's a deeply tanned, thick-waisted woman of maybe forty, wearing a clamshell bra and clumpy blue eyeshadow. The water bobs at her waistline and is slick with seaweed, obscuring the place where the tail merges with her torso. Even so, it is easy to see that she is a fake. The silver scales strain across her thighs, revealing a seam. Her fins twitch back and forth on wires, stirring the murky water.

A group of middle school wannabe skater punks lace their fingers in the chicken wire, trying to get Lela to admit she's not really a mermaid. 'What do you eat?' one of them asks, and Lela drawls, 'Clams.' Her voice has a grating edge, as if she spent years as the ring-toss barker, and has only just stepped into the mermaid tail this morning.

I feel Howie slump with disappointment that, despite having prepared for, I share.

'Hey,' I say, squeezing his arm. 'It's okay. We didn't expect anything, remember?'

Light pierces the room, and the tent swells with noise as people spill in from the outside. 'It's the Puzzle Pieces!' someone says. Lela looks up, peering into the darkness beyond her cage.

'Let's get out of here,' I say. We squeeze past the tweens towards the exit sign. I lift the tent flap and drop it again, feet frozen.

'What's wrong?' Howie asks. 'Let's go.'

'Everyone and their kissing-cousin is out there with a camera,' I whisper.

'So?' he asks. 'We've done it before.'

But this disappointment feels too private. I can't think of giving the world my face in this moment.

The voices get louder behind us. I brace myself. Beside me, Howie stiffens. Then a voice at our elbows says, 'Hey. Come this way.'

I look around, confused, then down. A heavily pierced dwarf gestures to us from a slit in the canvas I hadn't noticed before.

'Or you can just stand there with your thumbs up your asses,' he says. 'Whatever.'

Howie lifts his eyebrows. So I lead.

The dwarf's name is Lester. He leads us out into the dazzling sunlight, a small clearing sheltered by the backs of the freak show tents. A man and a woman perch on folding chairs nearby, smoking cigarettes. She's in camouflage from the waist up, with patches of black hair glued to her arms and cheekbones, and has her legs propped up in the man's lap. I recognise the man from a poster: THE LIVING DRUG ADDICT! HE'S DONE HEROIN ... THROUGH HIS EYES!

'You can go out that way,' the dwarf says, gesturing. 'Lela's got homeboys running towards the tractor pull.' He sniffs. 'They'll forget about you by the time they get to the butter sculpture.'

I have never talked with a dwarf before. I am not sure where to put my eyes. This must be how people feel talking to me.

'Thanks,' I say.

Howie lingers a moment, clearly not ready to go.

'What do you do here?' he asks.

Lester adjusts his belt. 'Blockhead stuff,' he says. 'Also some penny magic tricks – dollar bills in balloons, pulling quarters from ears.'

'Sounds pricier than pennies,' I say.

Lester smiles. It's a real sucker punch of a smile: devastating, impossible to see coming. 'Smart girl,' he says.

Howie glances back at the tent. Lester says, 'Don't bother asking for your money back. Woody runs a tight ship. Zero refund policy.'

'It's not the money,' Howie says. 'We were just hoping ...'

We look at each other, unsure what more to say, but Lester waves a stubby hand. 'It's all right,' he says. 'I know who you are. Lela's the one what recognised you, actually. She reads all that *People* magazine shit. Puzzle Pieces, right? She's been talking about you all week. Says you're just the cutest things.'

I look away. The air is a surreal blue over the white tent tops.

'We were hoping to find someone, um, like us, you know, to talk to,' Howie says.

'And you came here?' Lester's eyebrows droop like lazy

reddish wings, exhausted from a long season's migration. He shakes his head. 'Forget this stuff. This is family fare. You kids're barking up the wrong tree.'

'Do you know anything about Helen Rhees Boyle?' Lester looks blank, and Howie clarifies, 'The Angel of Appalachia?'

'Oh, her,' Lester says. 'Jesus. There's some ancient history. That old broad's still alive?'

'We think so.'

'My grandad saw her once when he was a kid,' Lester says. 'He told the story every Christmas. She was something else.'

'So she's real?' I ask.

'Real as they come,' Lester says. 'Maybe real dead, though. Who knows.'

'We're going to visit her this weekend,' Howie says.

Lester's eyebrow lifts. 'Really?'

'Do you want to come?'

I try to catch Howie's eye, but Lester's already waving him away, coughing into a fist.

'You're a sweet kid,' he says, when his throat is clear. He reaches into his pocket and pulls out a roll of tickets. 'Go enjoy the fair,' he says, pushing them into Howie's hand. 'Quit wasting your money. Just don't come back here, all right? Bad for business.'

We emerge behind the Expo Building into a rare patch of stillness. Before us, and all around, the fair beckons: tired families, brightly coloured tents, the painted animals of the carousel. I think about the frozen circus parade in the Loblolly gallery: the immobile acrobats and clowns laughing at some great joke I couldn't hear.

Beside me, Howie asks, 'What do you want to do?'

I close my eyes and stretch out into the warmth of the sun. My skin drinks in the jangle of music and barkers and show recordings mingling with the announcements over the loud-speakers. The clash and noise of life.

I laugh aloud. I can feel flight building in my toes.

'Everything,' I say.

We run down the fairway, shrieking like children. People shout and scatter; we slip between them, quick and nimble. There are the people leading ordinary lives, and then there is us: flying.

Later, in the papers, there will be pictures of Howie and me eating jumbo turkey legs and leaning over the railing at the blacksmith's shop in the Village of Yesteryear. We fling our tickets at rides, our money at games. We spend every penny on fried Oreos and the swinging pirate ship and the fun house where mirrors distort bodies even more than normal.

Outside of the agriculture tents, there's a pig that paints pictures by holding a paintbrush in its teeth. You can buy the paintings for a dollar. Howie suggests that I hang one at the end of my exhibit, and I laugh but feel depressed. I hug my scarf tighter against the chill in the air. The sun is drain-ing away, and with it, the dread reality of our appointment is dawning. Howie and I wander side by side through the twinkling midway. We don't look at each other. We are not ready for everything to be over.

'Screw it,' Howie says suddenly. 'One more ride.'

'We're out of tickets,' I say.

'Don't worry,' he says. 'I can get more.'

'Does this involve prostitution?' I ask. 'I can't let you debase yourself for my State Fair experience.'

He heaves an exaggerated sigh.

'You're sure you won't let me sell my body?'

'No more than usual,' I say.

Darkness has settled in by the time we reach the front of the long, quadruple-wrapped line for the Ferris wheel. The ticket-taker is supremely unimpressed with our empty hands. He points us away.

'Lela sent us,' Howie says.

The man says, 'Who the fuck is Lela?'

'The mermaid,' Howie says.

The man waves a hand. 'Get out of here.'

Howie stares the man in the face. Then he lifts his shirt.

I half expect the man to yelp, or swear, but he only rubs a hand across his tanned brow, looks exhausted. 'Just go,' he says, gesturing toward the car.

'I thought I said no selling your body,' I say to Howie as we step onto the car.

'It was barter,' he says. 'Screw capitalism. I would be remiss in my State Fair ambassador duties if I let you go home without riding the Ferris wheel.'

We settle into the cold metal basket, feeling the platform sway beneath us as a family of four squeezes in the seats on the other side of the car. The night is getting cold, and I shiver a little. Howie throws his arm across the back of the seat. I can feel the warmth of his body, how close his face is to mine. I can't turn to look.

We rise towards the sky in jerks and starts, our basket swinging as they load on more people below. I try to imagine all of the space between my feet and the ground, how it grows and grows.

'This ride is slow,' the little boy across from us complains.

'That's good,' his mother says. 'That means we get more time to ride.'

Howie and I say nothing. I can feel the heat of him on my skin, can sense the dark space in his chest in which his heart expands and contracts, sending the blood skittering through his veins. I sit very, very still, and I know he's feeling the same thing about me. I know that if I turn to look, I'll see something in his face that I'm not ready to see. Beneath us, the glowing world rocks and sways.

'I want to go on the Tornadoclone,' the kid is saying. The father tries to roll his eyes at me, as if to say, *kids*.

'I don't mind being up here a while,' Howie says, but softly, and only to me.

'Yeah,' I say, trying to diffuse the tension, and still the tingling in my stomach. 'May as well get your money's worth.'

He says nothing. Our car moves up another space, and

we're just one from the top. Then we inch up again, and we're there, hanging at the top, swinging. The world below us unfurls like a gem-strewn blanket: the swings tiny, the roller coaster far away. Despite all of the tallest skyscrapers, the mountain tops and airplanes, I am sure that we are the highest people in the world.

The kid says, 'Woah.' I look up at Howie, and find him smiling, and think, *damn*.

'What?' he asks.

'Nothing,' I say.

He's still looking at me. My breath catches. I don't know how to do what comes next.

I say, 'I was just thinking of this riddle I once heard.'

He says, quietly, 'I love riddles.'

I look back over the edge of the car, knowing we'll have to come back down, that in the morning I'll have to deal with this piece of myself that I am on the edge of giving away. But for the moment, everything looks safe and small and far away.

29

Howie picks me up early the next day, with a smile I feel too shy to return. We take our time driving, not speaking about what's to come. We're headed to a private clinic where we'll stay overnight for observation after the first round of gene therapy. We drive with the radio off and the windows cracked. The day is unusually cold, the sky a great flat muscle.

The press crew is smaller today, huddled in the parking lot and blowing into gloved fingers. Men with cameras climb out of idling cars to snap pictures of Howie and me as we run the gauntlet together. There are fewer mics, fewer bids for attention. Howie smiles and waves, but I don't bother. They don't need my consent to craft the story they want to tell.

We are met on the ground floor by our medical team. Dr Morse's hair glows crimson under the fluorescent lights. She is spoiling for a fight.

'We'll begin with a physical merging of the patients' bodies,' she announces. 'It's imperative that we have a sense of physiological compatibility pre-treatment.'

She stares us down. Howie and I stare at each other, at our bodies. A dizzy tingling flutters around the Hole like a storm of moths. Neither of us says anything. Dr Morse, who had clearly been bracing herself for an argument, continues, surprised and slightly disappointed.

'After that,' she says, more quietly, 'we'll prep you for treatment. This round consists of three injections each – for Morgan, cells modified with Howie's A436G, and for Howie, A436C isolated from Morgan's tissue. We'll keep you overnight for monitoring. You'll have access to medical staff at all hours. Have you had anything to eat or drink in the last six hours?'

We shake our heads.

'Let's head to the back,' Dr Takahashi says, startling me with his presence. He waits for most of the crowd to pass, then falls into step beside me, squeezes my shoulder. His gloved palm rides my scapula until I drift away to the changing room to don the gown that is, by now, like a second skin.

Everyone reconvenes in a large examination room, devoid of kitten posters. I want to go and stand by Howie, but I don't want anyone to know I want it, so I stand in a corner, hoping he'll come to me.

He does.

'It'll be okay,' he says.

'I know,' I say. 'It's just bodies.'

'It's just bodies,' he echoes.

But the air between us is troubled by tiny wings.

*

The Merge feels stiff and awkward. We stand toe to toe, inching our bodies together until Howie's Lump, lubricated, slips into my Hole like a key sliding into a well-oiled lock – so easily that we stumble the last half-step, and Howie's chin clips my temple. I gag involuntarily at the sudden warmth, the unfamiliar sense of being filled. I hear the pounding of Howie's heart, inches from my ear. He grips my elbow, ostensibly for balance, and I find my feet where I left them, beneath my knees, steadying myself.

I inhale, experimentally, and feel my organs swell around a hard foreign mass. We're both sweaty and too close to each other. My mouth is directly next to Howie's nipple. I try to pull back, and it pulls him forward. He stumbles a little, catching himself on my shoulders. He lets out a little huff of laughter, and it jumps inside my intestinal tract, and the sensation is so strange that I start to laugh, too. We laugh into each other's faces, tears streaming, guts locked together. 'That's enough,' Dr Morse calls, but we can't stop. We are hysterical. We are so relieved that this is all there is. No magic sparkle, no transformation. Just two bodies in an awkward, human position: the answer to all of our questions a completely ordinary blank.

I don't watch as Taka administers my injections. 'This might pinch a little,' he murmurs. There's a prick, then a sudden burning flow. I cringe, trying not to squirm. I focus on the colour of the wall. I think, *wall, wall, wall*. On the next table, I hear Howie take a sharp breath.

They settle us into hospital beds, plastered with electrodes and hooked up to an array of humming monitors. I've had nothing to eat since noon. Dr Morse settles into the chair beside my bed, clipboard in hand, muffin on a plate by her side.

'What are you watching for?' I ask.

'Symptoms,' she says, tersely. As though my body is not my business.

'Like boredom?' I say. 'I am currently suffering an overdose of boredom. Also hunger.'

'Do you want me to put the TV on?'

'Are you going to watch me watch TV?'

'It *is* called observation,' she says.

It's going to be a long night.

We watch *Animal Planet* while nurses brush in and out, checking and adjusting. Periodically, Dr Morse asks how we're doing. Do we feel nauseated? Warm? Are we experiencing pain? She eyes the Lump and the Hole, as though hoping, against her professional judgment, to see them shrink away on the spot.

'Irritated,' I tell her the sixth time she asks how I'm feeling. She closes her eyes and visibly counts to ten. Then she steps into the hall.

'You should give her a break,' Howie says softly, after she leaves the room. 'She's not all bad.'

'Really?'

'I know she can come off as kind of intense,' he says. 'She's just really passionate. There's been a lot of criticism of her work. I think it makes her more hostile than she needs to be.'

I fold my arms beneath my breasts and stare at a rhinoceros beetle having sex with another rhinoceros beetle on television. 'Is this another I-was-a-quiet-kid-on-the-outside-of-things observation?'

'No,' he says. I can feel his eyes on the side of my face. 'We've talked about it.'

'Your doctor told you that?' I think of Taka, always locked away behind gloves and glasses.

'She's actually a very kind person,' Howie says. 'I didn't know anyone when I first got to New York, and Parker took me under her wing. We have dinner together about once a week.'

'You and *Parker*? Are these dates?'

'What? No,' he says, irritated. 'We just order in Chinese and talk about her work, or my classes, or whatever.'

'Does she wear nice perfume, and excuse herself to slip into something more comfortable?'

'Quit being jealous,' he says.

'I'm not jealous,' I scoff. 'It's just weird.'

He shrugs. 'Think what you like, I can't stop you,' he says. 'She's been a really positive influence in my life, and a great advocate for me. Besides, I think it's good for her to get out of the lab every once and a while. I think she gets pretty lonely ...'

His voice trails off as Dr Morse comes back into the room. She walks briskly, eyes down, and crosses back to the chair between our beds. Her shoe catches the floor and she stumbles a little, her neck going pink as she crosses her legs and resettles her clipboard in her lap. Suddenly I can see, as plain as day, the word *insecure* tucked into every pore. I think of these weekly dinners, and how excited Dr Morse must be for them: picking out ingredients days before, cleaning house before he arrives. She spends a little more than she is comfortable with on ill-fitting sale blouses, dabs on a little lip gloss, allows herself to wonder intellectually if he'll notice. She never lets herself get beyond that word *intellectual* – he's too young, it would be unprofessional, but still. That pocket of excitement grows in her stomach, day by day, until Friday mornings are a haze of snappish excitement.

Or maybe not. Maybe she's just a type-A bitch. But now that I've sketched this picture of her for myself, I'm having trouble seeing past it.

'Howie, any troubling symptoms?' she asks, and he says no.

Poor Parker, I think. No wonder you hate me. You brought Howie here so you could cure him, and instead you're watching him drift away.

'None here, either,' I say, though she doesn't ask me. But I see her make the note in her chart: *9.45 MS no change*.

Dr Morse goes off-shift at eleven, and the nurses take turns filing in and out, checking our vitals, asking if we need anything. The lights stay on overhead. The hands of the clock press on towards two, three in the morning, and we lean back into our pillows but don't sleep. I'm grainy with exhaustion, but too charged up to relax. Every time my eyes meet Howie's, something leaps beneath us, an electric plea: *don't go yet.* He says, 'Do you know when I gave up on surgeries?'

I shake my head.

He says, 'We were driving home from the pre-op for yet another excision, and I looked at the Lump through my shirt, and I was like, "Mom? Can we just *not* any more?" The shirt was bright green ... the Lump looked like a little tree underneath it, like something growing naturally. I just had this sense that the Lump was *here* for something. Why else wouldn't it go away? It must have some reason to be on my body, we just hadn't figured it out yet.'

'It brought you here,' I say.

He looks at me, a strange expression on his face. 'Yeah,' he says. 'It did.'

An aide comes in, and we fall quiet. She tries to hide the little smile floating on her lips. The nurses all think we're a couple. I wonder if Howie knows this.

We don't say anything for a long time after she goes. The air in the room feels crookedly charged. All of the molecules swirling, confused and hungry.

'So, the Merge,' he says, hesitantly.

I stare at my feet, protruding from the thin clinic blanket. 'Yes?'

He speaks carefully. 'You were kind of freaked out about it. In the beginning.'

I think about Handsome Chad leering at me in the dark, the tentacles of his fingers writhing in my gut.

'Can we actually not talk about it?' I ask.

'Yeah,' he says. 'Of course.' But he sounds a little – hurt? I can't tell.

'Sorry,' I say.

'You don't have to be sorry for not telling me things,' he says.

'It's not because I don't trust you,' I say.

'It's okay,' he says.

'No,' I say, feeling everything rise to the surface. 'I really—'

'Look, snow,' Howie says.

He points. I turn to the window. The air is filled with white flakes spinning off into the blackness, silent on the other side of the glass.

'It can't be,' I say. But it is. I climb from bed and stand as close as I can to the window, straining at the wires hooking me to the monitors. From the far bed, I hear Howie rustle to do the same.

The flakes glow like fireflies in the streetlights, speeding down into the dark. I have the fleeting sense that the snow is holding still and the earth is rushing upward.

'Let's go down there,' Howie says.

I turn to look at him and he is wearing a mischievous smile that glows like the sun. Despite the IV drips, the beeping, the potential cancers spinning through our veins, I feel suddenly, gloriously warm.

We unplug our monitors from the wall, and then from ourselves, to avoid the shriek of a flatlining alarm. We leave the TV on. There's a low murmur of voices from the break room down the hall, so we pad in the opposite direction on bare feet, with the solemnity of children. The halls are eerily silent, lit with the humming flat daylight of fluorescent bulbs, and it occurs to me that hospitals never sleep. I wonder how much money is being sucked away, reserving this building just for us. How many dead dinosaurs burning silently up in the fixtures.

We creep from one external door to the next until we find one that's unlocked and then, clad only in thin hospital gowns and scrubs, push the door open and let ourselves out into the night.

I gasp at the cold. The sound is immediately swallowed by the silent landscape. There's a dusting of snow on the sidewalk beneath the overhang as fine and thin as sand. A few feet away, the exposed ground disappears into solid white. The snow glows eerily in the spaces between the streetlights, blanketing the empty parking lot and coating the branches of the distant pines. The trees sheltering the spaces, still in autumn splendour, droop heavily. It is too early to snow. We are so far south. And yet, somehow, in these last days of October, winter has found us early.

Howie drops his head and curses. I look at him in surprise.

'We were going to go see the Angel tomorrow,' he says. 'So much for our Tour de Freaks.'

'It's not over,' I say. 'We'll go next week.'

He sighs fog.

'Will we, though?' he asks. 'With your show coming up? With our next treatment?'

'Okay, fine. The week after.'

He turns from me so he's half in profile. The Lump disappears from my sight, and he looks like any normal boy in a white hospital gown, slump-shouldered against a brick wall in the snow.

'It was crazy anyway,' he says. 'We didn't think it through at all. Who says she'd even want to talk to us? What if we drove five hours just to find out that she'd moved? Or died?'

I wrap my arms around myself. The cold air sits in the Hole like a heavy block, but I try to smile. 'You're seriously going to give up, just like that? No hope, no crazy Howie philosophy? Every cloud has a silver et cetera, the whole world smiles with you?'

'I know the way the world works,' he explodes. 'It's just like this. All the time. Someone thinks they found a cure for you. But oh wait, there's no funding, but wait, there might be funding, but wait, they just have to clear the paperwork. Or they got the paperwork, but the patent's not accepted. Or it's all fine but the doctor's cat died, and so they can't see you after all.' He violently kicks at the snow. 'There's just always fucking *something*.'

271

I want to touch him, but I'm afraid of this anger, and where it came from. I don't want it turning on me. I grip my gown to my sides and wonder what the hell I'm doing here, barefoot in the snow, with this broken and breaking boy.

The snow melts silently in his hair, crystals turning into water. 'She's probably just a washed-up circus performer, anyway,' he says. 'A glamour girl with strap-on wings.'

I speak lightly. 'It's not like we thought she was really an angel.'

'I did,' he says. 'When I was a kid, I did. And maybe – I don't know, maybe it's for the best we don't go looking for her. Maybe I'm not ready to stop believing.' He laughs, short and harsh. 'I'm sorry,' he says. 'It's late and I'm tired, and cold, and hungry, and gene therapy is mutating me into a jerk. We should head back in.'

'You're not a jerk,' I say.

He looks at me beneath his damp flop of hair, plainly unhappy.

'I just thought it'd be different this time,' he says. 'With you.'

The words hang between us, heavy.

'I'm just some girl,' I say.

'You're not,' he says.

'Fine. I'm less than a girl.'

It's the wrong answer. I can see it as soon as I say it. Howie's face folds neatly: putting himself away again behind his eyes.

'Howie—'

'Let's just go inside,' he says.

The snow-blanketed earth stretches away from us, glowing in the light-polluted night: an endless white canvas, waiting for my mark.

'You know those collage paintings you saw?' I say. 'Even though Mother has completely co-opted the whole show, and I should be so angry about it, I still have them hanging up all over the apartment. I can't stop looking at them. Do you know why?'

'Can you tell me inside?' he asks.

'Because when I did those drawings, I thought they were done. I thought I knew the story they had to tell.' I dip my toe into the snow. It bites at first, and then the cold fades into a burning. An almost warmth. 'But then I added colour and the story changed. And changed again.' I look up at him. 'I never really got that before. The way you can change what you've got instead of starting over. One altered shade can change the mood of a whole piece. A few small lines can shift the axis of the earth.'

'That's great,' Howie says, exhausted. 'Can we talk about art in—'

I step out into the snow. The cold seizes my feet immediately, and the nerves shrill in response: my ankles tightening, muscles clenching. Snowflakes fall on my shoulders and back like icy moths. I step, and again, on frozen soles. I turn to face Howie, and smile.

'Our story needs an angel?' I ask. 'Let me make you one.'

273

I plunge backwards into the snow. The thin gown is instantly soaked through, cold shrieking through my skin. I fan my arms and legs. I open my mouth to the sky and let the unseasonal whiteness float down to me and turn to water.

When I can't bear it any more, I stumble up to survey my work. At the edge of the great white parking lot, in a sketch of white on white, a cartoon angel takes flight.

Howie laughs, despite himself. It is a sad sound.

'That's adorable,' he says. 'Now let's—'

But then he is paying attention, because I've reached behind my back and tugged free the laces on my top, and let it fall, exposing my body.

I dive again. A pillar of snow shoots straight up through the Hole as I fan my arms and legs. Everything is biting, everything is cold, and at my core a fist of ice shoots straight up to Heaven.

I rise, shivering, and study the new angel. *Yes.*

An angel-girl just my size stretching out her new-found wings. Piercing her middle is an ice-crusted cone of snow: the surface powder melted by the Hole, already beginning to refreeze.

It is smaller than I thought it would be.

I hear a whoop next to me, and look, and there's Howie, shirtless, face-down in the snow, angeling. I laugh, and flop down again, and again, numbness beginning to blunt my freezing skin. I am cold everywhere but my face, which is warm with life, laughing.

I finally feel young. I finally feel not-thinking, laughing, whooping the way I never could, leaping shirtless through the snow with a stranger. One of two lost children making an army of angels, mapping the strange geometry of ourselves over and over onto the unlikely night.

I stumble to my feet and turn towards Howie as he rises from his last angel, beaming at me.

'That was amazing,' he murmurs. 'You're amazing.' And he presses his lips to mine.

There is no hallelujah, no explosions. But there's a warmth, a steadiness, that lifts me. It's a kiss that sweeps like a current back into the past, lighting up moments with electric finger-tips: *that time you thought you'd always be alone, the time you cried, the time you thought you might end it because you didn't know this could be waiting for you.* A kiss that is a quiet promise: *I will catch you when you fall.*

Our faces part. He holds my eyes with his, our features fogged with breath and shadow. He whispers, 'Sorry. Was that okay?'

I think, *my whole body is cold except where you are.* And then I say it. 'My whole body is cold except where you are.'

He folds me to him, his skin on mine, and it's impossible to tell where his shivering begins and mine ends.

We run back through the hallways, numb feet slapping the linoleum. There's no one in sight as we slip back into our room, doubling over in silent hysterics. I race for the closet, pulling out blankets and towels. We rub our reddened skin dry, not looking at each other. Howie flips off the light. Outside, street-lit, the snow still swirls.

'I'm freezing,' I whisper.

'Come here,' he whispers.

'To your bed?'

'I won't try anything.'

'I wasn't worried about that,' I whisper-lie. I climb awkwardly underneath his hospital blanket and we shift around, the paper-coated bed crackling beneath us, a tangle of elbows and knees in the narrow space. At last we settle into a spooning position. The only alternative, sleeping Merged, feels too raw and exciting to mention. When we're not facing each other, his Lump pokes into the solid part of my back, so I have to be the big spoon. I tuck an arm beneath my head, wrap the other around his body.

'Are you comfortable?'

'Yeah. Are you?'

'Yeah. Are you getting warmer?'

I shiver and cuddle closer. 'I think so.'

'Good,' he says. The heat of his back soaks slowly into my chest. Gradually, our shivering subsides. I can still feel his heart pounding in my arm. My hands are curled in careful fists.

'You know,' Howie says. 'I've never slept with anyone else before. I mean, not – I mean, you know, just sleeping.'

'Really?'

He shrugs, a ripple against my chest. 'Have you?'

'Yeah. My mom. Caro when we were little.' The Hole is still freezing, feeling the echo of the snow. I press closer to Howie's back. 'Never a guy.'

He murmurs, 'Welcome to your first time.'

I laugh and push him a little. 'Shut up.'

'Shh,' he says. 'Quiet. You'll get us in trouble.'

My fingers brush across his stomach, experimentally, and I feel, rather than hear, the quick intake of Howie's breath as I graze the Lump. He reaches up and winds his fingers through mine, guiding my hand away. A warm tingling sifts through my fingertips and thrills up my arm. I want to fight it, but I'm so tired; it's been a lifetime of hoping and disappointment and heartache, but I'm so tired, I'm so tired. Just for once, I want to fall and not have to pick myself up again.

30

We wake the next morning shirtless and dry-mouthed, blinking into a room of angry doctors. We separate and sit on different beds, sleepwalking through the follow-up tests. Dr Morse presses unnecessarily hard against my ribs with the partometer. Even Taka looks displeased.

'You need to take this seriously,' he says. 'Something could have gone extremely wrong in the night. You could have stopped breathing. We don't monitor you for *our* health.'

Dr Morse says nothing, in a fury over the lost data. Nobody congratulates us on surviving.

Amanda winks as she hands me the bundle of my street clothes. I realise, belatedly, that she must have been the night nurse on the final shift, letting the two of us sleep in peace. I want to thank her but remember Taka's face and worry she may lose her job.

Outside, the snow has shifted into a dull grey sleet. In the freshness of daylight, Howie and I keep a respectable distance from each other. It doesn't seem to be a certain thing, what passed between us last night. But then, alone in the elevator, he kisses me, and I feel light flood every pore in my body.

There are no paparazzi awaiting me when Howie drops me home. They've been driven away by the terrible weather and the Southern certainty that an inch of snow on the roads means death. I wave goodbye to Howie and shuffle carefully up the icy steps.

Caro jumps when I open the front door. She's sitting on the sofa in a nest of crumpled tissues, weeping.

We stare at each other a moment. Then she stands, and I go to her, and she cries into my shoulder. We stand and rock a long time, wordlessly. The warmth of her body is a shock against mine for a second, but only a second. And then it's Caro, of course, it's Caro. My best friend since I was nine. I stroke her hair, breathing in the familiar smell of her lemon shampoo.

She snuffles and catches her breath, then says, 'Todd and I are breaking up?' Her voice breaks on the final word. Like she can't make it into a statement. 'I think?'

'Oh, sweetie,' I say. For the first time in my life, I feel like I have enough warmth and comfort in myself to be useful to someone else.

I make popcorn. We sit on the couch. She explains. The band is starting to pick up. 'Hole Girl' is a local hit; it's getting radio

279

play. They've begun booking some bigger venues. A&Rs show up on the regular. Producers have been calling. Nobody big, but still, it's something. Todd doesn't think it's the right time to leave.

'He doesn't want to do long distance,' she snuffles wetly. 'Does that mean he wants to date other people? Do you think he wants to get back with Sheila?'

'But Sheila's terrible,' I say.

'She's the worst,' she bawls.

'I'm sure he doesn't want to date Sheila,' I say, and then add, awkwardly, 'Hey, Todd loves you.' Once I would have choked on those words – would have welcomed her sadness, told her good riddance, looked forward to a glorious Thelma and Louise life. But now all I can see is my best friend crumpling.

'You'll work it out,' I say. 'Come on. It's you and Todd.'

'What if we don't?' she sniffles.

I don't know what to say. It's Caroline's job to be the positive one. I say, helplessly, 'You will.'

She sighs, wipes her nose, and goes to the kitchen sink. I come and look out the window with her, wrapping my arms around her middle, leaning my head into the cushion of her arm. We watch the cold grey rain fall from the cold grey sky, the snow sluicing away. It seems impossible to imagine that there is a sun anywhere. Caro heaves a heavy sigh.

'What if we don't?' she says. 'How can I go out and find someone to love me in this?'

*

280

Howie comes to visit the next day, bringing cheese sandwiches and apple slices in waxed paper. We climb through my window and eat lunch together on the damp roof of my building, far back from the edge and the view of any paparazzi who might be loitering in the parking lot below. We use the chill as an excuse to huddle close. My whole body is focused into those three places we're touching: shoulders, elbows and knees. It seems unbearable not to be closer, but I don't know how to close that gap, or whose job it is to do it.

The houses are small in this part of town, older and brightly painted. Up until a few years ago it was poor families and empty doorways, but it's turning slowly to gentrification: white hipster kids, then students, the first few young professionals. Grass still grows in cracks in the asphalt, the neighbourhood clinging to some faint remnant of decay.

'I'm supposed to ask you to go on the *Today Show*,' Howie says at last.

'So ask,' I say.

'Morgan Stone,' he says, with a shy smile, 'will you appear on a nationally syndicated talk show with me?'

I lean in and kiss him before he's done asking. It is long and soft and tastes of apples. He twines his fingers into my hair. I think, *oh*.

'Is that a "yes"?' he asks. His hand slides down my ear, to my chin. As if by touching me, he can memorise this moment.

'No,' I say, searching his face. 'I just wanted to kiss you.'

'Oh good,' he says, drawing me in. 'Me, too.'

I open my mouth to him, and he responds, hand tightening in my hair with a sharp sweetness that surprises me. I never would have expected this passion of him: this skinny boy with the too-honest eyes who's pulling me closer and I'm pulling him back, and I think this tingling in my stomach is going to rise up and choke me. Then my hand brushes the Lump, and everything becomes very serious and still.

'I'm sorry,' I say.

'Don't be,' he says. 'It's okay.' He reaches for my hand, to place it back, and I draw away.

'I'm sorry,' I say again.

'For what?' he says.

I chew my lip. 'Um, for casually putting my hand on the source of your years of otherness-related body trauma?'

'Who says I'm traumatised?' he asks. 'Besides, I trust you.'

I say, slowly, 'I trust you, too.' I don't know when this became true. But it is.

His eyes are dark in this light, shaded with green. 'So why not jump in with both feet?' he asks.

I try to conjure up dread and loathing. Chad's fingers. The invasive shock of Dr Morse. But it's not that. All I feel are butterflies.

'I've waited for trust my whole life,' I say. 'I want to let it be sacred for a few more days.'

He nods, but I can see he doesn't really understand, and this quashes something in me.

I say, 'I've spent a lot of my life thinking that once I found the right person, everything would be complete and perfect and I'd never be lonely again. I think I'm kind of afraid of what will happen if we … you know –' *have sex? Shag? Have intercourse?* '– get together and everything's not magically complete.'

'It probably won't be,' he says.

A laugh jumps from my throat.

'I'm just being honest,' he says.

'Is that the way you talk a girl into bed?'

'No,' he says quietly. 'I wouldn't talk anyone into bed if they didn't want to go.'

I wonder, in a flash, about his past: how many other conversations he's had like this, how many other girls' hands he's softly held, with this promise in his pale face. But then he leans forward and kisses me, and I understand that it doesn't matter, none of it: there is something between us unquestioning and living and true. I can't imagine fitting with some other person better than this.

'I'm meeting my family for Mexican,' he says, rising to go. He pulls me to my feet. 'Want to join us? Tyler's totally got a crush on you. If you're there, he'll be too embarrassed to smear beans in Riley's hair. Probably.'

I duck my head to hide the smile twisting at my lips. 'Thanks, but I can't,' I say. 'I'm hanging out with Caro tonight.'

Concern lowers his voice. 'How's she doing?'

'Better,' I say. But I'm not sure. Her mood drops when the sun sets these days. Some new sticky notes appeared around

the bathroom mirror this morning, containing the uncon-
vincing words *strong* and *moving on*.

We cross the rooftop, fingers tangling.

'Think about the *Today Show*,' he says. 'Parker would really
love it.'

'Which is reason enough for me not to go.'

'I wish you two would make peace.'

'She hates me,' I say.

'Well, you are kind of a brat to her.'

I shove his chest lightly. 'Asshole.'

He catches my fingertips and kisses them. My body is a
shiver of wings.

'Hole-Hole,' he says.

I laugh. The sound catches and chokes out strange, but he
doesn't laugh at me, and I feel safe. He just kisses my fingers
again until I break away, so full of tingling that I fear I'll
explode.

We climb back in through my window. We both look at the
bed: the soft tangle of sheets.

'Let me know if you change your mind,' he says in a low
voice.

We both pretend we are talking about the *Today Show*. I
shake my head.

He ends up going on the *Today Show* without me, and does
a few other appearances and interviews. I stream the videos
through my laptop and let Howie's voice wander through

my mind as I paint, tickling the edges of the pieces for the show. They're all in the finicky artistic hinterlands of near-completion: that tenuous space where a single brushstroke could just as easily ruin a piece as finish it. 'Leave them alone,' Caro tells me, watching me wearily over her geometry flash-cards. 'You're going to drive yourself nuts.'

But I feel, with every stroke, that I am painting myself into my own skin. I let the hours melt into one another. On the radio, Howie says: 'Of course I think about my body a lot. Don't you think about your own body all of the time? Everyone does. Mine's just more remarkable. In the literal sense. People remark on it.' I loop my signature into the bottom corner of the many-handed weaver painting, joy balanced in my chest like a brimming cup of liquid.

At times, my happiness is so great that it feels claustrophobic. The universe has been so clear: Here You Are! Made For You! Completion in the Form of Another Person! Out of stubbornness, I begin to look at other men. I perch in the Java Jane window, staring at every man who comes down the street. Women, too. The manager keeps the press out with an iron fist, leaving me peaceful hours to study old men, pregnant women, women with strollers, scruffy students in busted-knee blue jeans, construction workers inhaling steaming Thermoses of coffee before sunrise like oxygen. I imagine myself loving each of them: the dinner, the wedding, anniversaries, growing old. Holding wrinkled hands as we watch *Masterpiece Theater*.

It is not a difficult or special thing to love somebody, I think. It is just a guard that we let down. My eyes are open to a new kind of logic: in the person you love, you find the most obscenely mundane things beautiful. There are obscenely mundane things in everybody. And so everybody is lovable.

I understand I can love everybody because in the last few weeks, I've started to think I love Howie, and he has a lump the size of Oklahoma sticking out of his torso.

I haven't said *love* to Howie yet. He hasn't said it to me, either. We keep talking around it.

'I like you so much,' he'll say, playing with my hair.

'I like you, too,' I'll say, nuzzling his cheek. 'So much.'

'You too,' he'll say. 'So, so much.'

Or other synonyms: I adore you. I'm falling for you. I just *feel so close* to you.

Every time one of us says the word *love*, the other jumps. You can feel it beneath the skin, a bright flinching of desire. 'I love this band!' Flinch! 'I love that restaurant!' Flinch flinch! Sometimes I feel like we sneak the word into conversation where it isn't warranted, as though hoping that if we say it enough, the other will finally capitulate, take the plunge and say the thing we're both too afraid to say: 'I love potato chips.' 'I love you, too!'

Some nights I stay awake late, staring at the ceiling and swimming with anxiousness. It's peculiar. I never thought so much of myself could be invested in the specifics of how another person felt about me. Strange things can plunge me into misery: long gaps between his text messages, or that time he thought I was a vegetarian, and I explained that no, I wasn't, and a puzzled expression flashed behind his eyes that I spent the rest of an afternoon analysing (*who was he thinking of? An ex-girlfriend?*).

But in the full light of day, I fear nothing, and my feelings for him become steady and sure. Not because *love* is a word I am comfortable using. But because it isn't, and it still feels comfortable to use with Howie. Because he is the only person in the world who can step into the small and lonely room I've spent the last seventeen years peering out of and know, without looking, where to find the box of tissues, the chair, every last book on the shelf. Who I can trust when he pulls up the blinds and lets the light in, smiling, saying, *see? Look at the view out there. Here, let me show you the door.*

The internet is in love with us, too. The list of fan fiction titles on Public Scrutiny has more than tripled since we began treatment and became 'official'. The bulk of the stories follow the media's Missing Piece storyline: Howie and I meet. Eyes sparkle. Things are said breathily. There is, without fail, a soft-focus attention paid to 'The Fitting', the cyberlingo term given to the fitting together of the Lump and the Hole. Some writers clearly find this titillating; for others, it is intensely emotional, a reaffirmation of the truest, purest kind of love.

I perch at the counter at Java Jane with my laptop and read aloud to Caro: the noir-style 'Black Hole' vignettes; a circus-themed story called 'Never Reveals Her Tricks' featuring Hole Girl pulling comical plot-necessary objects (soup, underpants, a sword) from the Hole, like a magician. We giggle like children over confusingly written sex scenes. 'His mouth is *where*?' I ask. 'Wait, how can it be *there* if his face is *there*?' Caro snorts behind the espresso machine. Her boss, Cindy, comes out to fuss, and gets caught up in the story of a man named John who turns to liquid and pours through my Hole, filling me up.

'Just try to keep it clean when the customers are around,' she says at last, disappearing into the back. An older woman, waiting for a latte, eyes me with a sniff.

Somewhere between 'Holey Night' and 'To Scratch an Itch', the stories begin to lose their surreal quality. The Hole Girl in them resembles me closely enough sometimes that I should be seriously creeped out. But instead I'm fascinated by the possibilities unfolded by all of these other Hole Girls. They are bright, smart, angry, traumatised; crime fighters, damsels, professors of fine art in Holland. If they share my name and Hole and haircut, why not these other things, too?

I wonder what Howie thinks about the fan fiction, or if he knows about it at all. He found me through Public Scrutiny, after all. I imagine him in a hotel room across town, stretched on a germ-ridden floral print duvet. The blue glow of the screen illuminating his face as he dreams his own dreams, or some ones spun for us by strangers. Both of us wondering what our own dreams are, and when, and how, we might make them true.

31

We return to the hospital weekly for our injections and overnight observations. Even though the shots are unpleasant, I find myself getting excited, counting down days. We haven't made any more daring escapes in the last few weeks, but Dr Morse stays in our room at all times anyway, nodding in her chair over endless cups of coffee. The message is clear: No More Night-time Shenanigans. Nurses come in every hour on the hour, and Amanda is no longer among them.

We still begin our appointments with a Merge, carefully avoiding each other's eyes, frightened by the excitement we might see there. Each time laughing a little less. Each time lingering a little longer when the doctors say, *okay, that's it, we're done.* I wonder if Howie also thinks about forever. We have careful conversations over Dr Morse's head, and everything feels fraught with meaning in a way that fades away in the unchaperoned morning. Morse occasionally takes notes, or pretends to watch TV. I spend 90 per cent of these nights wishing she'd go away. I catch her glaring at me when she thinks I'm sleeping. *Don't worry, lady*, I think. *The feeling is completely mutual.*

One night, Howie's fallen asleep over *Bake Off* and I blink awake to an aching bladder.

'Jesus,' I mutter. The clock on the wall shows a bleary 3.03 a.m. I trudge through the math. The nurses come in on the hour, giving me approximately fifty-seven minutes until—

My bladder lurches like a ship and I groan. I lean towards the machines to unhook myself, and the plastic lining of my bed cracks like a bone. Dr Morse blinks awake. Her face, soft and open in sleep, hardens.

'What are you doing?'

'I have to—'

'Have to what?'

My eyes flick to the bathroom.

She says, 'Void?'

'Pee,' I say.

Her eyes check over my body, professionally. 'You can hold it until the morning.'

'I *promise* that's not true.'

'Well, you'll just have to try.'

'Lady,' I say, 'I am going to void all over this bed unless you let me get up.'

Howie stirs in his sleep. Morse and I both start. The TV is showing an infomercial for wrinkle cream.

Dr Morse sighs. She reaches for my IV pole.

We scoot across the floor together. I'm dizzy from the hours in bed and stumble a little at the doorframe, but sink into the bathroom with a sigh, tugging at the hospital gown. I pull the door shut, and it pops back open with a merry *clink*.

I pull. The door clinks open.

'Um,' I say. 'Dr Morse?'

An exasperated whisper. 'Morgan?'

'The door won't stay closed.'

There's a pause.

'I'll hold it for you,' she says at last. 'Knock when you want to come out.'

The door clicks closed. I stare at it for a brief, self-conscious eternity, then mercifully collapse on the seat. I've never had to pee this badly in my life, and for a moment, I'm certain that I won't be able to stop: my entire body will dissolve into liquid and cascade down into the bowl below. A strange footnote in Dr Morse's medical career. *Gene therapy has power to turn patients into human urine.*

I stop at last, rise and wash my hands. I tap on the bathroom door. Dr Morse's face appears on the other side of it, pinker than normal. I am 95 per cent certain she heard everything.

'Thanks,' I say, flushing.

'It's the IV,' she says, not looking at me. 'It's an awful lot of fluid. We'll be more conscientious about that in the future.'

'If my bladder explodes, does that affect your funding?' I ask as she trundles me back across the floor.

She emits a noise that, from any other human, would be a

laugh. Howie blinks awake, his eyes crawling from one of us to the other.

'What's going on?' he asks. 'Is something wrong?'

Dr Morse takes a moment, hand clamped tight over her mouth. When she removes it, she's wiped all vestiges of humour from her face.

'No,' she says. 'Morgan was having trouble sleeping.'

But she helps me into bed with surprising gentleness. When her gloved hands brush the Hole, I resist flinching.

She still regards me with hooded eyes, her face jumping between mine and Howie's as we talk late into the nights, sometimes feverish with the strange genes flushing our systems. But she begins to permit us, at sunset, to drag our wired bodies as close to the windows as we can, to watch the sky falling down across the city like a baby's blanket.

I load the paintings into the trunk of my car the next morning and meet Marcel at the gallery. The show's opening in a little less than three weeks. The space isn't quite what I imagined, but to his credit, Marcel has given it a try. The entryway leads into an empty room, with a spotlight on one wall, blank but for the stencilled words: *what am i missing?* Marcel leads me into a long, low-ceilinged hall, frigid and womb-dark. He flicks a switch and the whole thing startles blindingly to fluorescent life.

Marcel's lips wince into a perfect half-Windsor. 'We'll change that,' he murmurs.

We argue over small things: the order of the paintings, the location of the coat check, Garamond vs. Helvetica for the placards, 'soft' versus 'natural' lighting. Marcel handles these details, and me, with infuriating ease. There is a sense that the show is already out of my hands, and I want badly not to care. But I see Marcel setting aside the portrait of the many-handed weaver, and I blurt, too loudly, 'Where's that one going?'

The question strikes Marcel at an awkward angle. He grimaces slightly as he straightens.

'You've already got an extra-hand painting.' He lifts an unframed piece: an auditorium of people, delighted, clapping and clapping and clapping.

'So?'

'So,' he says, patiently. 'This is doing the same aesthetic work as the other one.'

'I like the other one.' I sound like I'm five years old. It is mortifying.

'This is a better choice,' Marcel says simply.

'I want to hang both.'

'Miss Stone,' he sighs. 'While I appreciate your opinion—'

'Do you?' I ask. 'Or do you just pretend to listen to my opinion because my mother pays you to?'

'Mostly the latter,' he says.

A paper cut stings across my thumb. I ball my hand into a fist.

'You're kind of an asshole,' I tell him. He pauses. I can

see him assembling the air around him before he proceeds: making sure it hangs it neat and straight as a well-pressed suit.

'What I am, Miss Stone, is a well-regarded professional being paid an exorbitant sum to produce a show for an impatient child with illusions of artistic grandeur,' he says. 'If you want emotional validation, ask your mother to buy you a therapist. Although,' he adds mildly, turning back to the wall, 'I'm surprised she hasn't already.'

I'm not sure whether to slap him or call my mother, and I hate that these are the first two options that come to mind. Something hot and bright twists up in me, but I can't think of a thing to say that's both hurtful and true.

I drive home and open and close my hand around the tiny cut, making the bead of blood rise to the surface and subside again. More than anything, I want to find the right words. To find the message. To have legions of people step into that hall and find the real *me*.

I just don't know who she is yet.

Caro, too, is remaking herself. She sits with me at night, and sometimes cries. In the daytime, though, she is building herself back up again. We travel to our old haunts, and I can see the uncertainty in her as she picks through skirts at Goodwill – is this the new her? Is this? What can she be, what can she become, in this world without a boyfriend? At Java Jane, she smiles and jokes with the customers, like always, but there is a new weight to her, a certain sad gravity.

I'm giggling over the phrase 'palpitating Lump' one day when I realise I'm laughing alone. I look up to ask Caro what that even means, and see that she's leaning against the sandwich bar, reading *The Invisible Man*. She catches my eye and lowers the book, holding her place with a finger. She is wearing lipstick for the first time in two weeks. She's still picking up the pieces of herself, but the girl I see is beginning to look like Caro again: healthy, smiling. Our bathroom mirror has become plastered with new notecards: *I don't need anyone to build me up, so no one can break me down*, and *no matter what happens, I'll always have me.*

'Do you ever look at these with Howie?' She shapes the words delicately, distantly, as though handling wet paper.

'What?' I close the laptop on 'Puzzle of Love'. 'Ew, no. That'd be weird.'

'Weirder than sharing them with me?'

'What? That isn't weird,' I say. 'You're my friend. That's what friends do. You know? Talk about relationship stuff.'

'We never talked about *my* relationship stuff.'

'That's different,' I say.

'How?' she asks.

'You and Todd were, like. You know.' *Boring. Terrible.* 'Established.'

'Not always.'

I open my mouth and close it again. Remembering how I listened and burned with curiosity and shame when Caro told me about losing her virginity to Todd, the boy she'd been seeing for six months but whom I still thought of as *new*. How later she'd bring up stories casually, with a blush, beginning, 'So we were in bed and,' and I'd change the subject, the way one might, in polite society, steer the conversation away from politics, or from the massive shit that the old and arthritic family dog was taking on the living room carpet.

I say, 'I didn't have any sex stuff to talk about then.'

'Yeah,' she said. 'Well, I did.'

A man at the counter taps the service bell. Caro ignores him, keeps her eyes on mine. I hold her gaze as long as possible, not wanting to be the first to look away. But I blink.

'You had other friends you could talk to,' I say. 'They knew about those things.'

'You're my best friend.'

The man taps the bell again. Caroline says, 'In a minute.'

My mouth feels dry.

'I'm sorry,' I say.

'Yeah,' she says. 'Thanks.' Then she goes and takes an order for an egg salad sandwich.

I bike home, face tightening in the chill. In my backpack, my laptop hums, and I realise, stupidly, that I forgot to turn it off. All those sex dreams of strangers spinning themselves out into the dark.

I never realised Caro noticed. Or, I guess I did. But I never realised she cared.

But ... I realised that, too. I just didn't think she'd ever call me on it.

I'm thinking I'm a little frightened of this new Caro when I see the first of the flyers.

They are in five colours. They litter the telephone poles on Wade Avenue, on Hillsboro Street, weave their way through the small neighbourhoods between. I pull my bike to a stop, pluck one from its staple with a gloved hand. The photographer in the car beside me slows, pulling up to the kerb, and I turn my face away as I read the text: four words, in block print.

HOLE GIRL I'M SORRY

I glance up, feeling the camera's eye slide away from my back. Traffic streams by, unaware. Above my head, polychromatic flyers flutter the rest of the way up the pole: HOLE GIRL I'M SORRY HOLE GIRL I'M SORRY I'M SORRY HOLE

There's a URL in tiny print at the bottom: www.myholestory.com. I turn the paper over, looking for a note, a signature, anything. But it's blank.

I stuff the flyer into my backpack, and then yank down all the others I can reach. I stop at the next pole to do the same. It takes me an hour to get home from Java Jane, the bag on my back crackling, heavy with crumpled paper.

Safely in my room, I tap out myholestory.com with trembling fingers. The page loads nearly empty: just an image of a hammer, and a line of text, Story under construction. Check back in 15 days.

I mouse over it, but there are no links or even hypertext. Just the words, flat.

I head to Public Scrutiny to see if anyone knows anything, and that's when I see the news, a flashing announcement pinned to the top of the screen:

MANSION CONDEMNED!!

32

I bike frantically back to Java Jane and then, when Caro's not there, to her second job at the pharmacy. I burst across her counter, breathless. 'What are you doing here?'

'Filling in for Jasirah. I'm trying to make some Christmas money.'

'Don't you have ... whatever. Caro,' I catch my breath, 'the Mansion's closing.'

'What do you mean?' Her eyes dart to the photo counter, where her workmate, Jeanine, glares pointedly. Jeanine's been working here for a year. She has aspirations of assistant managership and a passion for ratting out colleagues. I pick up the weekly coupon mailer, and wave it generally towards Caro's face.

'It's been condemned,' I say. 'They're closing later this month. It's going to be bulldozed and turned into condos.'

'That's urban development for you,' she says, straightening the gum display. I catch her hand.

'Caro, it's the Mansion,' I say, pleadingly.

Her fingers squeeze mine, a butterfly kiss.

'I'm sorry, Morgs,' she says. 'I know that place meant a lot to you. But you haven't even been there in weeks.' *Not since Chad*, she doesn't say. She says, 'Maybe it's good that it's going.'

But I think about the dusty cherubs drowsing open-eyed on the ceiling. Think about Frank and his umbrellas. Think about the magic melting upward through the floor and filling my bones.

'It was so much more than that,' I say, softly, pointing to a coupon for diapers. 'It's where I came out.'

'And now you're out. I know you love it, sweet pea. I'm sorry. But maybe you don't need it any more. And maybe that's okay.' She studies me, and her brow furrows. 'Do you have a fever? You look flushed.' She reaches for my forehead to test my temperature.

'It's chilly out.' I shrug her off. 'I just wish there were something I could do.'

'Then do something,' she says, and then, 'I am sorry, ma'am, that expired a week ago.'

I turn. Her manager, Tricia, is right over my shoulder.

'This is a *ludicrous* price for ChapStick!' I proclaim loudly, and duck from the store.

I bike home in the dark, stopping at every telephone pole and ripping down the I'M SORRY posters as though that will make it all okay.

'It's not exactly shocking,' Howie says the next day. He's

lying on my bed with my portfolio, flipping through the pages. 'I could have told you that building wasn't up to code, and I only vaguely know what *up to code* means.'

'Mmm,' I say, clicking into my email.

An email pops up in my inbox. Lately, I've been letting everything go to spam. It's overwhelming – the messages from agents, scouts, producers, screenwriters; the fan mail and hate mail from people who still haven't forgiven me for snapping at Howie on the news: bitch you dont deserve him you should go die you cunt. I delete most things without looking. It's not worth the blood pressure.

My cursor is hovering over the spam icon when the subject line of the message catches my eye. It reads, simply, 'Lunch?' I open it, and read:

Morgan,

I'm coming into town for your show and I was wondering if you'd like to get lunch. How about the day before it opens? I'd love to catch up, but I understand if you say no. sincerely,
Archie

'I like these texture collages from freshman year,' Howie says. 'Why did you quit doing them?'

'My dad wants to have lunch,' I say.

Howie drops the binder on the quilt.

'When?' he says.

'Right before my show.'

'Thanksgiving?'

I blink through a mental calendar. Marcel's planned a Black Friday opening, banking on the foot traffic from the City Market nearby. 'I guess.'

My hands are trembling, and I don't know why. Howie opens his arms. I come and nestle in them, the Lump poking me gently in the back.

'I never really knew him,' I say. 'He left when I was so little.'

He runs his fingers through my hair, making all the motions of comfort. His actions seem to pertain to something far away and unrelated, and I realise, distantly, that it's me.

'Well,' he says, softly. 'It's your call. Do you want to see him?'

'Maybe,' I say. 'Should I? I'm supposed to, right?'

'I don't think there is a "supposed to".'

We lie still a long time. My eyes trace the cover of my binder. I stare blankly at the name *Morgan Stone* like the letters might collapse in on themselves at any moment.

'I don't know what I would even do with a dad,' I say at last. 'What's it like?'

He shifts against me. 'What?'

I say, 'Having a dad,' and my lips jump hotly closed, the world blurring.

Howie turns my face towards him and I turn away, wordlessly. He lets me keep my face to myself, holds and rocks me, thumbing circles in my hair.

'He's ...' he pauses, considering. 'I think he wants to be a lot tougher than he is. It was always Mom who grounded us and stuff.' He shifts. I can feel his voice in my back. 'He always talks about how every time one of my aunts brought a guy home, my grandpa would get him alone and tell him, *if you break her heart, I'll kick your ass.* He brings it up every time Riley even says a boy's name.'

'Did he ever do it?' I ask.

'Do what?' he asks.

'Kick their boyfriends' asses.'

He laughs. 'Maybe once or twice,' he says. 'Though if they were that bad, my aunts usually gave them the boot themselves. They raise tough women in my family.'

I think, if Howie broke my heart, Mother would probably rip his body to shreds with manicured nails, then boil the bits down, distil them into perfume and market it under the name *Heartbreaker.* Or *Ladykiller.*

Or else she'd tell me, disinterestedly, that she told me so, and turn back to her planner.

I lift my head.

'Howie?'

'Yeah?'

'If you ever break my heart, I'll kick your ass.'

He laughs, and clasps my hand in his own. 'I know,' he says. 'That's what I like about you.' That word *like* yawning under its own weight.

*

After he goes, I try to paint out some answers. I've been working up a new composition on a huge canvas: double-stranded DNA topped with emergent human faces, Howie's and mine; the two liquid bodies twisting around and around each other in a dance. I stretch as I survey the piece, wincing. My joints feel swollen and achy. It's been an exhausting week.

In the kitchen, I pour a glass of nearly flat ginger ale, make popcorn. I mix up olive oil, cracked pepper, seasoned salt, reaching for comfort in the familiar smell. I check Public Scrutiny while my Netflix tab loads, neatly avoiding the email inbox where my father's unanswered message sits. There's a photo of flyered phone poles with a brief blurb on the main city events page: Street art? Viral marketing? Tell us your take on the Hole Girl posters! But nobody has weighed in with anything definitive. I go to the site again: Check back in 14 days.

A pinch of fear curdles somewhere near my descending colon. I hope to drown it out with television, but it drags on through three and a half episodes of *Twin Peaks*, and I finally pause the episode and log into my email. I don't know what I'm hoping for, but there it is, still. *Lunch*.

The pain abruptly sharpens and I rush to the bathroom. My insides seize, and popcorn and ginger ale surge violently up my throat, into the toilet. Hooray. I've barfed a circus.

I lean my forehead against the cool porcelain, flush with my eyes closed. My heart is racing.

I hear a door close downstairs, the sound of footsteps.

'Morgs?' Caro calls. She stops outside the bathroom. 'Are you okay?'

'Yeah,' I say.

She lingers in the doorway, looking worried.

'You look like hell,' she says.

'Yeah, I just threw up.'

'No, I mean generally,' she says. 'You look like George Romero and Tim Burton had a baby, and it's directing your life.'

I rinse my toothbrush and scrub at my tongue.

'My dad wants to get lunch,' I say indistinctly.

'Holy shit,' she says.

'My life is exploding,' I groan into the toilet.

'Maybe you should talk to Taka and Dr Morse.'

I lower the brush from my mouth, feeling dizzy. Not an overwhelming, swimming surge. Something less obvious and therefore more insidious – a sense of things moving half inches to the left and jumping back again, stealthily, each time I blink.

'Morgan?' she says.

'Yeah,' I say. 'Maybe.'

Her eyes meet mine in the mirror, and we both wait a minute for the joke; for some sarcastic snark about how terrible Dr Morse is, how evil and conniving. But I don't say anything, and the line in her brow deepens. She turns to go get the phone, leaving the silhouette of her concern hanging in the air behind her.

33

I wake up the next morning to a chill rain, still feeling nauseated. Curled in bed, I make a list: people who could be sorry.

Dr Morse, for turning my life into a media circus
Marcel, for being a douche
The YYSers for ignoring me at their shitty parties
Todd, for making Caro miserable
Creepers on the internet
Gallery woman for passing me over
Darcie McGill in sixth grade for calling me a skank
Father
Mother

I stretch for a red Sharpie. Then I go down the list,
appending:

Dr Morse - def not repentant (but maybe doesn't
hate me now?)

Marcel - ditto

YYSers - maybe?

Todd - posters should say Caro, not Hole Girl

Creepers - would be nice, but will never reform

Gallery woman - maybe?

Darcie - we're Facebook friends and she still sucks

Father - maybe

Mother - never

I study the list, considering. Then I pull on a sweater and start with the most straightforward place: the Loblolly gallery.

It is just as empty as before. Few people care to drive halfway into the country for art on a weekday. I park and jog across the rainy lot, holding a creased Hole Girl flyer tightly against my body. The flyers do have the feel of an installation piece: the scope, the boundlessness, the simplicity of the five colours against the variegated cityscape. The sense of a great deal of work and complication for very little profit.

I wonder if the gallery owner will greet me with her copy-and-paste smile, or will have forgotten who I am. But there is no one behind the low, sleek desk. I leave my dripping boots by the door, and check around, but Karen is nowhere to be seen. The elephant is also gone.

The scene in the middle of the vast cement floor now is of a full-scale cocktail party, complete with bar and buffet: backlit polycrylic drinks glowing in martini glasses, glistening wax shrimp and lemon tartlets on silver serving trays. The floor is covered in gumballs. There are hundreds, possibly thousands: an impossible number of pink gumballs. A graven sign reads, neatly, *please do not disturb the gumballs.*

I stare at the scene, wondering what in the world the artist was thinking. And then feeling a stab of envy: this artist got to think. This artist got to say, *I want to put gumballs on the floor at a cocktail party,* and someone else did not say, *that's nice, but let's make it blood, and let's make it at the White House,* but instead said, *yes, awesome, I love it,* or *I am not sure but let's do it anyway, because I trust your vision.* Even though it's kind of a seriously stupid vision.

The whole thing feels flimsy, arbitrary – the faux-rural barn, the horse names over the stalls. It's hard to believe I looked up to this place so hard just a couple of months ago. I step away from the gumballs. The envy-stab sharpens, and then becomes excruciating. I force myself to breathe slowly, realising that what I feel is not envy, but pain. A voice behind me says, *excuse me* through syrup, and my hands are grabbing at my stomach. Then my body flies apart, and I am flung into darkness.

When I open my eyes, Dr Takahashi is holding my hand.

He says, 'I came as soon as I could. Dr Morse is here, too.'

My lips are swollen and cracked. My tongue is bone dry.

'Where—?' I ask.

'Hospital,' he says. 'You've been here three days.'

I lift my head, examine my body. I'm in a strange hospital bed, covered in a thin sheet and pleasantly numbed below the chest. A rubber garden of tubes and blue wires springs up from the fertile flesh of my arms. I try to summon panic, but can foster nothing but a vague, fond interest. As in: *is that a catheter? That's nice.*

Taka lifts a plastic cup of ice chips to my lips, and I lower my face to it, carefully tonguing one into my mouth. My parched mouth blooms with liquid.

'Am I dying?' I ask. It is the pertinent thing to ask. I feel calm. I feel like an A student.

'No,' Taka says.

'Are you sure?' I ask.

He smiles, gives my fingers a squeeze. 'Of course I'm sure.'

'But you're not wearing gloves,' I say.

The smile fades from his face.

The door swings open, and Dr Morse bursts into the room. Howie lags behind her, a pale, floppy-haired shadow. I try to catch his eye, to make him come to me, but he won't.

'How long has she been awake?' Dr Morse asks Taka. Before he can answer, she thrusts a thick folder at him. Her hands tremble, the papers rattling and whispering.

Taka's face empties of emotion as he reads. Dr Morse watches him with visible strain, mouth jumping from smile to frown to composed line and back again. Behind her, Howie gazes out into the hall, his bangs a drawn curtain. Why won't he look at me?

'Howie?' I ask. He continues to stare through the narrow window with intense absorption. I lick my paper lips, turn to the doctors. The room seems too small. I want to rip the tubes from my arms and run anywhere, anywhere. 'What's going on?' I ask, more loudly. My voice cracks.

Taka turns another page. Dr Morse, who has, as always, the bedside manner of a silverback gorilla, blurts, 'It's working. The treatment is working. Morgan, your Hole is shrinking.'

34

For a long time, my breath feels too big for my body.

'Are you sure?' I ask.

Dr Morse nods. 'The interior perimeter has contracted a full quarter-inch. The resulting relocation of your organs—'

I reach down with a drug-thickened hand and peel back the sheet. Taka moves to stop me, but it's too late.

Puddled in my middle, where a peach-sized pit used to be, is a plum.

It's the same me: same pale stomach, same freckles. But with the Hole smaller, the perspective seems off. I fight the sense that I should be averting my eyes from this stranger's body, with its strange, small hole.

'Is it going to keep shrinking?' I ask, aware of the cold vagueness of that word *it*.

'We don't know,' Taka says, lowering the folder at last. 'We'll continue monitoring you.'

Dr Morse says, 'You realise we'll want to begin a second round of testing, as soon as possible.'

Underneath her chatter is a terrible quiet. I look away from my stomach and back toward the door, where Howie is trying as hard as possible not to be.

'What about Howie?' I ask.

Dr Morse falls quiet.

Taka says, 'Howie's condition remains unchanged.'

I say, 'Are you sure?'

'Yes,' Howie says. He looks me in the face, then, and I realise where I've seen this person before: the day I shouted at Howie on the street. Shoulders caved, eyes bruised with helplessness and hurt.

'Howie,' I say, but he turns and walks from the room. Despite the numbness in my chest, I feel a pang.

I turn to the doctors, helplessly. 'It could still work, though, right? It could just start shrinking. Mine did.'

'Morgan, we took samples while you were unconscious,' Taka says. 'The oldest cells there are several weeks old. They've been growing since the night you began treatment.'

'Howie could have them, too.'

'He doesn't,' Taka says, gently. 'We've tested him, too. The Lump shows no signs of reduction of any kind.'

I look at Dr Morse. She says, 'Any number of factors could be at play. There are still more things we can try.'

She sounds buoyant as ever, energised by the words *test*, *samples*, *immune repertoire*. Her mind already projecting ahead to data charts and cell slides and PCRs. But there is a heaviness to her jaw that I hadn't seen before, unhappily anchoring her to the room.

They keep me overnight. I stay up for hours: playing with my Jell-O, staring at the blank television. I see Howie's face again and again in my mind. How he looked like a dog, cruelly kicked and left out in the cold.

They let me go home after the anaesthesia wears off the next morning. Taka's given me muscle relaxants to prevent the spasms that accompany the Hole's shrinking. 'It's also a stool softener,' he says, deadpan as ever. 'Be careful.'

Mother's in the UK, tending to the child called Career-Before-Family, so Dr Morse takes me home. She helps me into a Volvo older than I am with a shuddering engine and a heating system that takes ages to warm up, and then blasts heat like a minor sun – a car for a person who lives just outside the realm of the body and its comforts. A steady stream of talk radio jabbers beneath audibility.

'How are you feeling?' she asks.

'Fine.'

'No pain?'

'No.'

'You're expected to check in hourly.'

'I know.'

I watch her face as she drives. She seems distracted, less than half here. Exhaustion stretches in the hammocks of skin beneath her eyes.

'What's wrong?' I say.

She glances at me, forces a smile. 'Nothing,' she says. And then, 'I was thinking about Howie.'

She runs a hand through her hair and sighs.

'It is intriguing that the treatment doesn't work on Howie. We'll want to do some more tests, some tissue samples. There's a lab in Toronto doing reverse osmotic sequencing, I'll get in touch with them this evening. And there's all the new data to review ...'

'It could still work,' I say. 'You never know.'

She shakes her head, but says, 'It's possible.' She pulls up to the kerb in front of my building to let me out. The parking lot is empty.

'That's weird,' I say, reaching for the door handle. 'No camera crew.'

'I told the media we were moving you to a secure facility,' Morse says.

Our eyes meet. I smile, but she doesn't.

'Congratulations,' she says.

'Congratulations to you,' I say. 'You must be thrilled.'

She stares at the road, the wan November light staining her eyes the unhappy colour of newsprint. 'I don't want him to be alone,' she says quietly.

Then she turns and stares out the driver's window as I say *who* and *but he has you* and finally *thank you for the ride*. When I call in an hour to report in, she asks about my bowel movements, and we say nothing more.

*

By five that evening, the paparazzi has figured out Morse's ruse and are back at our apartment building, in more of a frenzy than ever: someone's leaked the news that the cure is working. Caro comes home from work, grumbling. 'I swear I can hear them audibly sigh about the fact that I'm not you whenever I go outside,' she says, pulling a knit cap from her hair. 'This is wreaking havoc on my self-esteem.'

I take my phone into the bathroom and skim through Public Scrutiny. I've never seen anyone use the word *weep* so much. People are weeping out of joy for me, out of injustice for Howie, or a self-pity that seems unbelievably inappropriate. I know I'm supposed to be happy for her but I just can't believe she would want to change, write people with names like AprilMoon and PieIsAwesome86. I just feel so betrayed!!!! ;_;

I spend the evening and next morning calling Howie, but get no reply. I try to compose a text, but am interrupted by a call from an unidentified number, and then another. After the third, I stare at the mangled message in frustration (Cn welk?) and delete it.

The phone leaps back to life immediately, and I automatically press IGNORE, realizing seconds too late that the screen said MOTHER. My thumb hovers over the SEND button. Where's the emoji for *too little, too late* and also *I need you so much right now?*

A voicemail pings through.

'I'm on my way,' is all she says.

Then I'm alone again with the shrilling phone, a hungry

315

mob pressing against the outside of my building, and nothing to keep me company but the weakening of my body and the knowledge that somewhere out in the empty air is someone I betrayed without even trying.

35

I sleep and wake at odd hours. There's a knock at my door at 6 a.m. one morning. I'm lying on the couch while my latest painting dries, flipping through a trashy paperback called *Unchained Lust* that I found under the bathroom sink. I haven't been able to sleep, kept up by the atomic shrinking of the Hole. Taka insists that it's impossible to feel the growth, but alone in the dark, I am unable to shake the sense that my body is a clock, and that each passing second adds another cell, and another cell, and another ...

I've been painting to get away from myself. The enormous canvas, with its entwined DNA portrait of Howie and me, is turned to the wall. I'm working on a new piece: a solitary girl on a park bench, gazing up at the sky with overlays of yellow and blue blooming out around her. It's a gift for Caro, for Christmas. I call it *Joy*. It dries, glistening, in the lamplight.

I jump at the knock on the door, tucking the book beneath the couch cushion. I shuffle to the door feeling sticky and overfull, as though I've eaten a bag of candy in one sitting.

'Would you wear a fragrance called *Anaphora*?' Mother asks when I open it. She shows no signs of the early hour, serene and makeup free in a soft, grey tailored suit. It takes me a moment to spot the dot of colour in her outfit: a tiny pearl pin in mint.

I rub my eyes. 'If I were a middle school goth,' I say. 'Who stole it from my mom after my dad picked it up on sale on Christmas Eve.'

She sighs, pulling out her Blackberry. 'I know,' she says, typing. 'It just screams this-or-a-gift-card. But Srivani won't let it go.'

'Mother, it's super early,' I say.

'Oh, I'm sorry,' she says lightly, 'I'm still on London time. I didn't wake you, did I?'

We haven't talked since she dropped the bomb about my father. She sent me a gift basket earlier this week from a spa in Bath – tea, bath salts, lavender body oils – presumably to apologise for destroying my semblance of near-adulthood, but there's no telling. The accompanying card merely said *Mother*.

'No,' I say. 'I was up, working on some things.'

She embraces me abruptly. It is crushing and formal, the dictionary definition of a hug. She steps back, holding me at arm's length, like a garment.

'Are you okay?' she asks.

'Yes.'

'Are you in pain?'

'No.'

'And the—' She makes a distasteful motion with her hand. 'Shrinking.'

She relaxes then, body slumping into organic lines.

'Good,' she says. 'Finally. Well, are you going to invite me in, or do you want to stand in the doorway all day like Jehovah's Witnesses?'

She follows me into the living room and stands precariously in its centre, equidistant from all of the furniture, as though she fears she will catch some sort of disease. In the east, the sun is pinking the sky. I switch off the lamp, let the infant light crawl into the room.

'How was the UK?' I ask.

'Damp,' she says, tersely, perching on the edge of the brown sofa. 'The beds were too soft, and the room service was uninspiring. Thank God *Union Jacked & Ripped* wrapped. Everyone was so British it made me ill.'

She sounds so much like herself that I want to crawl into her lap, lean on her shoulder. I wonder what she smells like today.

I go to the kitchen, put on the kettle for tea. As the water grinds to life, I peek back into the living room. My mother is studying Caro's painting. The blue is a little off, but the yellow is just the colour of Caro's blonde hair. It wreathes the canvas, twisting and shimmering. Mother reaches out to touch the wet paint, and then sees me watching and lets her hand drop.

'So, I heard from Dad. About coming to my opening next week,' I say, placing two steaming mugs on the coffee table.

'Mmm,' she says absently, but I see her eyes flick up to me, dark.

I sit on the sofa, cup a mug between my cool hands. 'What's he doing here?'

'Nothing good, I imagine,' she says, sinking down in the chair at my side. She tugs at the tag on the teabag. 'I thought this was loose-leaf. I wouldn't have bought it if I'd known otherwise.'

'Mother, it's fine. Did you invite him?'

'Not actively,' she says, briskly, taking a sip. 'He saw a story about you on the news. He contacted me and I mentioned the show. I guess he decided to get in touch.'

'I just don't get it. Why now?' I ask. 'It's not like he couldn't find us before. You have a protein shake named after you.'

'Only if you shop in the fitness aisle,' she says. 'Which I'm sure he doesn't.'

I fiddle with my teabag, unsure of what to do with this information. The scent curls up fragrantly into the air, all black leaves and bergamot.

'He wants to have lunch the day before the show.'

Her nostrils flare slightly. 'On Thanksgiving?' She tilts her head back and stares at the ceiling. 'Ridiculous,' she says. 'Nothing will be open. That's just like Archie.' She reaches for her phone. 'I'll get in touch with him.'

'No,' I say, surprising myself with my vehemence. 'Why?'

'To tell him to reschedule.'

'I can handle it.' She's unlocking her phone, entering numbers. 'Mother, stop. Let me handle this.'

She lowers her phone with a shade of irritation. 'Fine,' she says. 'I just don't want him to interrupt our dinner.'

'So we *are* having Thanksgiving dinner this year.'

'Of course we're having Thanksgiving dinner,' she says. 'We always have Thanksgiving dinner.'

'We didn't last year.'

'That's one year.'

'The year before that you got snowed in at JFK.'

'Right,' she says, remembering. 'That ghastly blizzard.'

'I'm used to being a Thanksgiving orphan. Caro's little brothers have probably already made a seasonal placemat for me.'

Her knuckles are white on her mug. 'Not this year,' she says.

We sit in silence for a moment. I sploosh my teabag up and down, up and down, staining the water bitter and dark.

'So you have his phone number?' I ask, avoiding her gaze.

She shakes her head. 'Just an email address,' she says. 'He got in touch via my management a month ago.'

'Why?'

She says, carelessly, 'As I said, I believe he saw you on the news.'

I remember the footage of me screaming at Howie about freaks, and cringe.

'He asked after you,' she continues. 'I gave him your email.'

'Did you know . . . ?' I'm not sure how to finish the question. She answers it anyway.

'Morgan, I quit expecting things from your father long ago.'

The early light is grainy, still ethereal. The barriers in the air between us seem imagined, as thin and filmy as curtains.

I set down my mug. My childhood pet name for her comes creeping shyly out of its kennel, lays its head on my mother's knee.

'Ma,' I say, 'what happened?'

She says, 'You know what happened.'

I know the Wikipedia version. The stripped-down facts, potentially biased: the kind English teachers tell you not to base an essay on – married at eighteen, pregnant at nineteen. An astoundingly successful and revolutionary series of *Pregnant Fit!*™ shows. A plan for a *Mommy 'n' Me Cardio* video, plug hastily pulled when I emerged into the world with a Hole, and Mother shut the press out of her personal life. I've seen the tape, even, leaked to the internet by some too-dedicated fan: my young, glowing mother, just a little older than I am now, sporting a baby bump and a yellow leotard, encouragingly leading mommies-to-be of the nation through Gentle Stretches.

I say, 'Tell me why my father left.'

She purses her lips. 'Morgan, now's not the time to get into that.'

'Really?' I ask. 'You really came to my door at six in the morning to complain about teabags.'

She sighs, wringing her white hands one at a time, slowly,

like old towels. When she speaks, she doesn't address me but, rather, addresses the middle distance that has always lain between us: between home and Los Angeles, New York, the ashrams in India and martial arts training centres in the Negev; between what we both knew to be the truth, and the things we actually said.

Then she says, 'You know I never wanted children? It was all Archie's idea. He wanted a huge brood. He wanted eight.'

She says, 'And then you were born and he was horrified.'

I go very still.

'The night we brought you home from the hospital, I woke up and he was gone. I found him sitting on the couch in the dark. I said, "Archie, what is it, come back to bed," and he said, "Everything I touch breaks." I said, "Our daughter's not broken," but he was inconsolable.'

Her finger absently circles her lips. 'I think maybe he really did try to overcome it. But it wasn't enough. He never wanted to hold you. I would come home from working long hours and find you in your crib, diaper overflowing, because he couldn't bring himself to touch you. We never had a nanny in those days, of course. Archie was certain that word about your deformity would get out if we let any strangers in. He wanted to hide you from the world.'

'And then you hid me from the world.'

'I hid your Hole from the world,' she says. 'To give *you* a normal life. He would have kept you in isolation. He would – there's no telling.'

323

I sit up, barely hearing her.

'The show,' I say. 'You planned it *after* you found out Dad was coming to town.' I lean forward. 'That's why you bought the gallery.'

She pinches the ends of her long purple fingernails. 'I'd been considering something similar for some time,' she says. 'But yes. I raised you to be somebody worth being proud of. I wanted him to see that.'

I shake my head. 'The mirror at the end of the exhibition was for him. The *what am I missing?* mirror.' I run my hands through my hair. 'No wonder you liked Marcel's idea so much. You wanted Dad to see himself in it.'

For the first time in my life, my mother looks helpless. Her body still rigid but her skin tired.

'I'm a proud woman, Morgan,' she says softly. 'I know I haven't always been the perfect mother, and I'm sorry. But I gave you a life without a man in it who would tell you that you were broken.'

We stare at each other across the space of the living room. There is something fierce and unyielding and exhausted in her gaze.

'I'm not sorry for that,' she says. 'I'm not sorry.'

I imagine her, eyes closed, pinching the bridge of her nose off set in Hong Kong, in Rio, in Seoul, in all of the hotels of the world. I think of all the times I wanted her to just be my mother, and I imagine her wishing she could reach across oceans and touch my cheek.

So I cross the room, and touch hers.

She reaches up and I crawl into her lap. She wraps her arms around me, nestling me close. I breathe in the warm skin of her neck, and she smells like nothing but my mother.

36

After Mother leaves I take forty-five minutes to draft an email to my father. In the end, it is just eight words. I can't do Thanksgiving. How about Saturday instead? I agonise over the signature – *sincerely? yours? best?* definitely not *love* – and eventually send it off with just my name.

I try calling Howie for the eight hundredth time, but it goes straight to voicemail. I finally drive to his hotel and climb the external staircase to his room, breath clacking around in my chest. There's a light on in room 217, but no one comes to the door when I knock.

I try calling again, look around for something on which to leave a note. I finally go to the lobby, steal a napkin from the stack next to the coffee pot, and a complimentary pen. You don't want to be alone and I don't either. No good. I ball it in my fist, try again. Just because we don't fit doesn't mean. Crumple.

The woman behind the reception desk is beginning to look at me askance, so I steal just one last napkin. I write, I miss you. - M

I wedge it in the crack beneath his door and head back to the car. A chill is creeping into the air, and a wind already beginning to pick up. As I drive home, I imagine that every piece of trash whipping by is my letter to Howie, the shoulders and drainage ditches of Raleigh repeating *I miss you, I miss you, I miss you.*

There's an email from my father when I get home: Sure, that sounds great! What about Gypsy's at noon?

So at least there's that.

I rehearse our conversation in my mind as dusk falls, and the photographers outside thin, huddling closer to the competition for body heat.

I walk into the diner. He is sitting in a corner booth, impossibly large for just the two of us. But when I scoot in beside him, it somehow feels intimate.

He says, 'Morgan, thank you for meeting me.'

No, I think, paging through Caro's well-worn copy of *Tiny Beautiful Things*. Too formal. Too much out of a mobster movie. The language of a father with a Glock under the table, a father who, in the heat of the moment, would shout, 'Leave the gun, take the bottomless coffee refills!'

'Morgan, it's great to see you at last.' He studies the tablecloth. 'It's been too long.'

'Has it?' I ask, casually. 'What took you so long to get in touch?'

But the fantasy breaks down there. I can't figure out what perfect thing I want him to say. I try on hurt, screaming rage, reconciliation, idle threats and understated composure.

But the imagined conversation always spins itself out, dissipating sometime between the departure of the waitress and the arrival of the food. Again and again I catch my mind wandering the nooks and crannies of Howie's face, the gentle bones of his hands. I try to reel it back in, but I can't seem to set myself straight. I stare out the window at the November clouds scudding by, lumpy and cold and promising nothing.

Friday arrives: our weekly overnight at the clinic. The thought of seeing Howie makes me jittery. I wake up too early, agonise over what to wear. 'It doesn't matter,' I rage to Caro, trying on and discarding blouses and earrings. 'They're just going to put us in hospital gowns.' She agrees, but brushes my hair anyway, dabs rouge onto my cheeks until I glow, a feverish Pollyanna in a pixie cut. She grips my wrists.

'You'll be great,' she says.

'Yeah,' I say. 'It doesn't matter. It's just a doctor's appointment.'

'That you look totally hot for.'

I hold her tightly. 'Caro, how do you have room in your broken heart to take care of me?'

She examines me critically, pushes my fringe out of my eyes. 'I guess I'm just a goddamned superhero.'

On the way to the clinic, Yum Yum Situation's 'Hole Girl' comes on the radio, and I switch it off.

Howie's nowhere to be seen when I arrive. Dr Morse has a literal stack of papers for me to sign, consenting to a ream of new tests on my growing tissue and shrinking Hole. 'The reagents won't come in until next week,' she says, eyes bright, already seeing beyond, as though the small details of time and physical reality are a minor stumbling block in her plans. I sign my name on dotted lines, glancing up at the door and wondering when I'll see Howie.

I don't get a chance until after I've changed and been led into the examination room. He's waiting, arms crossed, perched on the bed furthest from the door. I say, 'Hi, Howie,' and he says, tightly, 'Hey.'

Dr Morse wants us to begin the appointment with a Merge, to see if we still fit. It seems a hateful and impossible request – but then, somehow, we do. It is tighter this time, harder. There is a terrible squeezing sensation in my ribs as the Lump, lubricated with cold, clear jelly, slides inexorably into place, Howie's hand tight on my shoulder, my palm at the flat of his back, pressing. But then my breath seizes, and it's there.

A shaking sigh escapes Howie and reverberates in my gut. The nurses break into restrained applause. Dr Morse's head is down, eyes two fringed slits as she scribbles on her clipboard.

I peer up towards Howie's face, trying to read his reaction. But I'm standing so close, I can only see him in pieces: elfin chin, knob of shoulder, arching tendon of neck. I want to say, *see? It's okay! We're okay! We can still fit!* But I'm standing too close to see the whole of him, and the pieces don't add up to the person I want to comfort.

After we separate, Howie turns and leaves the room. I look to Dr Morse, questioningly.

'Howard requested to stay in a separate room tonight,' she says, ducking her head as she follows him. 'Sorry.'

I sway my cloth gown and rouged cheeks as the nurses step in, dab away the lubricant with warm, damp cloths. I can feel him, clear as a blip on a radar screen, moving away down the hall, somewhere in the bowels of the building. I trace his arc away from me as a nurse guides me to the lonely second bed and begins the business of hooking up my breath and blood to project brightly across a screen.

The sunset that night is beautiful, and I can't help myself: even from the depths of my self-pity, I mix and name the colours: *ultraviolet. Rescue flare. Lemon dream.* I name *orange-peel-all-in-one-piece-and-flung-over-the-shoulder*, and *orange peel broken*. I name *still-beating heart*.

At some point, against all odds, I sleep.

They unhook me in the morning, take notes. Dr Morse comes in with her thousand too-personal questions, and I answer them as honestly as I can, enervated but rushing, hoping to catch Howie in the parking lot. I only have a few minutes before I have to go meet my dad, but all I need is a look from him, a hug. Even a simple word: *later.*

I get to the parking lot just in time to see him pull away. The cameras eat up my disappointment in precise, happy clicks. I wave them away half-heartedly. I climb into the car and sit a long minute, watching the clock. It ticks from 11.47 to 11.48, and the air drains from my body. I crank the engine to life and head to the diner where my father waits, and to some uncertain future.

Then I pop an illegal U-turn on Tryon Road and speed towards Howie's hotel.

37

I pound on the door of room 217. There is a flutter of floral drapes. Then Howie opens the door, face steeped in weariness.

'Come with me,' I say.

'To meet your dad?' he asks.

'No,' I say. 'Screw that. Get in the car.'

He rubs his forehead. The skin bunches beneath his hand like laundry.

'You should go,' he says.

I step directly into his space. We are toe to toe, chest to chest. We are breathing each other's breath.

I say, too quickly, the words crunching together. 'I'm in love with you.'

'Stop,' he says.

I reach up and pull his hand from his face and say, again, each word clear and right and true: *'I'm in love with you.'*

He catches my wrist. 'Stop it,' he says. 'Okay? It's not magic. We're not puzzle pieces. We're not mystically, genetically meant to be together or whatever.'

'So?'

'So please leave me alone.'

I am inches from him, feeling the warmth that rolls off his skin. It seems impossible to be so close to a person and to still have them say *no, you can't, you've gotten this close but I will not let you further.* To have everything stop at the skin.

I stoop and put my shoulder to his stomach. Then I lift.

Howie yelps in surprise as I stagger with his weight. My spine crunches together. He pounds on my back, but the blows are light, useless. Fists like summer rain.

'Morgan, what the actual hell,' he shouts.

A deep ache of dizziness wells up in my middle, and I push it down. I say, 'I am going to get you into this car if it kills me.'

And he must believe me, because when I stagger and nearly drop him on the walkway several steps later, he gets up and walks the rest of the way to the car by himself.

Howie doesn't speak as I steer onto the Beltline and west out of the city, staring out the window at the weak-tea sun. But as the exit numbers decrease, I can feel his mood lighten: from sullenness to irritation to curiosity. We stop at a service station so I can vomit and put gas in the car. When I emerge from the bathroom, wiping my mouth, he looks at me with a mixture of sympathy and jealousy.

'Where are we going?' he asks at last.

I try to click the nozzle off right on forty dollars, but miss, spilling a few pennies over. Across the street, the sky stretches out over a bone-coloured tobacco field.

'Where do you think?' I ask.

'The Angel. Morgan,' he says. 'I get it. But you have to let this go.' He squints at me across the roof of my car. I hadn't given him time to grab sunglasses, or a jacket, for that matter. He was lucky he was wearing shoes when he answered the door.

'Why?' I say. 'Because we might not be perfectly physically matched?'

'Morgan—'

'Don't you understand that that's the physical reality for literally every other couple everywhere?'

'We aren't every other couple.'

'Fine,' I say. 'So the rules are different for us. We can't be together because my genetic deformity is slightly smaller than your genetic deformity. That sounds totally realistic and fair.'

'That's not the point,' he says.

'What is it, then?' I ask. 'I'm a Taurus and you're a Pisces?'

He turns away from me, staring out at the ragged pine fringe on the horizon.

'Just take me home,' he says.

'Where is home?' I ask.

The fight goes out of him. He slumps against the door of the car.

I want to be close to him, but I don't know how to execute the steps. I say, across the car, 'Howie, ever since I could talk,

I've been making excuses for not having what I want. But then, when I met you, I thought maybe I was done with that. Not because of anything you said, or did, but because you made me feel like maybe I could be a different person. A better person. If everything changed tomorrow – if the Hole healed and you never spoke to me again – at least we would have done this thing you've wanted to do your whole life.'

Howie says nothing, still staring out at the horizon. I rub my cold nose with my palm, fasten my seatbelt. He stares a long time at the stand of loblolly pine cupping the field across the street, and I wonder what it whispers to him, what he's reading in those tea-leaf shadows. I'm about to start the car, to turn on the heat, when he finally opens the door and climbs inside. I turn on the radio to drown out the silence between us as we head toward Appalachia and our Angel.

The directions take us through increasingly small towns. Eventually, the map prompts us to leave the highway, nudging our headlights onto smaller roads and then smaller ones, knotted mountain byways that go by numbers instead of names and change demarcation from town to town.

Dusk falls early in the mountains. Though the sky directly overhead is bright, darkness has stretched across our feet when we finally turn off the road and begin a steep climb on a narrow, wooded drive. The body of my car squeals through a quarter-mile of scraping limbs and then the cabin is there, on a flat patch of scrub carved into the side of the mountain.

It is small and weathered with a mossy roof, the white wearing from its clapboards. A ladder of wood smoke pitches its way into the sky.

Howie hasn't spoken in hours. When he says, 'Is this trespassing?' I jump.

'Maybe.' I turn off the car and cinch the emergency brake, climb cautiously from the door. The driveway is just rutted dirt, studded with stones too large to be called rocks and too small to be called boulders. The air outside is sharp and cold, with a damp smell that is simultaneously strange and familiar. I can hear water running around us, an early snowmelt snaking through leaves.

Howie follows me across the dirt yard. We both hesitate at the front porch, then I knock twice, loudly. A light within sets a curtain aglow, a faint pink.

I'm lifting my fist to knock again when the cabin door cracks open. We're assaulted by yapping, and the smell of old paper, and an old woman peers out, withered and minute in a worn cotton nightdress.

She is impossibly tiny, blue-eyed and hollow-cheeked, with deep pockets on either side of her mouth. Her forehead, beneath the thin cirrus cloud of her white hair, is furrowed with so many lines that I am tempted to count them. The number would be prime, I feel, or a piece of the Golden Ratio.

'Helen?' I ask. 'Are you Helen Rhees Boyle?'

The woman says, 'Yes?'

I say, 'We're looking for the Fallen Angel of Appalachia.'

She starts to close the door, but I jam my foot inside the frame, bones squeezing painfully. 'Wait,' I blurt.

'Excuse me,' she says, with the sharp politeness of old Southern women. 'Do I know you?'

'No,' I say. Then, 'Yes.' I lift my shirt.

The woman stares at me a long time, stares at the mountains beyond and through my body. Her jaw works in her face.

Finally, she says, 'If I'd known I was getting company, I'd have put my teeth in.' She steps aside, leaving the door open behind her.

The house is stuffy, filled with dachshunds and ceramic figurines. When Helen steps into a rare patch of light, we see her wings: not feathered after all, but bladelike, fleshy protrusions that jut through slits in the back of her gown. They are hairless, liver-spotted and spider-webbed with veins. The skin drips from their edges in thin paper flaps.

Howie and I sit on a sofa lichen-spotted with antimacassars of unlikely sizes and colours, momentarily made a *we* again by the strangeness of our surroundings. The dachshunds sit in a very straight line and stare at us as the Angel rattles in the kitchen, finally emerging with three steaming mugs of Nescafé and a plate of pink wafer cookies on a tray, taking a neat and practised side-shuffle to get through the kitchen door. The dishes clatter as she lowers the tray to the coffee table, a noisy prelude to conversation. The dachshunds race around her ankles, barking, as she settles onto a wide, backless chair. She has pulled a thin cardigan over her gown, put in her teeth, applied the improbably bright lipstick elderly women sometimes wear. She says, 'I don't do the Angel shows any more.'

'We're not asking you to,' I say. 'We want some advice.'

'Certainly,' she says. 'Don't fall in love with a circus man.'

She folds her hands and smiles at us.

'It's more complicated than that,' I say. I turn to silent Howie, exasperated. 'Will you just show her?'

'Show me what?' the Angel asks. I note, with pleasure, that she pronounces the *h* in *what*.

Howie glares at me, but lifts his shirt.

The Angel hums. 'I see.'

I explain, as delicately as I can, our respective lifetimes of loneliness and isolation, our meeting, the news, my cure, Howie's Book. The Angel swirls sugar wafer cookies in her coffee, takes them between her teeth in precise, ladylike bites.

'So you're getting better, and he's not,' she says. 'And I was in this book of yours.'

Howie tugs at his hair. 'Yes, ma'am,' he says. Helen looks as though she isn't sure whether she's flattered or offended.

'We were hoping to ask you some questions,' I say.

'Is that right?' the Angel asks. A wire-haired dachshund has curled in her lap, and she rearranges his ears with care. 'Well, I don't know if I've got all that much I can tell you. But you came all this way; you might as well ask.'

Howie becomes intensely absorbed in stirring his coffee. I feel my temper rise to a breaking point.

'Howie,' I say. 'I drove your ass 279 miles. If you don't buck up and start talking, I'm going to ask if she can fly.'

'Why, of course I can fly,' the Angel says.

We both look at her, startled. She holds our gazes, steady, for a beat. Then her face lights up with delight. She guffaws, coffee spilling everywhere. The dachshunds leap up and begin barking again, and in the ensuing chaos, Howie accidentally catches my eye. I smile at him, and he can't help it. He smiles back.

'I loved being the Angel,' she says, three cups of instant coffee later. 'Oh, yes. Mr Wiley discovered me when I was just thirteen. I had – let's just say a hard childhood. My father was a difficult man. He didn't know quite what to do with me.'

Her papery face is serene, but I can hear the weight behind the words: the long decades it must have taken to whittle this story down to these few, non-judgmental sentences, to cut out the cold basements, the empty wells, hunger and beatings. Or so I imagine, watching her face.

She says, 'My parents were glad to have me off their hands, to be quite honest. There were too many of us at home already. And at the circus, there was my own car, warm food. They dressed me up every night in feathers and sequins, and when I came on the stage, people cried. Oh, they just cried. They thought I was really an angel come to earth.'

'Why did you quit being the Angel?' Howie asks.

The Angel smiles at him. 'It's not exactly a thing I can quit,' she says.

'No, I mean performing,' he says.

'Oh, shows. I got married,' she says. 'To my manager, Lou Boyle. He thought it wasn't proper to have his wife be a spectacle. And so I gave it all up.'

I'm about to ask how she felt about that, putting her career on hold, when Howie leans in.

'But that was in nineteen forty-five,' he says. 'You didn't quit until nineteen forty-eight.'

Helen's smile grows lean.

'Well,' she says, and though there's not an *h* in this word, she pronounces it, too. 'Someone's done his research.' She closes her eyes for a moment, considering. Then she sighs through her nose, reaches for her cane. 'You came this far,' she says. 'Come out back. I've got something to show you.'

In the sloping backyard, cutting upward through the forest, are four gravestones: three little ones and a big one. Helen stumps forward, her wing lumps pale in the last of the day's light. She brushes the leaves from the largest headstone.

LUCIUS ABERNATHY BOYLE. APR. 28, 1903 – JAN. 3, 1951.

BLESSED HUSBAND, FATHER AND SON.

'Lou was a good man, and he loved me,' she says, hardly to us at all: to the stone, the trees, the darkening sky.

'He never understood what it was like, the burden of having people stare. He adored the attention. At first, I think that's what he liked about me – when we were together, people stared at the two of us. I was a special something, and the made him feel like he was, too.

'But after a while, he got tired of it. He wanted it to stop. I used to tell him, *sweetheart, it doesn't stop. I can't hang up these wings.* But it was like he felt I *could* somehow. He was a good man,' she says again. 'He tried. But that was the wall between us. That he couldn't know what I was living through.'

She looks toward the smaller headstones. My breath hitches in my throat.

CLARENCE WILLIAM BOYLE. B. DEC. 1 1948. D. DEC. 1 1948.
MARY LUCINDA BOYLE. B. JUN. 30 1949. D. JUN. 30 1949.
ISAAC JAMES BOYLE. B. NOV. 3 1950 D. NOV. 5 1950.

She says, 'Losing them was the closest Lou came to understanding what it was like to have wings. To lose a child like that, that gross kind of tragedy. It's an awful spectacle you can't get away from. Everyone looking at you, wanting to touch you, to tell you their story.' Her voice is husky, walking the delicate tightrope of composure. 'It undid him.'

Howie shifts, leaves crackling underfoot. The Angel turns to him.

'And now here the two of you are,' she says. 'Put onto this planet with someone else who knows exactly what it's like to be the way you are. Isn't that something?'

Howie says, pained, 'But Morgan's getting better.'

Helen says, 'And you're not happy for her?'

'Of course,' he says. He looks at me: at my stomach, at my face. He says to me: 'I just don't want to be left behind.'

There's a wind in the trees. I look out over the three little gravestones. All the space between.

'Howard,' the Angel says, sounding weary. 'Do you really believe this girl's going to forget her entire life story just because she grows a new stomach?' She shifts forward, her cane staking out familiar territory as she turns towards the house. 'You'll have to forgive my language, but you've got someone in your life who understands all the supreme and beautiful horseshit of your existence. That's not a thing to let go of.'

She turns back to look at us one last time. Then she lifts her wings, and lifts into the sky.

No, not really. But wouldn't that be amazing?

Really, the Angel announces that it's long past time for supper and, pointedly, that she's only done the shopping for one. We nod. We take our leave. I think she might hug us, but she just waves us through the door, brushing off our thanks.

We sit for a moment in the car. Then Howie says, 'I can't believe you asked if she could fly.'

'I can't believe I drank so much instant coffee. I think I'm going to explode.'

He says, more quietly, 'I can't believe you drove me all the way out here.'

I want to say, *I can't believe you sulked the whole way*. But he leans forward and kisses me, instant coffee breath and all, and nothing else needs saying.

The mountain air is cold, but Howie cranks his window down; reaches for the radio and switches it off. The car fills with the buffeting of wind, the chill familiarity of old times.

I ask, 'How come you never listen to the radio in the car?'

'So I can listen to you,' he says. He gives me that grin: daring, mischievous, bright. My cheeks, despite the chill air, warm.

'What about when I'm not there?' I ask.

'Then, too.'

'Your car must be really boring ninety-nine per cent of the time,' I counter.

'Not at all,' he says. 'I just listen to you from far away, that's all. I've got a pretty simple system rigged up. That's why I keep the windows down. It's amazing what you can hear. Try it – listen.' He cups a hand to his ear, squinting into the middle distance. 'Right now ... there's a storm blowing in over Kansas.'

I play with a penny in the cup holder. 'Uh-huh. And how do you know?'

'All that wind,' he says, simply. 'Don't you hear it?'

'That's because we're driving fifty-five miles per hour.'

He just shakes his head, looking sad. 'Ah, such cynicism in one so young.' I take my eyes off the road for a second and find myself squarely in his gaze: the prime meridian in a world of soft brown. 'You know what I hear in your voice?'

I flip the penny over. Heads, tails. Heads, tails.

'What?'

He slips his hand in mine, takes the penny. 'I hear the voice of someone who's always had people in her life to listen to,' he says. 'Someone with friends. The rest of us, we're just wind-listeners.'

I think about the first time Caro ever saw the Hole at age ten: walking in accidentally while I was changing into my nightgown at her house. I blurted, *you can't tell anybody*, and she said, shakily, *I won't*. I gulped, *I mean it, it's a really big secret*. Staring at the floor while I waited for her to send me away. To run crying to her mother. But she just folded her little arms across her chest. *I said I won't. So I won't. Duh.*

'Why do you say that?' I ask.

'Because if you hadn't had friends,' he says, 'you'd have a much more active imagination.'

'Why do I get the impression you're speaking autobio-graphically?' I ask.

He shrugs.

'Well,' I say. 'You've got at least one friend now.'

He toys with the tips of my fingers. 'At least.'

He falls asleep at some point, leaving me alone with my jangling brain. I sort through the component thoughts, smoothing and folding and putting away. *Bailed on Dad. Show next week. Mansion closing for good.*

The ripe full moon follows me down the highway, bathing

fields in silver, jumping in and out of puddles and ponds. The huddled lumps of trees and barns shift darkly as we pass, magical in the graphite-thin light. I catch a flicker of movement out of the corner of my eye and my brain flashes a million answers (*cat car bushes tractor hay*) before I focus and see, improbably, a horse galloping in the moon-painted pasture beside us, soft and mutable in the in-between light.

Graphite light.

I brake, pulling to the side of the road. In the passenger seat, Howie jolts awake as we bump to a stop on the shoulder.

'What's wrong?' he croaks, alarmed.

'I'm thinking about oils.'

His gaze fumbles for the dash. 'Is the car low?'

'No,' I say. 'Graphite and oil paint. They're both mutable media.'

I lift my cold fingers from the steering wheel and reach up toward that cool coin of the moon. I press my thumb out against the sky, squint my eyes. I'm remembering mindthegap's first drawing, a simple sketch in pencil; remembering my erasures, and how they bloomed to life when I added paint. The way that collage can change the context.

The way things come together and find a whole new voice.

Howie's voice crosses from worried to irritated. 'Morgan, what are you doing?'

I say, 'Changing my story.'

*

345

I drop Howie off, then leave a voicemail for Dr Morse, asking her to call me back in the morning. At home, I flip my phone to selfie mode and snap a shot. It's a little dark, and I'm smirking a bit, but the Hole is clearly visible, and there's no denying it's me.

I log into Public Scrutiny as MissAbyss. I click into the 'WHAT'S YOUR HOLE?' forum. The original piece has inspired a slew of independent threads. There's a section for eating disorders, for depression, for grief, for the miscellaneous lonely and sick and sad.

I start a new thread. Title: SHOWCASE YOUR HOLE.

This week, the place I learned to live my life openly is clos-ing its doors for good.

This is the first place I showed the world the Hole. It changed my life. Let it change yours before it's too late.

FINAL DANCE PARTY AT THE MANSION. 25 NOVEMBER. COME BARING YOURSELF.

I attach the photo. Then I wrap up in gloves and a hoodie, and head back to my bike. There's one more thing I need to do.

Boring Todd does not look bored when he opens his apart-ment door. He looks terrified.

He opens his mouth, but I cut him off.

'There are at least fourteen reasons for me to kick your ass right now,' I say. 'But I need to ask a favour.'

*

I conduct my first official interviews with the press over the next few days. Dr Morse is displeased when I elect to ignore the national media, focusing on local television stations and a handful of radio shows. As soon as I open my mouth, the interviewers are even less pleased. The pretty blonde host of *Your News, Your Life* is visibly disconcerted when I refuse to talk about my budding romance with Lump Boy and stick instead to my own message.

'So it's a benefit concert,' she says, uncertainly. Her name is Ella Jaronowski. She landed the job just after college, her fresh face the gem of local cable-access news shows. She's still new enough to the profession that she's easily knocked off balance. She walked me around the studio when I arrived, and I could see bright red spots on her heels where her shoes rubbed.

'It's not a benefit, necessarily,' I say. 'We're not collecting money for anything. It's more of a tribute to a place that helped me become the person that I am today.'

She leans in, ears perked, sensing a good sound bite. 'And who's that?'

I smile at her up to my eye teeth. I say, 'Morgan Stone.'

I see the myholestory flyers again leaving the WKNC college radio station with Frank, who came grudgingly with me to talk with two student DJs about the Mansion's closing and the final party, a conversation that meandered into a list of every drug Frank did in the 1980s (most of them) and that the hosts had done in their first year at college (Frank snorted and looked away, unimpressed). I've got a two-hour break before I'm due for a more sedate interview with another university station. I could spend it working on the press release but my blurring eyes focus on a telephone pole of bright pink flyers, fluttering in the wind.

These are different from the last ones, with dark grey squares in the middle. The square resolves into an image as I catch one and pull it down: a black-and-white photocopied photograph of a sequined bikini top, bearing stars and a moon. Beneath, in small print: *Get the Hole story at myholestory.com*.

'What is that?' Frank asks. 'Goggles?'

'It's a shirt,' I say. 'My shirt.'

Frank snorts. 'That's a shirt?'

'Hey,' I say. 'It's a bikini top. It's a thing.'

'Ah, Jesus,' he says. 'You kids.'

'I'm sure you've seen worse,' I say.

He studies the shirt. 'Is that a moon?'

'And sequins.'

Chad.

Frank rubs his eyelids with a thumb and two fingers. 'I've got to get to work,' he says.

He chugs away on his Harley and leaves me there with the whole of my future fluttering in the wind around me. Then I know what I have to do.

I don't have his phone number, and I am half afraid, if I go public to ask, Chad will be swept up and bundled onto talk shows, that someone will press a book deal into his hands while I'm shouting, *I need to explain to you how you violated me.* So I do the only thing I can think of. I drive to Chad's apartment complex and knock on his door.

After a long minute, he answers. I wordlessly hold up the pink flyer, and at least three emotions flicker though his face. Maybe one of them is surprise. Maybe not. He closes the door and returns, moon-and-stars bikini top in his hand.

We sit on his stoop. He folds the pink flyer into an airplane, neatly, and chucks it. It loops and dives nose-first into the bushes.

'There were definitely easier ways to find me,' I say, breaking the silence.

He shrugs. 'I've always been an elaborate kind of guy.' He flashes me the dimpled grin that once made me melt. 'The posters were my roommate's idea, actually. He's studying advertising. He thought it would get your attention.'

'Attention got,' I say.

Chad lets his head hang. He sighs, a man with the great burden of feeling feelings.

'I don't know,' he says. 'I mean, I felt kind of shitty when you ran out like that. I thought you would be into it, being touched like that. Turns out you weren't.' He passes me the top. The sequins throw light over my fingers like water.

We sit and stare out over the parking lot. The sky is aging.

'You should have asked,' I say.

'You could have just told me,' he says.

The air is saturated with all of the things I want to say to him. *You can't assume* and *consent works both ways,* and *I hadn't found my voice yet.* But I feel a deep-down, peaceful kind of tired. I turn the sequined top over in my fingers. Dry Clean Only, it informs me in small letters. The wind picks up, and I pull my coat closer.

'Did you know I'd never been with a guy before?' I ask.

He looks at me. I have lost all feeling for this boy, but his eyes are still arrestingly blue. It seems unfair, that someone can mean so little to you and still be so handsome.

'No shit,' he says. It is half a question, and half not.

'Zero shits,' I tell him.

'Huh,' he says. He laughs. I look at him. He says, 'You know, that actually explains a lot.'

'What's that supposed to mean?'

'I dunno. I guess I thought you were some experienced chick or something, playing these messed up head games.'

'No,' I say. 'I just didn't know anything.'

I laugh. It's a bright, painful, unfunny thing, twisting up into the air. He laughs too, and I know it is only because I am laughing. That he doesn't get it at all.

'What were you going to put on the website when it went live?'

He rumples his hair. 'I dunno. Probably just something dumb. Like that dancing banana gif.' He grins at me, but it is a check-in grin. Do I think this is funny? I do not. I also suspect it is not the truth. 'I guess you want us to take it down, huh.'

'No,' I say. 'I want you to take it live.' And I reach for a pen and paper, and explain the rest.

I don't know if he'll do it. I'm not even sure he gets entirely what I mean. But he nods a lot, and in the end, no matter what I feel he owes me, I guess I can't ask for more than that.

'Hey,' he says, as I stand to go. 'You're still a virgin?'

'Yeah.'

He squints blue up at me, and I hope, for a minute, that he'll say, *well, if you ever want to try again* – make me some offer that I can turn down, firmly and proudly. So I can say, *I don't need you, Handsome Chad! I have real love now.* And smugly watch the disappointment dawn on his face.

But he doesn't. He just looks at me until the wind rattles the flyer in the bushes, and then he looks at that.

'Life's funny,' he says, at last.

'Yeah,' I say. 'I guess it is.'

I pick up my bag, then turn back towards him, impulsively. His legs are too long. They fold up around him, spring-like, ready to propel him into some next chapter of his life that doesn't have me in it.

'Do you want to keep the shirt?' I ask.

He looks bemused. 'What am I going to do with it?'

'You know,' I say. 'Just hold on to it. A memory of the time you almost slept with the Hole Girl.'

'You're funny,' he says. But he takes the shirt, stands. I look for him in the rear-view mirror as I pull out of the parking lot, but he has already disappeared inside, taking a small, sequined remnant of my story with him.

38

I was hoping to make a quiet entrance, but a roar goes up from the crowd outside the Mansion when we walk up on 25th November: Howie, looking self-conscious, me with the Hole exposed to the world. Caro follows in a blowsy skirt and bikini top, beaming, serene in her own skin. The cameras are there, as ever, but they're lost in the shouting, smiling sea of humanity. People grasp my hand, wrap me up in hugs. I fight back a wave of claustrophobia and lean my cheek against the sticky skins of strangers. The crowd is a seething mix of bodies: large, small, dark, light, scarred, smooth, abled and dis-. People wear white paper circles taped to their stomachs. ADDICT, reads one. ANOREXIA. LOST FAITH. ASSAULT SURVIVOR. HAVEN'T COME OUT TO MY MOM. Some contain long, complex messages: drawings, poems. You'd have to spend a long time with the person to understand their Hole. I watch a man peer at a woman's stomach for a long, confused time. She regards him quietly, confidently, waiting. Ready to field the answer to his question.

There's a folding table set up to one side with markers and tape, and a sign pinned to it: THE WHAT'S YOUR HOLE? PROJECT. I wave to the two girls tending it, and they – mind-thegap and janeyz, I know, though I'm not sure which is which – break into smiles, wave frantically back. One of them, a broad-shouldered high schooler, excitedly flashes me five spread fingers and mouths, *five hundred!* Five hundred Holes already out among the crowd.

When we get inside, Yum Yum Situation is just taking the stage. The dance floor is packed, the bar completely mobbed. Frank complained when I dropped by earlier to drop off supplies. 'I was hoping for an easy last night of work,' he said. The drinks of the crowd roiling around the bar are dotted with pink and lime umbrellas.

Caro puts on a brave face as the band launches into the familiar opening chords of 'Go-Go A No-No'. I slip my hand into hers and squeeze her sweating palm with mine. Then we throw ourselves into the fray, losing our bodies and building them back up out of sound. Sweat drips down my back and runs through the Hole, and my arms are leopard-spotted with the flashing blue and green lights. My ears are ground away into white nothing; I am throbbing, I am pulsing, I am the beat surging up through the floor and setting me alight. Around me, hundreds of people give themselves up to the sound. Lost Holes cover the floor, the adhesive in the cheap masking tape relinquishing its hold on people's sweat-pearling flesh. No art is perfect.

Howie finds me toward the end of the last set, sitting on

my favourite stool. For the past hour I've been shaking hands, hugging, shouting into microphones. By my elbow is a growing pile of Holes that people have taken off and given to me. 'Thank you, Hole Girl,' one girl said. Another couldn't stop crying. People drift away from me and then to each other, eyes creeping from stomachs to faces. I've noticed knots forming, groups swelling and growing bigger. And, too, couples pairing off shyly, LONELINESS scrawled across their stomachs.

I'm slapping the back of my neck when Howie comes up. Every time I turn my back, Frank's been squirting me with a lemon wedge. Howie shouts something in my ear, but it's lost. His blond hair is slick with sweat, and his body is pale and thin and glistening and shaped exactly like him. My whole body throbs in one painful, sweet heartbeat. There's an E-chord from the stage, and a scream goes up from the crowd. A spot-lit Todd sings, low into the mic: '*Hole Girl, Hole Girl . . .*' The crowd choruses back, '*I'm falling for you.*'

Or is it *Whole Girl*? I watch Todd's face as he searches the audience, and wonder. Is he looking for Caroline? Is she looking back?

Howie slips his arm around my waist, and I lean against his sweaty body. I look out at the floating sea of holes. The dusty cherubs. The many arms around many waists.

'I want to stop our treatment,' I shout to Howie.

He doesn't seem to hear me for a second. I start to say it again when he says, 'I don't think this is the right place to talk about it.'

'I do,' I say.

'You're getting better,' he says.

'No, I'm not.'

'The Hole's going away.'

'That doesn't make me better.'

Todd launches into the chorus, and the crowd screams: '*Reach on down and fall right through!*'. Howie's arm tightens around my waist.

'Think about it,' he says.

'I have.'

He turns and leans his damp forehead against the side of my neck, and we lose ourselves in each other.

The song is winding down. People are beginning to look our way again. And I say, for the second time ever to a boy in a club: 'Do you want to get out of here?'

Howie's eyes jump to mine and away and back again: little leverets of hope.

'Yes,' he says quietly. 'I would.'

He twines his fingers into mine, and we hold each other in this way, dizzy with happiness, while all around us people, still hurting but no longer lonely, scream for an encore.

Caro stays behind. She hugs me tight, says she needs to take care of a few things, that she'll get a ride from Arquette. In the background, the band slowly packs up their equipment. One lone silhouette stands at the edge of the stage, tense and searching.

Howie and I climb into my car. The air between us vibrates like a plucked chord, the reverberations thrilling in the Hole.

We don't look at each other. Our fingers dance together and apart and together again.

'I need to make a quick detour,' I say, eyeing the rear-view mirror. Howie, dizzy and distracted in the passenger seat, barely notices until we pull up in the alley behind the gallery.

'Did you want to—' he asks. 'Here?'

'What?' I laugh, and scarlet. 'I just need to run inside for a minute. Wait here.'

I grab a towel from the trunk of my car and unlock the gallery's back door. I deactivate the alarm and pass through the office and into the main hall without turning on the lights. The words *what am i missing?* nibble at the corners of their vast wall, glowing blue in the dark. Everything's in place, intact, ready for the Black Friday opening. My footsteps echo emptily as I pass through a hall of my own lonely, wild making.

I round the corner, come to the final room. It's empty except for the mirror in its antique frame. It takes less than a minute to pry the clasps loose and slide the glass from its moorings. I wrap it in the towel, lean it against the wall, and stomp-kick through it. It gives way with a sickening crack, slumping down within its terrycloth skin. I step on it again, and again, until I'm satisfied. Then I collect my bundle, tucking in the edges carefully, and go.

I leave the frame where it is, hanging empty on the wall. What am I missing? the exhibition asks as I leave.

And the answer: nothing.

*

We drive home with the windows down and the radio off. I listen to the wind and hear nothing but the sounds of two hearts beating.

We climb the stairs to my room carefully, quietly, the edges of our bodies touching. I want to melt into him, for the whole thing to pick up momentum and snowball us forward, but we are both so nervous that even kissing is difficult, complicated by bumping noses and hyperawareness. The entire night has leaned towards this one moment and now that it is finally here I am terrified and he is terrified and neither of us knows how to go forwards and neither of us wants to stop.

We undress each other. My shirt gets caught on my nose and he gets tangled in his jeans but we make it work somehow, and then suddenly, we are in our underwear, facing each other.

And then in our skin. He reaches for me.

Here are the options for our first time together:

Option A: The whole thing is ecstatically, blissfully perfect. We come together like the lost human puzzle pieces we are. We clash against each other again and again; we cling to one another and ride the waves of ebbing bliss. We are turned inside out by passion. We hold each other, gaze into each other's eyes and know that this is it, this is the great true love that people spend their whole lives searching for. Everything feels like eternity.

Option B: It is sweet, but awkward. We fumble, virgins in the dark. Words and ideas like *between the sheets* cease to be ideas gleaned from movies and dreams and become a thing concrete and moist and real. We can't figure out elbows. My leg cramps. We laugh, and we stop laughing, and suddenly everything is quiet and candlelight.

It hurts, both more and less than I was expecting. Howie comes almost immediately. The whole thing lasts about three minutes, so short that we didn't even get the Hole figured out, and the Lump just sort of pressed into my side the whole time. He jumps up and gets me tissues, dabs between my legs at the mess I don't want to see and can't believe is finally mine. I feel suddenly shy, tell him, 'Don't.' I reach to take the tissues away and our fingers brush, and our eyes lock in the candlelight. And that's when I realise that it is all going to be okay: that this thing that just happened happened with Howie, and he is a person that I know and trust, and this fact is enough to keep me awake in the dim light long after the sound of his gentle breathing has begun to fill the room.

Or maybe the options aren't mutually exclusive.

I climb quietly from bed around five in the morning. The house is quiet, Howie still sleeping. I leave a kiss in the soft hollow of his temple, a piece of the broken mirror by his shoes. I pause to prop another by Caro's door as I pass. It's closed, but I hear the low murmuring of breath inside. I strain a moment to hear if it's one person or two. It's hard to know definitively, but I know that no matter what, I don't need to worry. The sticky notes marching around the bathroom door are just one word, again and again, that she posted last night before we left: joy, joy, joy.

I got an email from my dad just before the party. He didn't

say anything about being stood up, which makes me wonder if he bailed, too. He apologised for having to leave town before Thanksgiving, but said he was eager to get back to Michigan, to spend the day with his family. He sent me the pictures, and I looked at the grimacing smiles of two children who have nothing to do with me but blood. He assured me, though I did not ask, that their torsos are perfectly whole. I haven't replied.

The other pieces of the mirror chatter in my bag as I pad down the stairs into the quiet morning. The street outside is still – people sleeping in on the holiday, the paparazzi gone home to their own families. I lean my forehead against the glass and think about the still-dark houses in the neighbourhoods waiting to be transformed by the warm smells of turkey and pie. I reach instinctively for emptiness, but for once, find none.

We're having Thanksgiving dinner at Mother's later with Howie's family. Mother was going to have everything catered, but Howie's mom insisted on home cooking. Their family car will roll up to my mother's enormous house at noon with a back seat full of kids and dogs, and a trunk stuffed with casserole dishes: mashed potatoes, green beans, corn bread, sweet potatoes heaped with marshmallows and ready to go into the oven. I asked Mother what I should bring and she said, with a pained glance toward my kitchen, 'Napkins.'

I lay the remaining pieces of mirror on the windowsill. I've marked them out in my mind for Mother and Taka and Frank, plus a few extra for strangers I haven't met yet. But right now, the *what am i missing* mirrors reflect only pieces of sky.

I go to my easel, examine the painting there. It's the DNA portrait of Howie and me, and it's wrong, all wrong. I cut it gently from its frame, let it collapse to the floor. Then I stretch a new piece and begin again.

The painting pours out of my brush in rapid, urgent strokes. It is nothing I know and it is also everything. There is the dancing umber of Howie's eyes, the bright honey colour of Caroline's hair. I see the crooked line of Frank's grin, the cool, elegant strokes of Mother's fingers. And colours and shapes I don't know. Or maybe will, but don't yet.

I cut the still-wet canvas from the frame and wrap it around myself, again and again. The paint is thick against my skin like mud, a sticky rainbow of black and blue and goldenrod.

I stand by the window. Far away, slow-moving cars trace the veins of the city in tiny white and red lights. There is a blushing of the sky in the east, the world shuddering into dawn. I think the city seems exhausted, waking again to find that it is still, inescapably, itself. But also, incredibly, itself.

I let the canvas wilt from my waist like a flower. In the last glimpse of my reflection, pale in the glass before the first ray of sun strikes the window, I see myself smeared in the tones of the people I love. And, framed in my middle, a small clear ring. For a second, in the morning light, it doesn't look like a hole. It looks like a tiny picture, a slice of the room: a pitcher. A canvas. Someone coming down my stairs with a smile.

The rising light wipes me from the glass, and I turn to meet the future.

ACKNOWLEDGMENTS

This book is dappled with the fingerprints of friends and beloveds. I owe gratitude to perhaps more people than I can count, but let us try:

Enormous thanks to my fierce and feisty agent Molly Ker Hawn, who never stopped believing, and to my brilliant editor Sarah Castleton, who had a vision. You are the first and second real, not-obligated-by-blood humans to extend a hand to this project and say *yes*. You have changed my world forever. And to everyone at team Atom, and to copyeditor Fraser Crichton and German translator Fabienne Pfeiffer, for understanding this text, and me, more deeply than I could have dreamed.

To my Clarion classmates and instructors, who came into my life after the writing of this book, but who have celebrated it more thoroughly than my glad heart can fully comprehend: teachers Kelly Link, Ted Chiang, Andy Duncan, Victor LaValle, Delia Sherman, Ellen Kushner and Shelly Streeby, and classmates Emily Cataneo, Maggie Cooper, Giovanni De Feo, Jaymee Goh, Jenn Grunigen, Marykate Jasper, Jen Julian, Kathleen Kayembe, Alan Lin, Sunil Patel, Ryan Pennington, Jordy Rosenberg, Grant Shepert, Ben Sloan, Mackenzie Smith, Derek So and Jack Sullivan. Watch them, world. They're going places.

To my New Writers Project and Michener classmates and teachers, who saw this novel in its earliest, shaky-leg days, particularly teachers and mentors Elizabeth McCracken, Ed Carey,

Jim Magnuson and Pete LaSalle, and classmates Sara, Thomas, Ben, Hsien, Antonio, Karim, Anushka, Mary, Greg, Catherine and all the rest. Also to the rare and assorted geniuses in my life: Heather and Corinne, for their kind hearts and honest feedback; Aly and Aubri, my passionate first readers; Brandon, whose curiosity and knowledge of immunology comprised the entire scientific backbone of the novel; my auntwoman Kate, who helped me muddle through the medical; and Jason and Elliot, who dreamed with me of a pop band called Yum Yum Situation at the Stonebraker Ranch in the River of No Return Wilderness during our AmeriCorps service there.

To my "family," Kim, Mikey, Craig and Betny, for loving me despite my prickles.

To my real family: my parents and grandparents, who are genetically responsible for this glorious mess, who never told me what to be or not to be, and who imbued me with a love of language and puns. For my sister Ivy, who lends her initials to the ICF-3 gene, and who helps me feel like I'm never missing in the world. And especially for my grandfather Arnold, who treated me as a serious storyteller when I was three years old, and has never stopped.

To Blake, my partner and be-my-best-selfer and stubborn delight. Thank you for throwing that brick through that window. Some things truly are obvious.

To myself: thank you for always being there.

And to all of you.

362